THE
ORIGINAL
SIN

"Wrath is cruel, anger is overwhelming; but who can stand before jealousy?"

—Proverbs 27:4, RSV

THE
ORIGINAL
SIN

Bonnie Chavda

Treasure House

An Imprint of

Destiny Image® Publishers, Inc.

P.O. Box 310

Shippensburg, PA 17257-0310

"For where your treasure is, there will your heart be also."
Matthew 6:21

ISBN 0-7684-2181-0

For Worldwide Distribution
Printed in the U.S.A.

This book and all other Destiny Image, Revival Press, MercyPlace, Fresh Bread, Destiny Image Fiction, and Treasure House books are available at Christian bookstores and distributors worldwide.

For a U.S. bookstore nearest you, call **1-800-722-6774**.
For more information on foreign distributors, call **717-532-3040**.
Or reach us on the Internet:

www.destinyimage.com

TABLE OF CONTENTS

DEDICATION

This book is dedicated to my mentor and apostle, my husband, Mahesh, and to my children, Ben, Anna, Serah, and, Aaron. You are the highest joy of my life.

FOREWORD

You are on a quest. In you is a God-given desire to achieve inner peace, joy, and fulfillment. Yet, you confront obstacles and inner conflict. This conflict is reflected in present world affairs. Today we see the clash of civilizations, with nationalities and ethnic groups in violent struggles—even leading to destruction and genocide.

In a world tossed on the waves of suspicion, mistrust, anger, and broken relationships, God in His mercy gives us revelation and enlightenment and provides a way of escape and deliverance. This book bears such a light. If you lay hold of these revelations, they will enlighten you and change your life. They certainly have impacted my life.

What are the roots of this conflict inside our hearts and in the world? How did it begin? Bonnie Chavda has woven together dramatic biblical stories with powerful prophetic truths that give a refreshing insight into the mystery of iniquity. Over many years, I have seen the life-changing results of these insights. Whether speaking to an audience of thousands or counseling a married couple in crisis, many have been set free as Bonnie has shared these truths.

I believe the stories you will read in the next pages will provide amazing clues that will make the missing puzzle pieces in your life suddenly fit together. In addition, you will be helped to avoid big pitfalls at strategic times in your life. These powerful tales are also full of adventure and excitement.

The truths they portray have been gleaned from twenty-five years of vital involvement in every aspect of ministry, an amazing life of prayer, and, above all, a Holy Spirit anointing. The Bible promises: "However, when He, the Spirit of truth has come, He will guide you into all truth" (John 16:13, NKJ).

Bonnie is my life partner and friend. After 26 years of marriage and four children, we continue to remain in revival, joy, and love.

Dr. Mahesh Chavda
Senior Pastor, All Nations Church,
Charlotte, N.C.

ENDORSEMENTS

Bonnie Chavda's book is a unique spiritual work which should be read by every Christian. It deals with the key weapon that the evil one uses to distort the work of God's Kingdom, jealousy. Jealousy is the most destructive force at work in the Church today and sadly Christians are not exempt from being caught in its evil web. The imaginative way in which Bonnie Chavda has managed to weave this book into the narrative of Biblical figures who succumbed to this temptation makes this work an enthralling and essential read.

Canon Andrew White
Director of the International Centre for Reconciliation
Coventry Cathedral UK

I have been so blessed by Bonnie's ministry of prayer and her tremendous teaching gift. By her artistic insight into jealousy, the enemy of every man's soul, Orginal Sin opens a new chapter of triumph for everyone seeking the likeness of Christ.

Ricky Skaggs

"THE ORIGINAL SIN" is a message that was in the heart of God before it was put within the heart of Pastor Bonnie Chavda.

In this book, she shares how the sin of jealousy, which then led to rebellion, was the reason the Lord cast the angel Lucifer out of His presence, and how it continued to be a stronghold in other people's lives in the Bible.

The anointing of the Lord and the impartation through this book can and will break every yoke of bondage in our lives if we embrace these truths.

3 John 3:2 says, "Beloved, I wish above all things that you will prosper and be in good health, even as your soul prospers."

Because of the sacrifice of the Lord on the cross and through the blood of Jesus, we can know freedom from jealousy and walk in complete deliverance.

Suzanne Hinn

Snakebite!

Have you ever witnessed wonderful things happening to someone else and, though you expressed outward happiness for that person, inwardly you felt a cool reservation? Perhaps you compared yourself to the one being blessed or promoted and questioned that individual's integrity or worthiness to be so honored. They may have wronged you in the past, or you may be aware of weaknesses or past failures which make them undeserving. Perhaps you're convinced that the person being exalted came to their blessing unfairly. Their blessing makes you uneasy. Beware. The serpent is waiting to strike! Irrespective of your history, position, influence or affluence, jealousy lurks at the door of your heart.

In thirty years of Spirit-filled life and ministry, I cannot recall witnessing a single break up of a marriage, family, church, ministry or business in which jealousy was not a primary factor. Webster defines *jealousy* as "the passion or peculiar uneasiness that arises from apprehension that another enjoys some advantage we desire for ourselves; suspicious that we do not enjoy the affection or respect of others, or that another is more respected and loved than ourselves."

Years ago, a renown pastor came to our leaders with a thick syllabus he had compiled containing testimony against the leaders and associates of a new church in his city. The new church was gaining national and international influence eclipsing his own. Having mailed the syllabus to leaders everywhere the accused were known, the pastor asked our leaders to censure the church and persons named in the syllabus, people who were our own spiritual "family." I was astounded to find our leaders respond to the accuser, taking his side when it was apparent that the man was jealous of those he accused.

In the aftermath I received a clear vision. In it the accuser was one of several schoolboys dressed in Sunday clothes all sitting side by side on a long bench. The leaders to whom he had come for reinforcing were the other boys on the bench. The accuser gripped the edge of the bench and began to anxiously kick his kegs back and forth in a peculiar rhythm. Before long the boy next to him unconsciously imitated the rhythm and movements of the first. As the spirit of the accuser was passed all the boys on the bench picked up the vibration. Soon they were rocking and kicking in unison like tuning forks on a plane! I was reminded of Lucifer, the great worship leader who became jealous for the throne of heaven. Lucifer persuaded one third of heaven's hosts to harmonize with him and led a revolt against God.

Jealousy is the poisonous kiss of the accuser. It is the influence of Satan crouching at the door of the heart. It is the slide down which Lucifer's pride and great knowledge flew headlong to destruction. The first betrayal, the very first war, the first abdication from destiny by God's creation, and the first murder, all started from jealousy.

Jealousy is the original sin!

His jealous heart fully corrupted, Satan continues his orgy of wrath against God. Satan is determined to take as many as possible with him to eternal judgment. In his wake Lucifer has carved a wide path of deceit, being himself deceived, seduction, revolt and murder. One of the sharpest examples of jealousy in our day is international terrorism lurking in every nation.

My first memory of jealousy was in the seventh grade. A girl I considered a best friend tried out for cheerleader. I was elected and she was not. She found new friends, a gang of bullies. The gang began to harass and threaten me. One day I received a note ordering me to "meet her in the restroom." Every girl in school feared getting "a note" from those girls. They carried knives and were famous for physical fighting. Terrified, I went to the appointed place. Several rough, scowling, girls loitered to guard the door. I wanted to run but thought if I went in I could reason with my former friend, restore our bonds, and free myself from oppression by this evil gang. Trembling, I passed through the gauntlet.

I was shocked and disheartened when I came face to face with my former friend. Taller, larger, and more extroverted than I, she immediately blocked the escape and began to shove me, accusing me of acting "like I was so smart" now that I was a cheerleader and she wasn't. I had never been in a physical fight in my life and felt certain I hadn't a chance against her. I knew the gang outside was only waiting to let her get in the first punch before they made their entrance. In an adrenaline rush inspired by my own terror, I lunged. The next thing I knew the huge girl was on her backside, surprised, hurting, and afraid *of me!* She and her gang never bothered me again.

Jealousy has 13 phases from inception to destruction. They can happen over a period of years or overnight.

• *Peculiar uneasiness.* A tiny internal twinge of passion is aroused as you witness another's promotion, blessing, or receipt of affections you desire or deserve. The individual who arouses that peculiar uneasiness becomes the victim of your jealousy.

• Suspicion. Your mind is plagued with untenable thoughts about the motives, character, words, actions or circumstances of the victim.

• *Criticism and confusion.* Your feelings waver between rejection, pride, and guilt, as more questions arise in your mind and emerging evidence reinforces your negative feelings about the victim.

• *Deception.* Your mind becomes filled with false impressions and lies, which seem to be true, and your former blessed knowledge of or confidence in the victim is broken.

• *Accusation of the victim begins.* These accusations can be overt or covert, hidden in the heart or spoken from the mouth in public or private, including gossip.

• *Alienation of affection and respect.* Cordiality between you and the victim of your jealousy dissolves leaving a vacuum that will be filled with more lies and false charges as the relationship breaks down.

• *Obsession.* Thoughts of the victim and every scenario surrounding him or her become foremost in your mind. The mention of his or her name or the sight of the victim stirs a negative emotional/physiological reaction. Unrecognized and unrepented of, jealousy takes over from here. It will spin out of control, consuming lives and destroying relationships and people.

• *Distressing spirit.* You feel agitated and oppressed when you think about or enter the presence of your victim. Your emotions, decision-making, and even physiology (heart rate, body temperature, sight, hearing) are effected by anxiety that fills the void left when bonds of affection or respect dissolved. A spirit of jealousy takes hold.

• *Delusion.* You abandon yourself to belief in the lies supporting your jealous feelings. Your ability to draw the correct conclusions is impaired. Those who fellowship with you can be infected, being convinced of your delusion, just as a tuning fork sends its vibration to the others on its plane.

• *Fraternizing.* You seek the support of others to justify yourself, defend your own character, or enforce your claims. At the same time, you appear innocent, as if you are sincerely seeking "the truth" or "the good" or "justice" based on religious or legal grounds.

• *Resolution.* The urgent need for satisfaction from your victim gives way to frustration and anger. A resolution is demanded.

• *Plotting.* You begin making plans to get the upper hand in the situation; your primary purpose becomes exposing or removing the victim in order to gain control. In the more benign circumstances the jealous party makes plans to "disappear" from the conflict. You leave feeling defrauded and take with you those who sympathize.

• *Confrontation and Hijacking.* "Red rage"—a state of being emotionally hijacked by jealousy's negative feelings and false beliefs—drives you to take action. At this point jealousy becomes proactive. No longer is anything too sacred to risk: not relationships, friendships, fortunes, reputation, or legacy. Murder is at the door.

Jealousy becomes a spirit that cannot be appeased with compromise or gifts. The fire of jealousy will consume everything and every one in its path. It is bent on destruction of its victim. If left to fester jealousy creates delusion. Lies will be received as truth. Heaped upon that first peculiar uneasiness, suspicion and religious or legal arguments about the insufficiency of the victim breaks bonds of fellowship. A relational vacuum is formed. In it jealousy forges new alliances among agreeing parties who have been offended by the victim. Deception and vain imagining twist every act, word, or circumstance, transforming them into evidence to prove the accuser's case.

Down through the ages men and women of destiny have become victims of this worm we call jealousy. Lucifer, Cain, Abraham, Moses, Samson, Elijah, David, and even Jesus, who was crucified because of the jealousy of the Pharisees', were vessels or victims of jealousy. The spirit of antichrist is a jealous spirit! It is the opposite of our "jealous God" who ultimately manifest His zeal for mankind by laying down His life for the object of His love.

The Bible says *"Love is not jealous."* Our greatest example is Jesus Christ. Though equal to God, He refused to grasp His rights. Christ became a mortal and humbled Himself as a Son before His Father, becoming an obedient vessel of the will of God in order to obtain salvation for us.

His example is the prescription for jealousy. Jesus' conduct was the exact opposite of Lucifer's, the anointed cherub who first felt the peculiar uneasiness of jealousy and set about to usurp God, the victim of Lucifer's jealous passion. The anointing, (*christos*), the power of Christ is the believer's strength over the spirit of antichrist. In the same way love (*agape*) is our antidote for jealousy.

—Bonnie Chavda

Brother's Keeper

Woe to them! For they have gone in the way of Cain...

—Jude 1:11, NKJV

Cain, confident as the elder and heir, not to mention the champion promised to Eve, felt a peculiar uneasiness at the very sight of his lazy, disheveled younger brother. The feeling started on the day that Adam knelt down and showed his *b'kowr*—his firstborn—his new baby brother.

That wet scowling thing became the center of Eemah's[1] attention for weeks. And Abba[2] insisted that Cain allow the squalling, hairy-headed baby to share his lap, often forcing Cain right off of Abba's knee whenever the squirming bundle fussed. Abel had even been the reason Abba and Eemah first scolded Cain.

The second son of Adam grew up as a root out of dry ground. He hadn't the form or comeliness of Cain. From the

1 – mother.
2 – father.

beginning, Cain felt a need to exercise his status as the elder son and set things right. As Abel grew and Abba and Eemah spoiled him, Cain's suspicions of his sibling's indolent nature were confirmed.

From boyhood Cain prodded Abel, trying to make him change into something useful.

"If you don't mend your ways, you'll surely starve once you've grown up and don't have Abba and Eemah to take care of you!" Cain wagged a stubby finger at Abel. "They should make you work in the fields like a man." Standing up straight, he puffed out his chest: "A man like me!"

Abel ignored the comments, which only infuriated Cain. He chose instead to live in a world of his own invention, one that he imagined in his head. Occasionally, Cain's sense of superiority would spike Abel's temper, and he would strike back with a word or a threatening fist. But his size was not threatening at all, and ultimately Abel would run away scowling while Cain laughed.

Cain—His Parents' Pride

It had been twelve years since Cain's[3] birth. Abel[4] was two years younger. Cain was the pride of his parents. With red-brown hair that gleamed with sun-bleached golden streaks from days spent working the fields with Adam, and hazel eyes that shone with kindness and wonder over every green growing thing, the tall, lean boy was already at eye level with his father's shoulders. His own shoulders were beginning to broaden. Cain had the same thin lips that Adam had, and his ready smile lit up his face. He seldom laughed out loud, though Eve often cajoled him by saying he had once laughed readily and heartily.

3 – Cain: Hebrew to acquire, purchase; to provoke to jealousy.
4 – Abel: Hebrew for vanity, emptiness.

The boy just had begun to sport the slightest shadow of hair over his upper lip, a wisp accompanying the change in his voice. Once bold, his voice now squeaked uncontrollably at unexpected moments, embarrassing him and indicating passage into young adulthood was upon him. Cain's hands and feet were like his father's, used for tools as much as anything. His wide, flat feet deftly tramped the ground around new plants, and his great rounded fingers easily plucked even the most stubborn thistles.

Cain and Adam had a running discussion of soil, seed and earth while they were working in the field, and they kept it up even when they came in for supper. They talked and planned in the evenings while the family sat at the hearth, until sleep finally overtook them and they stumbled off to their beds.

Much was expected of the boy. Cain was *b'kowr*, firstborn seed of the mother of all the living. Jehovah had promised that this seed would crush the head of the treacherous serpent that had caused the expulsion of his parents from Jehovah's garden.

Cain was the perfect son. A boy of pleasant countenance, serious, obedient, and studious, he was never far from his father the gardener. His mild nature and consistent habits made him a joy. His mother's steadfast hope according to the prophecy was in him.

Every morning Eve put her lips to the boy's ear.

"*B'kowr*," she would whisper quietly. The dew of promise was on her sweet breath. "You will crush his head!" It was the secret promise of Cain's birth.

There was bitter enmity[5] between the serpent and the woman. Eve rejoiced in the anticipation of her son's striking back at the one who tricked her and caused their banishment. Every morning as she shook him awake, Cain's mother vowed to see the prophecy fulfilled.

5 – To hate as one of an opposite party or tribe, hence to be hostile as an enemy

Abel—Free and Wild

Eve turned to the pallet of her second son thinking how very different they were. The natures of the two boys were as opposite as their appearances. The second son of Adam had none of the budding bulk of his brother. His limbs were as thin as sticks, his hands and feet delicate and beautiful like his mother's, seldom devoted to any useful work. His clothing hung on him like a rag on a scarecrow. But he cared little about his appearance. Abel cared only for the wild.

Unlike agreeable Cain, Abel was almost impossible to wake in the mornings. Half asleep, the ten-year-old scowled angrily, eyes tightly shut, kicking and batting away his mother's affectionate urging to get up. He pulled his coverlet over his head of coarse curly black hair, hiding from her and the light.

As always, he obstinately stayed beneath the wrap until Eve had gone away.

Finally sitting down at the table for a breakfast of figs, bread fresh from the hearth drizzled with warm, wild honey, Abel's attitude was as foul as his morning breath.

His black almond eyes glared behind thick puffed lids, still shaded by a fringe of long curling lashes only half-visible beneath the bangs of his shaggy hair, which he refused to comb for weeks on end. He would avoid both gaze and conversation of the others as they ate their meal.

Even as a child, Abel spoke very little—not because he couldn't, but because he cared little about mingling with his family. He was only animated, polite, or loving when he was hungry or afraid. As soon as his needs were satisfied, Abel turned away again. But he was not always silent. Alone in the wild, Abel mimicked the sounds of every bird and woodland creature. He sang while he was away from his parents and brother, inventing the words as he went along.

It became his habit to stay away from their dwelling long after sundown, in spite of being regularly rebuked by Adam and begged by Eve not to do so. He disappeared and reappeared eerily, like a vapor or a sprite, often silently coming up on his parents or brother without their notice. Abel delighted in standing in the shadows and silently watching, listening. If they remarked about him, thinking him to be out of earshot, he would growl a terse reply and startle them half out of their wits. With an insolent look amusement and a mocking laugh, Abel would be gone again as quickly as he had come, running free as the wind and just as fast.

Abel was interested in every four-legged creature, especially the woolly wild sheep and silken long-haired goats that roamed the countryside in flocks. The sheep often leapt nimbly into the low branches of the squatty wild pine and olive trees that dotted the untended fields around the boy's home. The rams in particular climbed the low-reaching arms of the trees to perch like hairy watchmen. They mischievously spied out their surroundings with their keen eyes as they grazed on the tender leaves overhead. As sentinels, they would bleat warnings if danger, man or animal, approached. With no playmate other than his sober, arrogant elder brother, Abel would imagine the sheep and goats to be his real family. He pretended he was really a woolly-fleeced ram trapped in a boy's body.

As he wandered the wild fields, Abel studied the spindle-legged creatures for hours. He could recognize any one of the animals from afar, by the shape of their head or the color of their coat or the sound of their bleating. He often spoke to them as though they could understand and talk back. Abel certainly preferred these wild creatures to Cain, who always displayed a superior attitude toward him.

Cain and Abel were often at odds, though not overtly. They were locked in the smoldering tension of hopeless

competition that occurs when one sibling is congenial and
the other obstinate, when one is industrious and the other
distracted, when one draws near to those who care for him
and the other pulls away.

A Terrifying Miracle

One day in the heat of the afternoon, while Adam and
Cain were laboring over the last of the summer grain harvest, Abel roamed the wild environs across the river from the
cultivated fields. The lad stole upon one of the wild flocks
he had been following for several days. Through the nodding heads of yellow grass, his attention fell upon a sheep
that had grown very fat and laggard in the past weeks. The
heavy-bellied animal had fallen behind the rest and was left
alone, panting and puffing, as if each step was nearly impossible to make. Whatever illness had overtaken it, Abel was
concerned that the animal could fall prey to a hungry lion
or jackal.

Abel lay flat on his belly, hardly breathing, almost invisible in the cover of the high grass. Motionless, he watched
the distressed sheep. Its steps finally halted completely, and
at last it hunched down, mouth open, and succumbed to the
spasms overtaking its rounded form. A fly buzzed noisily
around the Abel's head and landed just above one eye. The
bothersome insect darted about his brow and crawled down
the bridge of his nose, buzzing as it went. But Abel refused
to let its tiny tickling feet make him move, even to brush it
away. Any movement might frighten and further distress the
suffering animal two body-lengths away. Abel stayed perfectly still, blowing fiercely, his bottom lip contorted to
direct his breath at the insect.

"It's dying," Abel told himself, his eyes locked on the
heaving woolly body before him. "I should fetch Adam!"

But just as Abel rose up, a wet, dark, bloody, leggy form suddenly emerged from the suffering animal's body. Horrified, Abel froze on all fours. He was stunned at what happened next. Within minutes a second animal, a tiny, weak replica of the first, was being pushed about on the ground by the larger one. Its hair was matted to its long dark body. The boy's eyes grew wide in disbelief as the larger animal, its contractions over and its labored breath now quiet, managed to pull itself upright. It inspected the new sheep, then licked it all over. The attention of the first animal forced the tiny new thing to finally stand up on its own legs.

It let out one frail sound. "Baaah!"

Terrified and confused at the strange thing he had witnessed, Abel bolted. The tired sheep turned its woolly head at the flurry of movement and dully watched the boy go. Abel ran as fast as his legs would carry him—down the hillside, splashing heedlessly through the shallow river that cut through the valley, and up through the fields, until at last he burst into the house. There he found Eve sitting, washing and cutting great red, yellow, and purple fruit from Cain and Adam's garden.

"Eemah!" The boy knocked aside her work and crashed into his mother's arms, wrapping his own skinny, sun-darkened ones tightly around her. He buried his face in her neck.

"Oh, Eemah!" he cried.

Eve laughed and basked in the opportunity of his rare attention. She pushed her nose into his hair.

"Umm. You smell like the fields, the open sky and wild grass!" She hugged her son until he pulled free. His countenance fierce with confusion, he sat back upon his feet.

"Where have you been all day?" she asked. "Abba and Cain are working hard at the wheat harvest and should have your help."

Eyes wide and hardly able to speak for his rapid breathing, Abel exclaimed, "Something terrible has happened to

one of the wild sheep!" His words died in his throat, unable
to explain what he had seen. His long delicate finger hung
in midair, pointing in the direction of the fields across the
river. It was the land that Adam had set aside for his second
son to cultivate when he grew old enough to care for it. "I've
seen the most awful thing!"

Eve grew serious and looked her young son straight in
the face.

"You must be careful, Abel. There are many dangers
afield." She was thinking of jackals and lions…and the serpent.

She took him by the shoulders. "What is it? Tell me!"

In the best words he could find, Abel reported the scene
across the river. As his tale unfolded and it became clear
what he was describing, Eve broke into gales of laughter. She
pulled her eager son close. Stiffly, he allowed her to embrace
him while he waited for her explanation of what he had seen.

"Oh, Abel! Dear, silly thing!" She tousled his wild hair
and pushed it out of his eyes. "That is how a new life appears!"

He gave her a confused look with a deep frown across
his brow.

The mother of all the living patted her own belly.

"From within!" she said. "The Lord Jehovah has
arranged it so!" She paused to watch his expression. "It is the
way you were made!" she whispered.

Abel screwed up his face and pulled free of her embrace.
He looked down at his own very flat stomach.

"Out of my belly?" he asked.

Eve reached for him and pulled the boy up on her lap.

"Well, not exactly," she said. "But one day your wife will
make fine sons for you, just as I have made for Abba."

"Wife, Eemah?"

"When you are much bigger, twice as old as you are
now, we shall find a wife for you. She will be your helper, as
I am to Abba. Then you shall have children of your own."

"But I don't want children!" he insisted. Then he paused. "Who is my wife, Eemah?"

"Abba will find her. One who is beautiful and who will love you very much."

Abel frowned.

"But you are beautiful, Eemah. And you love me, don't you? Why can't you be my wife?"

Eve laughed again. She explained things to her young son as best she could, using words she thought he would understand. She told Abel again about genesis, the beginning of life, and how Jehovah made the stars and the fields and each of the animals. She also explained how He had taken her from Adam's side.

As Eve went on, Abel quietly rolled the delicious word *genesis* around on his tongue, repeating it softly and imagining the time that everything first began.

"Genesis!" he whispered.

"Abba gave each of the creatures its name," she said.

"Am I as smart as Abba?" he asked.

Just then Cain came into the house carrying a large bundle of wheat from the field, which he balanced on his muscular shoulder. He eyed his brother sitting in Eemah's lap. The two years separating them emphasized the vast difference in the boys' habits and natures. Cain was just beginning to express an acute awareness of his own journey toward manhood.

"You'll never be as smart as Abba!" Cain threw the bundle onto the table. "Where have you been all day?" He glared at his sibling. "While Abba and I toil, you are off chasing the wind and the wild goats!"

Cain stooped over a large, standing clay pot and removed its lid. Drawing out a ladle of water, he turned his head back and drank; trickles of water ran down his dark, sun-browned neck.

"Goat Boy!"

"Abba is going to get me a wife!" Abel stood up quickly.

Cain wiped his wet mouth on an arm. Dropping the ladle back into the jar, he put a hand to his burning shoulder to rub out the deep crease from the strap of the bundle he had brought in.

"Here, son." Eve handed Cain a piece of the sweet fruit she was preparing.

Cain took it with a brief soft smile for her. Then he looked at his brother.

"What are you saying? A wife?" Cain laughed. "Ha! First you'll have to learn how to work!" Cain spied the collection of miniature goats Eemah had fashioned for Abel from twigs, bits of leather, and tufts of wool. The toys always cluttered the hearth and floor. "Goat boy!" Cain danced around his little brother. "Goat boy! Goat boy!"

"Make him stop it, Eemah," Abel said through clenched teeth. He stood up defiantly and took a half-step toward Cain.

Cain was immediately by Eve's side.

"Eemah," he said, stroking her arm, directing his concerned remarks at his sibling, "you should make Abel work as I do! He will shame us all." Cain turned and gazed into her eyes. "What will become of him left as he is?" Cain turned around again. "Always away chasing dreams." Cain leaned against Eve and bit into the fruit, and it muffled his words. "And you encourage him!"

Eve smoothed Cain's silken hair and smiled at her two sons. Each was aptly named. Cain, *I have acquired*, was the fulfillment of the Lord Jehovah's promise. He had come to her through great pain, which had also been promised by the Lord when they were expelled from the garden. During her labor, she had thought she surely would die. Abel—her eyes fell on the younger of the two—was still fuming, his fists clenched. His name meant *Vanity*. She had given it to him as memorial of the emptiness she felt deep inside after she and her husband left Eden and the companionship with Lord Jehovah.

"Abba did not take you with him to the fields until you were eight summers old. Don't you remember? And Abel is small compared to your size," she reassured Cain. "Abel will help soon enough. Let him be."

Cain looked at Abel. She was always defending him.

"He is a baby. Abba spoils him as you do!" Cain grabbed the boy's skinny arm and tweaked it. "And he is weak! Weakling!" Cain taunted.

"Cain! Stop it!" Abel rubbed his thin brown arm.

"Let me see." Eve tried to kiss the insulted skin to soothe it but Abel yanked his smarting arm free. Already a light bruise had appeared where Cain had pinched his brother.

"Go back to Abba!" she barked at the elder.

The chafed first son tossed his half-eaten fruit on the table. It splattered wetly, making a mess. As he went out, Cain could hear the kind melodic voice of his mother returning to her story. Abel sat on the floor, distracted, playing with his sheep toys.

Eve repeated the part of the story where Adam had given names to each of the animals as they were paraded before him one by one. Carefully placing each toy sheep on the floor before him, Abel imagined that Lord Jehovah stood by as he assigned names to the woolly animals of the wild flocks he considered as his own. He used words he had heard from Adam and Eve; words for the things around him, like rivers and sky; and colors, like earth red, midnight black, dawn rose. No sheep or goat was left unchristened. The flocks brought Abel the only sense of purpose or joy he knew.

In the evenings, after supper, the first family sat by the fire. Abel's toy sheep were scattered about on the floor where he played. Adam drew illustrations of the way the seed emerges under the soil to show Cain exactly what was happening beyond the human eye to bring the plants up out of the ground.

On one such night Abel suddenly blurted, "What's sin?"

All three of the others turned and stared at him in surprise, as much for the fact that he had spoken as for what he had said.

Adam and Eve exchanged glances. She was always bringing up things Adam would rather leave alone. And now her son had begun to do the same. Adam would speak to her about it again, lest this kind of curiosity cause Abel the trouble it had caused them.

Adam cleared his throat.

"Where did you learn that word, son?" Adam asked.

Abel didn't look up from his flock. He shrugged.

Eve looked at the boy intensely then she looked at her husband. He turned away.

"Sin is missing the mark," she said. "That's the worst thing."

Adam wheeled and glared at her, knowing she was about to elaborate on something he would rather avoid discussing. But his wife avoided his look. She carded her wool and began to speak. After a moment she was fully animated, looking right through them all to a vista from the past, wide-eyed, the sound of her voice eerie and insistent. "Beware the serpent's cunning, my sons!" she said.

The hair stood up on the back of both boys' necks.

"He is full of deceit and guile. His scheme is to find a break in the hedge. A vacuum..." Eve spoke from the deep pain of her own experience.

Abel wanted to ask the meaning of the word but was afraid his interruption would stop the whole conversation. She explained it on her own.

"...a place of pride in which to sow his seed." Eve's eyes flashed in anger. "He sought to usurp Jehovah and is forever banished."

"Banished, Eemah?" Cain said carefully.

Abel shot him an angry look, afraid that Adam would halt the conversation, as he often did if they asked too many questions. But Cain could not see Abel's expression by the dim firelight.

"Expelled," Eve said. "He was called the son of morning, and he was expelled from heaven forever."

Adam mumbled uncomfortably under his breath. "Just as we were banished from the Garden."

Hot blood filled Cain's neck when he heard his father's quiet words. He wondered with disbelief if Adam had also fought against God.

Abel didn't dare move, pretending not to hear it at all.

"The serpent's time is ending, and he knows it," Eve said over her husband's remark. "The Lord Jehovah told him to his face before we came out of Eden."

Adam stood up and Abel thought he would stop her, but she ignored him.

"The serpent will use every device to turn the creation against its Maker." Her eyes shone with hope as they settled on Cain. "But you will crush his head."

The Serpent's Jealousy

Abel saw her expression and looked away. Cain only smiled a lopsided grin at her. A fire ignited in his heart. He had heard this from as far back as he could remember. Then he said triumphantly. "Yes, Eemah!" He looked at Adam, who was standing with his back to them, clasping his hands behind him, as he did when he had great things to think through.

Abel rolled his eyes. He was tired of hearing this.

Inwardly Eve groaned. She was thankful that with every morning she could recall fewer and fewer of the details of their good days in the Garden.

Adam suddenly walked across to the hearth. He poked at the fire fiercely with no particular intent. Sparks exploded and skipped up the mud chimney, up and out into the sky.

"But why, Eemah?" Cain asked. "Why would the serpent want to destroy things?" Abel's ears tingled.

"He is jealous," she shot back.

"Jealous?" Cain repeated. "What does that mean?"

Abel knew his brother was on the brink of getting this conversation stopped for sure now.

"Wanting what does not belong to you." Eve's eyes flashed and her mouth became grim.

"Who is the serpent jealous of?" Cain asked.

Adam noisily poked at the fire again. "That's enough talk of these things," he said abruptly, turning from the hearth. "It's well past time for us all to sleep." Adam eyed Eve fiercely. He raised his arms and stretched, with a wide yawn that Abel was sure to be only mock tiredness.

Saving Genesis

Adam and Eve were awakened by what sounded like the sudden frightened yelp of a child. Adam scrambled from his bed and fumbled in the darkness for his flint knife. Covering himself, he quickly went to check on his sons. On their pallets, he found Cain heavily slumbering and young Abel awake. Sitting up, Abel threw off his coverlet and leapt from his bed.

"Genesis!" He pushed past his father. His voice wakened his elder brother.

"What is it, Abba?" Cain muttered, rubbing the sleep from his face. He let out a deep yawn.

But Adam was gone, following Abel in search of the source of the cry. Cain scrambled after him once he realized he wasn't dreaming.

Adam came out of the house and quickly went around to the place where the noise had come from. There in the trees at the edge of the thick forest that stretched away behind their mud and thatch dwelling Adam could make out Abel bending over a skinny, longhaired ram. This animal had made a nuisance of itself for weeks. Following Abel home like a stray dog, it would dart away whenever Adam attempted to catch it. Otherwise, the ram loitered around just out of arm's reach, or perched on a low limb, grazing. Letting out an occasional bleat, it would bolt away following after Abel every time the boy left for the wilds.

The ram's hind leg was buckled cruelly under its body. The animal heaved in terrified pain, eyes wild and rolling in its head. When Adam tried to approach the animal it attempted to scramble up and escape, but its leg was clearly broken, causing it to fall in a confused, painful heap. Abel was trying to soothe the terrified animal when he heard Cain's voice.

"What shall we do with it, Abba?" Cain asked.

Adam shook his head.

"There is nothing to be done, son," he said. "It will die of its wound if wild animals don't find it first."

Abel imagined it helplessly dying, deserted, with the vultures that circled above him from time to time flying down upon it. He shuddered, his heart wrenching as he smoothed the silken coat and gazed at the ram's piteous, wild eyes.

Adam took the knife from his belt and stepped toward the animal.

"Move aside, Abel," Adam said. As he lifted the blade Abel screeched.

"No!" Abel threw his body over the injured animal. Turning his face into its hair, he cried, "You mustn't hurt him!"

"But Abel," Adam replied, "if the ram can't walk or climb, he will surely starve, or wild beasts will catch him. It will be worse for him then. It's merciful this way." Adam put a hand on the boy's shoulder. "Now, move aside."

"No!" Abel shouted defiantly, not budging. He clung to the ram. "Genesis belongs to me! I will feed him and protect him from the beasts!"

"Genesis?" Cain asked. "Who's Genesis?"

"It's the name I've given this ram," Abel said protectively.

Cain sniffed. "No wonder that smelly goat is always underfoot. He's made a pet of it!" he exclaimed.

"Please, Abba!" the boy pleaded, large tears rolling down his face. "I'll care for him until his leg has mended!"

Eve came quietly upon the scene.

"What is it, husband?"

"One of the wild rams has fallen and broken its leg," Adam told her.

"Abel wants to save it," Cain said. "But Abba knows it can't survive. We're going to kill it."

At Cain's words, Abel whimpered and clung even more tightly to Genesis, protecting its tiny life with his own body.

Eve looked at her trembling youngest son, with his body shielding the wounded animal. She put a hand on Adam's arm.

"Look at the child's compassion for it. Let him be for now, husband," she implored gently. "At least until the night has passed. We can decide in the morning."

He looked at his wife under the speckled moonlight, which was just coming through the leafy roof overhead. Silver shapes danced on Eve's alluring face, and the cool night breeze carried up her sweet fragrance. Like spring blossoms, she intoxicated him; her long, raven hair fell about her waist in between the shadows.

Adam resigned himself to her wishes. "I will let the two of you have your way…for now." He stepped back and put a hand on the shoulder of his eldest son as he turned around.

"Come, Cain. At least there is one man among us with my good sense." The two of them marched arm in arm around the house.

Eve took Abel by the shoulders.

"It's all right now, Abel," she said. "Come back to bed."

The boy pulled away.

"No, Eemah! I must stay here and protect my ram from wild beasts." He looked in the direction Cain and Adam had gone. "Since he can't defend himself, I'll do it."

"But, Abel…" she started.

"Please, Eemah!" the boy begged.

Eve looked up, listening to the soft sound of the night wind in the trees.

"All right then," she said. "I'll bring your coverlet. But you will smell like that goat by morning!" Amused, Eve laughed softly and went inside.

Abel hugged the neck of the animal. Genesis's warm breath, calm now that the others had gone, was like incense to the boy. In it he felt the wonder of life. The ram's heart beat rapidly against Abel's face.

"He's not a smelly goat," the boy said into the night wind, as hot tears dropped from his chin and landed on the animal's matted coat.

"Don't be afraid, Genesis," Abel soothed. I'll find a way to make your leg as good as new; you'll see."

The wild ram's quick puffs of breath stirred the dust under its head. With one round eyeball it stared at the lad lying over it.

⸎

While Adam and Cain returned to the fields the next morning, Abel and his mother considered how to mend the broken leg. By rigging a splint to hold the leg in place, and arranging a hanging sling over a tree branch, they could keep the animal from putting its weight on the injured leg. Happy with their ingenuity, mother and son set themselves to wait out the mending process, hoping the animal would be good as new in time.

Abel's new occupation was finding the ram all kinds of things to eat. He petted its head as he hand-fed it, thrilled at last to have real contact with one of the animals he so loved. Genesis became accustomed to the boy's presence and touch, so much so that if Abel left him to go into the fields and check on the rest of the flock, Genesis would bleat plaintively until Abel returned. The ram rocked gently back and forth in the sling. As Abel sat on his haunches beside it, relaying detailed reports of each member of the flock, he began inventing stories that he told for hours on end, as though the ram understood every word. The days passed. Abel asked his mother all kinds of questions about life, now that he had seen both sides of it—witnessing the birth of the lamb and saving Genesis from death. Meanwhile, the ram grew fine and fat.

A Wife for Genesis

When Abel realized that Genesis would never return to the wild, he became determined to bring him some company. Many times he lay in wait for the rangy herds on his side of the valley, ready to spring up and chase down a companion for the crippled ram. He finally managed to sneak close enough, and run fast enough, to tackle one. Though its sharp hooves planted several painful kicks on Abel's face and body, the boy held on for dear life, determined to have a mate for Genesis. At last Abel subdued and bound the captive with leather thongs he had carried in his belt for just such a purpose. Abel began dragging the new animal home with him, as it bucked and tried to bolt with every step he took.

Abel passed the rows of the vineyard where Adam and Cain were working. Adam looked up to see the boy and his bleating, kicking captive. He stood upright and called to his youngest son. "What do you have there?"

Cain looked up briefly and went right back to tying up the tendrils of a grapevine.

"Look, Abba!" Abel said proudly. "I've brought Genesis a wife to keep him company!"

Adam looked the new animal over as it bucked and pulled against the boy's grip. After squatting to see its underside, he laughed out loud.

"No, son!" Adam shook his head, eyebrows raised, and smiled widely. "That is no wife for your ram!"

Abel looked at the animal and back at his father, confused.

"But why? Genesis must be lonely!"

Adam left his work and came to where his son wrestled with the new animal. Adam grabbed the lead rope, firmly seized the bucking creature, and rolled it over on its side. Following his father, Cain came to watch the scene. His hands were black from working the earth.

"Look here, Abel." Adam pointed out the particular form of the underparts of the sheep. "This is a *he*, like Genesis. Genesis must have a *she* for a wife!"

Abel stood open-mouthed while his father explained that the sheep he had in tow could never be a wife for Genesis.

Cain doubled over in delight at Abel's ignorance.

Red with embarrassment, Abel realized the ridiculous mistake he had made. Scowling, he untied the tether from the neck of the new ram and chased it away, yelling loudly.

The next afternoon Abel returned with another prospect. This time it was a ewe, a proper wife for Genesis, and so began the development of Abel's flocks. Before long, he had built pens and a short lean-to shelter for them to retreat beneath when the rains came. Ultimately Adam made the boy move his sheep, and their peculiar odor, away from the family's dwelling and into the field that was to be Abel's inheritance.

Firstfruits of Promise

Abel named the ewe Dabar, or "Promise." In the next year Adam and Eve and their sons witnessed the birth of the first lamb from Abel's new stock. A male. Abel named him Bikkuwr, "firstfruits." Abel's interest in the sheep after the birth of Bikkuwr earned him new respect from his parents, especially Adam.

Cain, accustomed to being the apple of his father's eye, found Adam's sudden attention to his younger sibling disconcerting, to say the least. He scowled and followed along unwillingly, not wanting to be left out, whenever Abel urged Adam to inspect some particular matter in the sheepfold. But mostly Abel kept to himself and his animals. Bikkuwr was by his side day and night. It seemed to Cain that the animal was always underfoot, a smelly fixture in their home. Abel even sneaked the lamb into his bed at nights. Cain threatened to move himself into the orchard because of it.

One evening, as the family was gathering for dinner, Abel came in with a jar of sheep's milk. He held it out to his brother.

"It's fresh," he said, but Cain refused. Abel shrugged. "Suit yourself." He took a long, noisy drink. Just then the shadow of a gamboling lamb fell onto the place on the polished red earthen floor where the sun streamed in. A few seconds later Bikkuwr bounded through the open doorway. Like a huge cat, he bumped into Abel's legs, unsteadying him and sloshing the contents of the jar. Abel set the milk aside and picked up the spindly-legged lamb.

"Abba," Cain complained again, "I have had more than enough of this silly animal being underfoot all the time. Abel even takes it into bed with him. It belongs in the field like the rest of the flock."

Adam raised his eyebrows as he considered Cain's objections. He ran his wide strong hands through his wet locks, pushing them flat onto his head away from his face. His thick dark curls popped up again immediately as they all took their places at the table.

"Bikkuwr is no bother to me," Adam finally replied.

Unhappy with Adam's response to his complaint Cain stood up. "This house is too small for us all," he said in a low weighty tone. "As long as that lamb is here, you'll find me elsewhere." He shot Abel a black look as he exited.

Eve grabbed up Cain's breakfast and went to the door. "Cain!"

Abel appeared at Eve's shoulder. Handing her the lamb, Abel took Cain's breakfast and went after his brother. He found Cain cutting timber for his new house.

"I brought your breakfast," Abel said.

Jealousy Enters

The sound of his brother's voice made Cain's pulse quicken. Beads of sweat formed on Cain's face and his muscles bulged with every strike of his axe against the tree. Dark passion filled his thoughts. Frustration and a vapor swirled within when Abel appeared.

Abel set the food and drink on a rock. He picked up Cain's second axe and went to work.

After two hours of hacking in silence, except for the sound of their tools striking trees, Cain stopped. "I'll have that food now," he said. He reached for the loaf and held it out to Abel.

Abel dropped his axe and pulled off a piece of the bread. His eyes on his elder brother, Abel stuffed it into his mouth.

Cain jerked his head toward the clearing, richly planted with high heads of golden wheat. The two of them took their meal into the sun-drenched field. They passed the bowl between them.

"Eemah has some idea that she can preserve this as curd," Cain said at last, looking into the souring milk. "She says if she cooks it down and kneads it with salt it can be stored and eaten later. Perhaps even many days later!"

Abel heartily scratched the side of his curly dark head, yawning from the mixture of the sun on his back and the bread and milk filling his stomach. "What will Eemah think up next?"

"It's as if knowledge invents itself within her," Cain said.

Abel suddenly screwed up his face. "I remember a few of her ideas that weren't fit for the crows or porcupines!" He lay down in the field, his head resting on his arms. "Like the time she used those strange roots to make a stew."

Cain grabbed the sides of his stomach. "Everything we ate for days came out faster than it went in! I've never had such a storm in my belly!"

Abel glanced mischievously at his elder brother. "Except when you dream about the tribesman's daughter!"

Cain looked at him sharply.

"You talk in your sleep, big brother!" Abel kicked playfully at Cain's foot.

Cain dropped the bowl grinning foolishly. Its contents splashed them both. "I'll show you, tribesman's daughter, Goat boy!"

The brothers went down in the field locked together in horseplay. Squeals of the scuffle filled the air. They thrashed out a wide circle of Cain's proud standing grain as they wrestled.

Cain stood up and surveyed the endless orchard, breathing in the sweet fragrant air heavy with ripening fruit. Twelve years of persistent, patient, backbreaking, sweat since he first came to the field with Adam had come to rewarding fruition. This orchard alone would yield much more than they could eat or dry or stew. It would be the best harvest yet.

"Thorn and thistle indeed!" Cain thought of his mother. "I will give you back your Eden, Eemah," Cain whispered. "By the time my sons are chest high the whole earth will be under our dominion again!" He reached into the bough above his head and twisted off a round plum. "But first I need a wife." He imagined the scene: coming up the mountain to the tribesmen's village, the sentinels long since announcing the approach of Adam and his eldest son. The whole community would gather and the men would strike the arrangement.

Cain rubbed the warm fruit on his shirt and smiled as he bit into its soft flesh. Then the dark eyed girl would come to live with them, with him.

A sharp whistle sounded, signaling from the slope on the opposite side of the valley, followed by the soft tinkling of sheep bells. Abel's wild black mop appeared over the top of the ridge, a flock of wooly bodies flowing around him like bouncing noisy children, the shepherd and his sheep poured over the hillside and down to the water. A shadow crossed the elder brother's brow as Abel came into view.

The half clad young man plummeted down the hill, leaping over boulders and crossing the field. His vest flew up behind him like bird's wings.

"Cain!" Abel shouted. He splashed through the river, drenching himself without thinking twice, and crossed the field.

The brother's eyes met.

"By Jehovah's grace I'm glad you're the sober one, keeping to this tedious planting," Abel said as he approached.

He paused to snatch one of the sweet fruits from a bough. "Else I would have starved long ago!" he moved past Cain into the thick shade and sat down.

"Jehovah's grace and the toil of these hands," Cain reminded him, holding up both calloused palms. He frowned as Abel passed. "Whew! That dip in the river only wetted your stank. You smell of your ewes!"

Abel sniffed himself. "I don't notice it!"

"Abba will have to bribe a man to get you a wife when your time comes." Cain looked past him.

"Abba doesn't seem to think so," Abel said nonchalantly.

Cain turned sharply. His discomfit showed on his face. "When did Abba discuss anything so weighty as marriage with you?"

"The chieftain has more than one daughter," Abel's words were distorted as he sucked down the fruit. "And Abba has more than one son."

"But you're still a boy!" Cain snapped.

Abel laughed out loud. "Barely two summers less than you, brother!" He spit the plum stone back into his palm and wiped his mouth on the back of his arm. He tossed the pit at Cain. "You want this spore for replanting?"

Cain caught the plum stone automatically and then dropped the slimy thing in disgust. "It's not a spore," he said through tense thin lips. He wiped Abel's saliva on his shirt. Cain despised Abel's insisted ignorance of his cultivation arts. The continual teasing about it further rankled. Cain had an overwhelming urge to rush at his brother. He knew he could easily take him down. The tension between them was palpable. "I could crush your skull for that," Cain growled.

"Like you will crush the serpent's head?" Abel's voice was mocking. He had been well awake every morning all those years while Eemah crept in to awaken Cain first. He had heard her telling the *b'kowr* of his great destiny. No similar words were saved for him, and under his cover pulled tightly over his head, hot tears escaped Abel's young eyes. To hide them Abel batted Eemah's affections away until she left the room.

Cain did not know before this his brother had heard Eemah's words.

Abel stood up. "I'll leave the farming to your capable hands, big brother. It's much too tedious for me. I'll take my wild hillside any day. We're alike, my land and I." His dark eyes flashed. The sound of the stream rushing below whetted his thirst after the plucked fruit. "I promised Eemah several liters of milk from the flock by this evening."

Cain stared after him, stunned, as Abel crossed the river to his own side of the valley. The sound of the tinkling bells of the sheep gradually faded while Cain went out into the middle of his grain and lay down. He stared into the endless blue sky.

Scenes of his childhood, pictures of himself and recollections of Abel with their parents filled his mind. Abel had always acted so aloof, so uninterested in anything between Cain and his parents. But it was obvious now there was more to Abel than Cain had known. Recalling the sound of Eemah's words on Abel's lips made gooseflesh travel up Cain's back in spite of the warmth of the sun baked earth on which he lay.

What was Abel up to?

Eventually Cain turned on his side and pushed away the unhappy sense of insecurity and suspicion that something was about to be stolen from him. He turned his thoughts to the tribesman's daughter. Reaching out an arm he stripped a handful of grain from the stalks around him. He rolled the kernels about on his palm to break off the chaff and expose their bitter green heart. One by one, Cain crunched the unripe kernels slowly between his teeth.

A hawk circled overhead searching for carrion. It screamed down at him once and flew out of sight.

Suspicion and Division

The sun broke over the horizon to the west, and the whole valley was suddenly veiled in a smoky gauze of mist, which sparkled with all the fiery red and orange colors of dragonfly wings. Adam breathed in the cool wet air as the red-jeweled fingers of sunlight crept over the skyline and flushed his face with a warm orange glow.

"Eemah will have our breakfast waiting," Adam said, patting Cain gently on the shoulder. "Perhaps your brother will finally have made his way off his pallet."

Cain smiled stiffly in response to Adam's touch and remarks. They stepped into the grain field where they had been working since before daylight. Cain felt the heavy tops of the bending stalks, which signified that the barley harvest was upon them. Only days ago, they had finished stripping the orchard.

Cain was distracted as he pushed aside the thick plants. He sighed. Something in his heart had dulled since the revelation of Abel's budding close bonds with Adam. Cain no longer felt that his own relationship with their father as special as it had once been. A growing camaraderie seemed to be developing between his father and brother, and he didn't feel included. He was certain that Adam's affections were changing towards him. Even Eemah's whispers grated on him now. He hardly let her speak the words of the prophecy anymore; they made him suspicious and anxious, rather than excited, whenever he heard them.

Cain was also noticing a change in his brother's behavior. Abel was obviously scheming to innocently ascend to the position of *b'kowr*—the firstborn, the *chosen one*. The signs of it were increasingly irrefutable. Cain's mind swam as he thought about how Adam might be planning to find a wife for Abel before himself. The specter of Abel marrying first, perhaps winning the girl Cain had wanted for his own, was impossible to shake. Cain had dark dreams, and he consoled himself with his ability to see right through Abel's guise. The subtle words and insidious little gestures were designed to manipulate Eemah and Abba. Abel hung around Adam like a stray dog, underfoot every time Cain turned around.

"Did you set aside oil for the whetstone?" Adam asked his sullen oldest son.

Cain nodded, and they walked together along the edge of the orchard to where it turned in toward the house. "The blades will require an extra edge this season," he heard himself say, to fill the silence after his tardy non-reply to Adam.

Meanwhile, Abel stumbled out of bed, scratching himself and groaning.

"Even my fingers are aching!" he complained, stretching and feeling the soreness in his muscles from the hard work of picking fruit. He was used to being at ease in the fields as he followed his flock. "I think I hate everything about this time of year but what it puts in my belly."

Eve laughed at him as she set a bowl of milk and some bread on the heavy hand-hewn table that served as everything but a bed in the center of their house. Sounds from the birds excitedly welcoming the day came from outside. Abel looked at his breakfast, the only one placed at the table.

"Where are Abba and Cain?"

"Already in the field. It's harvest, remember?" She paused and said kindly, "They tried to wake you."

"I've dreamed of it again, Eemah," Abel told her. Their eyes met. "It's as if it is calling to me. A voice calling me to return for something lost."

Eve shuddered and drew in her breath. She looked around as if someone might be listening to them.

"You mustn't speak of it, my son," she said. "You mustn't think of it." She grabbed hold of both of Abel's forearms. "And you must never attempt to go there!"

Abel did not reply.

They rarely spoke of what had happened before Cain and Abel were born, before the man and woman followed the counsel of the serpent. The shame of it still hung on the parents of the first sons, much like the skin tunics God made to cover their nakedness. Abel wished they could return to the Garden. Abel longed to venture inside the magical place that was spoken of only in the rarest of moments. The Garden was where his parents had known only life and joy, and eternal goodness.

None of his family knew it, and he was sure to receive the severest of rebukes, especially from Adam, should they ever find out how Abel longed to visit the Garden of Eden. His sleep was often filled with dreams of it. He saw himself parting the thick hedge of briars encircling the old enclave where the river's mouth bubbled up from beneath the roots of *the tree.*

Eve put her hands around his face. Bringing it near, she said softly, "You are my consolation after the Garden."

Abel patted her shoulder in return. The lanky young man, now eighteen summers old, rubbed his eyes and lifted the bowl to his mouth. He drank several deep gulps of the tangy, tepid milk that he had drawn the evening before from his ewes. Eve had perfected her experiment with curd, and they regularly enjoyed fine cheese made from goat's milk with their meals.

Later that evening, following a day of work in the fields, Eve seemed unusually adventurous.

"The moon is full and bright!" She announced abruptly as they sat at the hearth after supper. "Let's go to the waterfall!"

It was a delightful idea. The rest agreed. As they went out of the house together and passed through the fields, the smell of freshly cut grain rising from the ground with the evening mist was satisfying to them all. They trekked along the bank of the gently flowing river until they came to the waterfall, where the river plunged down from the hills and formed a wide, deep pool. Beyond the high cliffs overlooking their valley were wilds into which they seldom ventured.

The magnificent falls and deep, cool pool were the first respite Adam and Eve had found when they were wandering, in regret and fear, after the expulsion. Following the swiftly flowing current of the river, they had emerged from the thick undergrowth and seen the river's roaring plunge over these falls.

The sound of the rushing water and the sight of the rainbow-colored mists that danced everywhere washed over their stripped souls. The man and his wife found a sense of hope at these headwaters.

They swam in the pool, at last smiling, laughing, and embracing one another again. They bathed themselves, refreshing their bodies and their hearts. It was here that they first experienced the seeds of hope. Since then, the falls and the clear pools had symbolized reconciliation and renewal for Adam, Eve, and their sons. Cain and Abel learned to swim before they could even walk, and the first family spent many hot afternoons lying on the sun-drenched rocks. Surrounded by the sound of crashing waters, Eve made up stories of adventure and wonder and wove crowns of water grass and field flowers for each of them.

"Look out below!" Cain shouted as he leapt from halfway up the cliff. He plunged into the pool shrieking.

Just before he hit the surface Cain doubled into a ball, his eyes clenched tight, an expectant look of pain on his happy face. He crashed into the pool, splashing huge waves of spray over the other three swimmers, drenching them all. The waters rocked with the impact of his dive.

Abel just watched.

"That was about as skillful as falling into a pit!" Abel jibed. "If you want form, watch this!" Abel's wet body came up out of the water. Deftly, he scaled the rocks, maneuvering between the handholds like a giant spider. Coming to the ledge, Abel stood straight, toes hooking the sharp edge, arms pointed into the night sky. Like a great bird taking flight, he pushed off from the wall and fell like a human arrow, cutting into the water's with scarcely a splash. When he came up he shook the water out of his hair.

Adam whistled in approval, and Eve clapped her hands.

"A fish! A great bird!" she cried.

"A lazy buffoon," Cain thought, "who spends his days lounging here while I'm in the fields working like a slave to grow the food he eats."

Adam and Eve, arm in arm, circled the dark pool peacefully, while their sons energetically tried to outdo one another. Shouts, laughter, and the splash of water mingled with the roar of the falls and filled the night. The moon came up behind the cliffs, forming a huge, silver-white face that peered down at them with curious gray eyes. As the great orb ascended in the blue-black sky peppered with points of light, it shone down on the swimmers until they and the entire earth around them were drenched in pale moonlight.

The Jaws of Death

In the midst of the splendor of that night a frightened bleat was suddenly heard above the sounds of the waterfall and the laughter.

"Baah!"

Abel was first to look up.

"*Bikkuwr!*" he cried, looking toward the voice of his lamb.

The lamb appeared on the side of the high rocks. It bleated plaintively again, its white spindly legs quaking, its frozen form clear against the black cliff.

Everyone was looking up now.

"What's he doing up there?" Abel dove toward the rocks at the bottom of the falls.

"Baah!" Bikkuwr feebly answered Abel's voice.

A rush of panic swept over Abel as he climbed out of the pool and started up the face of the cliff. The rest of the family watched him. The firstfruits of Abel's flocks looked confused and afraid. Trembling legs spread wide beneath the frail body bleached white in the silver moonlight. "Baah!" Bikkuwr waited for rescue.

"Be careful, Abel!" Eve admonished the climbing shepherd. Though it was too dark to see his expression, she knew that caution was far from his mind. Rescuing Bikkuwr was all Abel was thinking about at that moment.

Water crashed around Abel and fell over his shoulders as he reached the level of the animal. He began to make his way across the wall of rocks, clinging to the wet surface and passing behind the raging waterfall to the place beneath the ledge where the frightened animal stood. Several times, Abel's hands or feet slipped and he barely managed to catch himself.

Adam held his breath when Abel grasped a last handhold and swung himself onto the jutting rock.

A piercing scream cut into the fresh night air.

Eve shrieked below when she heard it. She grasped Adam with wet hands. Her voice was terrified and pleading. "A lion!"

Abel's bare feet and body had just dropped onto the ledge, within arm's reach of his lamb, when he saw the lion.

Crouched, fangs bared, furious now that it was cornered, the beast straddled the shepherd's dying ewe. Dark stains of fresh blood covered its muzzle.

"Promise!"

The sheep's sides heaved weakly under the bloodied mouth of the lion.

As Abel appeared, another eerie wail screamed into the night, as the lion slashed a menacing claw towards the shepherd.

"Leave it alone, son!" Adam ordered from below, scrambling out of the pool and running for a nearby tree. Cain followed on his father's heels. Adam wrestled the limb from the trunk to use as a defense weapon, though what he would do with it was a mystery. "Abel, get off that ledge!" he shouted as he struggled. Cain left Adam wrestling with the tree limb and headed toward the incline that led up the backside of the falls.

"Abel!" Eve cried. "Do as Abba says!"

Abel was not listening. His eyes were fixed on the snarling face of the lion.

"You'll not have my Promise or the firstfruits of my flock!" Abel growled back at the predator.

Bikkuwr was precariously close to the drop-off. His sharp hooves slipped on the wet granite. Crashing down, his jaw thudded heavily as he scrambled to regain his footing.

The eyes of the mortally wounded ewe rolled upward, pleading with the shepherd. The gash in her throat was wide and gaping, and her blood-soaked breast rose and fell in labored spasms, her life draining out of her with every beat of her heart.

Abel grasped the flint blade he always carried strapped to his hip.

From below Eve saw her son's arm raised to attack.

"No, Abel!" she screamed frantically. "No! Adam, do something!" Covering her eyes, Eve turned her head away, not wanting to see what was sure to happen. She wailed, her head of long, wet hair clinging about her face and body in crooked tendrils.

"You cannot fight a lion with your bare hands!" Adam roared.

Cain said nothing as he scrambled out of the pool. While his father still wrestled with the tree limb, Cain skirted the ascent, half-running, half-clawing his way up to the terrible scene on the ledge. Terrified, he had no idea what he would do once there.

Abel was oblivious to everything except the fact that a predator had attacked his sheep and was threatening her baby as well. Crouching nimbly, blade raised, Abel lunged toward the great cat. A clawed foreleg swung back but missed the young man's flesh. Unafraid now, Abel moved back and forth on his haunches, looking for an opening to the beast's chest and heart, or at least its throat. His eyes never left the lion's threatening glare. The breath of Promise was little more than a gurgling snuffle as blood filled her lungs. The smell of blood, metallic, sickening, was thick on the night air.

The strike of the lion strengthened Abel's impassioned resolve to defend his flock. He lunged again, and this time the cat grabbed him, digging its great claws into his shoulder, piercing his soft flesh with razor-sharp tips. The burning wounds were scored deeply. For a moment, Abel saw nothing but bright flecks of light swimming before his eyes. When he realized death might claim one or both of them before they left the ledge, he flew again into the flailing embrace of the lion.

Locked in mortal struggle, the beast's back claws curled on the end of his hind legs like living knives loaded on two powerful springs. Claws fully bared, the animal dug again into the flesh of Abel's belly. The shepherd's determined blade attacked the lion's neck and head as man and beast rolled about on the wet ledge.

From behind the falls Cain could hear the struggle. He could hardly distinguish between the angry, guttural screams. Did they belong to the beast, or were they the sounds of his brother pushed to his limit? Adam's frantic breath came up from below as he bounded up, determined to save his son. Another angry snarl came from the ledge, and then there was silence.

Below, Eve wept for the men she loved, all of them rushing into the lion's lair.

Cain was first to reach the scene, with Adam at his heels. There was Abel, red with his own blood, the blood of Promise, and the blood of the lion. The dead ewe was cradled in his arms; his flesh was torn, striped, and bleeding profusely. The body of the dead lion, its throat opened neatly by the blade, lay crumpled at Abel's bare feet. The young man's body trembled with the adrenaline still pulsating through his battered body.

"Promise is dead." It was all he said.

Adam knelt and gathered his son up into his arms.

Convincing Abel to leave the ewe, Adam inspected the wounds that were weakening his son by the second. Together Adam and Cain lifted Abel up to the top of the cliff and over the ledge. The moment he was at the top, Abel turned around. Cain stood beneath him. The moon was darkened by the heavy fist of a cloud, which looked as though it had a finger extended accusingly across its face.

"Give me the lamb," Abel told his brother weakly, his bloody hands stretched toward him.

As Cain stood looking up, two heavy drops of his brother's blood fell. One of them hit Cain directly in the middle of his forehead, the other dropped onto the wet rock at his bare feet. Cain wiped Abel's blood off of his face, and for a single mesmerizing moment stared at the thick red liquid. It sent a twinge through Cain's stomach.

"You're bleeding badly," Cain said. "I'll carry Bikkuwr."

Abel suddenly slumped to his knees. Adam grabbed his son to keep him from tumbling over the falls. Cain struggled up out of the lion's bloody lair after them, with Bikkuwr stiffly straddling his neck like a high woolly collar. Man and animal left predator and prey alike dead behind them.

"Adam!" Eve cried from the dark below. "Is Abel..." She was afraid. "Is he all right?"

"He's been badly slashed by the lion," Adam shouted down in reply.

Tears of fear and hope flooded her face.

"Lord Jehovah!" she whispered, her voice breaking together with her terrified heart. "Please!" Her legs buckled as she wept. "Please save him."

It was an ordeal getting down, as the two men carried the wounded shepherd and the frightened sheep in the dark over the rugged black terrain. The rocks were slippery from perpetual mists that rose from the raucous falls. Eve paced nervously below, stopping every few steps to peer up into the shadowy darkness. She could measure the men's progress by the moonlit reflection of the lamb's fleece against the dark cliff. Adam supported Abel's torso and Cain, with Bikkuwr awkwardly around his neck, carried Abel's lower body. None of them spoke.

A Dark Shadow Passes

Eve rushed toward the men the moment they neared the pool. Seeing Abel's wounds, she feared she would pass out. She nearly bit through her own tongue to stay conscious as she cried out and cradled him against her. Gently touching the deep gashes dug by the lion's sharp claws, Eve shook her head.

"It could have killed you, son!"

At that moment something dark and terrible, like a ghoul from the deep, an ancient dragon, cursed and awakened from its sleep, overtook Cain.

"What if it had?" asked a voice Cain knew but could not identify. For a fleeting moment, the *b'kowr* imagined his life, past and future, without Abel plaguing it. His gaze went to the bloody legs that hung over his arms.

Abel opened his eyes and squeezed his mother's hand as best he could.

"But it didn't, Eemah," Abel replied with a hoarse, dry throat.

Cain shuddered. Hot guilt tore at his gut. He looked around to see if they had heard the voice.

"Thank You, Jehovah!" Eve was praying again.

"Let's go home," Adam said. He and Cain moved forward, carrying Abel in their arms.

All the way home Eve said over and over again, "Thank You!" She kept touching Abel's matted hair. "Jehovah has spared my son!"

Once the trauma was past, Cain was overcome with exhaustion. The stars that signaled fainting passed over his eyes once or twice. The adrenaline, the memory of the wail of the lion as it devoured its prey, the smell of his brother's blood, all pummeled him. He was never more relieved to fall asleep in his bed than on that night.

Adam went alone into the orchard. Eve stayed by Abel's side.

By midnight, Abel was resting uncomfortably, an herb poultice wrapped tightly around his body to seal and heal the wounds.

Bikkuwr, tethered to one leg of the table, skittered about nervously, bleating weakly for his mother from time to time in the firelight.

That night, after Cain and Abel had fallen asleep and there were no sounds except heavy breathing coming from the room where they slept, Adam and his wife lay side by side, thinking of what had happened to them and their sons that day.

"The time spoken of by Jehovah has come," Adam said in the darkness. "We've taken in a plentiful harvest and Jehovah has spared our son. Cain and Abel must learn His ways." He shifted and remembered the Garden and how Jehovah had spared the man and his wife after they had sinned.

Abel Is Gone!

In the predawn light, Eve crept from her bed to check on Abel. When she came to his bed she found it empty. The lamb was there, wrapped in Abel's coverlet and sleeping peacefully. The firepan, used for carrying live coals to make fire outside or in the smithy where they beat out iron for tools, was missing.

"Adam!" Eve roused her husband. "Abel is gone! He has taken fire with him."

Adam awakened and sat up, pushing the sleep from his face and eyes. For a moment he thought the whole scene had been but a bad dream. But then full consciousness hit him and he came out of the house in three great strides.

"Foolish boy!" Adam railed at his son, with worry rather than anger. "He shall come to a sorry end!"

Adam's breath flowed into the cool, damp morning atmosphere like puffs of thin smoke as he came up the path and onto the crest of the knoll overlooking their valley.

The red-gold sun slipped over the dark horizon and pulled itself up by glistening fingers of light, which cast a purple-pink veil over the landscape. Adam's gaze swept over the vista, searching for signs of his son's whereabouts. In the distance across the river, a single column of black smoke made it way into the sky, dense and roiling in the early light. Adam started toward it.

When he came upon the place at last he found Abel there, leaning heavily on his shepherd's crook, one arm wrapped stiffly around his bandaged torso. Before him was a quickly arranged pyre and on it lay the burning body of the dead ewe, missing the hide and hair.

Abel painfully watched the form of the burning animal in the fire he had made. He didn't turn around at the approach of his father's footsteps. The two stood there before the pyre, saying nothing, until the legs of the altar were no more than crackling, crumbling black shards and the carcass of the ewe had been reduced to charred bone. At last the whole structure caved upon itself and fell into a heap, with one last burst of flying sparks and ash.

Abel let out a deep sigh.

Adam put a hand on his son's shoulder; his son was now more a man than the tall boy of days gone by had been. He had faced the lion. "Jehovah delivered us from death, my son," he said at last. "We worship Him for it."

Abel's angry eyes looked at him.

"Delivered us? What about Promise?" He was thinking of the poor sheep alone at the mercy of the lion. Adam saw it as Abel turned from the smoldering pyre.

"I would have gladly laid down my life for my sheep!" At that moment his weakness made him dizzy. Adam steadied him.

"Understand what I tell you, my son," he said kindly. "The life is in the blood." He was remembering the Garden and the coverings Jehovah had made for them after they had eaten of the tree. "A life for a life. Promise in exchange for you."

But Abel did not understand.

The two men made their way back to the river and crossed to the other side. Stopping just once as they crossed the wide field, Abel painfully stooped near the base of a boulder he often sat upon as he watched over his flock. From the crevice, Abel pulled out the fleece of Promise, rolled in a bundle.

"Eemah can make some use of it." His tone was sad and sullen. The weary young man, smelling of blood and smoke, limped toward the river.

They stopped in the waters to wash. Abel's strength was nearly gone, so Adam took the fresh hide and gave it a preliminary rinsing, squeezing out the thick hair while Abel regained the strength to rise and walk.

Adam stared down at the bloody animal skin. "It's like before. He spared once when He could have..." He fell silent.

"Could have what? Killed you instead?" Abel replied. The young man pulled the bloodied fleece out of his father's hands. There were no more words between them. When they were home again, Abel fell into his bed.

Before they slept, Adam spoke to Eve.

"Once the crop is in we'll build an altar," he said.

She waited for his next words.

"Abel burned the body of the sheep today. I was reminded of Jehovah and the Garden when I saw Promise on the burial pyre. Our sons must learn His ways."

He briefly imagined himself with Cain and Abel, walking and talking with the Invisible One as he had once done. A tear escaped his eye and ran down his face in the dark. "Perhaps we have waited too long," he told his wife quietly. His words faded away in the darkness.

"Jehovah is long-suffering," she said. "Hope in Him, my husband. And He has made us a great promise!"

Looking Back in a Dream

"We must bring Jehovah an offering," Adam said. "We will build an altar once Abel's strength returns." That night Adam dreamed an unusual dream. He and his wife were desperately trying to sew together the leaves of the trees of the Garden to make coverings for themselves. They had eaten of the tree whose fruit carried the knowledge of good and evil. The entrance of evil fouled their former state of innocence, and previously undiscovered vanity, strife, twisted thoughts, and overwhelming questions replaced the peace they had once enjoyed. Suspicion instead of trust filled them.

The man and woman now feared what they were now capable of doing. If that knowledge were fed with immortality from the Tree of Life, the eternal perpetuation of all those troubles would be inevitable. Ever-increasing darkness had entered creation because of what they had done. Creation's need for redemption condemned man to mortality until Jehovah intervened.

Dread of the future gnawed at their hearts. Everything had changed. They were ashamed to find themselves naked. For the first time Adam feared the presence of Jehovah. Impatient anger flared between Adam and Eve. Harmony was broken, and they argued over who was to blame for their predicament, each accusing the other and neither admitting his own part.

Adam could hear Jehovah as He approached. A wind stirred the leaves where Adam and his wife hid themselves, trying to make their own coverings before Jehovah saw them in their nakedness. Adam's heart beat faster and his hands shook as he continued tying the leaves together. Eve silently wept as she quickly fastened the apron she had made around her neck.

"Adam?" Jehovah called. "Adam, where are you?"

In a bright, hot flash, Jehovah appeared, and their self-made coverings instantly wilted, curling in dry, useless, brittle bits and dropping away. The man and woman were naked again. Their only covering was their shame.

Hot showers of terrible guilt and inescapable doom pelted Adam as Jehovah found him. Then, in the dream as in the Garden, Jehovah brought the man and his wife coverings He had made for them. Garments made from the skins of animals were given to both of them. Adam stirred at the overpowering smell of the bloody sacrifice. The knowledge that innocent life had been sacrificed for the sake of their sin pierced his heart with pain. He could feel the blood—warm, wet, sticky—between himself and the new garment that clung to his skin. He cried out in the dream.

Eve woke at the sound of her husband's muffled cry. She drew close to him, putting a comforting hand on his arm, and they slept.

❦

Abel rested for seven more days. With Eve's care, his wounds were healing quickly and his strength and mobility were returning, though he remained a little stiff. Each morning he gingerly made his way out to see that his flock was accounted for, concerned that neglect would induce them to wander. Adam and Cain cut the remainder of the grain.

For the next week, Eve was busy nearby threshing the heads of grain for roasting and milling. Seed for the next planting was carefully separated and set aside by Cain. All the while, Adam was considering the sacrifice to come.

After the harvesting process was completed, he turned his energies to plans for building the altar. He and Cain constantly reviewed it together. A sense of anticipation had settled on them. "It should be on Abel's land," Adam decided.

He thought of the wild expanse there and was certain by now that it would never be cultivated as Cain's land had been.

Adam excitedly sketched rendering after rendering directly onto the top of their table. He would throw a ladle of water onto the sketch when he changed his mind concerning this detail or that, swiping it away with his forearm. He seemed oblivious to the sludge pooling on the floor. Washing away the changes, he filled out the lines again with the tip of a green twig, finely sharpened, with a ridge cut down its spine to hold ink. Adam worked quickly, the pen plunging again and again into the pot of thick, wet ash, until he had satisfied himself.

Eve wandered near from time to time, her gaze floating over the table drawing, nodding approvingly.

The Altar

The square earthen mound was as high as it was in the length of its sides. Halfway up the sides Adam had drawn ramparts of stone mudded in with more earth. The top was flat, and on one side a ramp led up to the place where the sacrifices would be offered.

"We'll need wood," Adam said to his sons, "lots of wood, to make the offerings rise to heaven as pleasing incense." Cain exchanged happy glances with Eve. Abel kept to himself and said nothing.

Abel was the first to retire. When Cain came to his pallet he saw that Abel was still awake. They said nothing as Cain lay down and rolled a piece of his coverlet and put it under his head. The oil lamp flickered, casting soothing, dancing shadows up the wall.

"I've not seen Abba so excited about anything in a long while," Cain said.

Abel did not reply.

"I've already imagined the offering I will prepare." Cain turned on his side toward Abel.

Abel played with Bikkuwr's ears.

"What are you going to bring Jehovah?" Cain's question sounded faintly like a taunt.

Abel's eyes met his brother's without turning his head. He looked away and shrugged.

"Something of value," Cain told him. "It should be impressive. Important to you! Something worthy of Jehovah's notice and favor!" Cain rolled onto his other side for more comfort, turning his back to his brother. "Like Bikkuwr," he yawned.

Abel watched Cain's reclining form. "What did you say?"

Cain turned his head around and pointed.

"You could bring Him that lamb of yours. Its about the only thing you really care for!"

"What are you talking about?" Abel shot up on his pallet. Bikkuwr jumped and looked at him curiously. "Why would Jehovah want Bikkuwr?"

Cain chuckled. "Your *firstfruits*. Haven't you learned anything from Abba?" Cain turned back onto his side, facing the wall. "I will have the firstfruits of everything I have harvested this year," he gloated, subtly suggesting that the uselessness of Abel's life and vocation would finally be revealed to their parents.

Abel peered angrily at the reclining length of his preaching brother. He had lost one sheep already. He wasn't about to lay down another one willingly.

"It would get it out from under our feet anyway," Cain mumbled darkly. "Sweet dreams, little brother."

Abel was about to speak when he heard the soft snores coming up from Cain's pallet. His elder brother's words screamed down through Abel's soul. *"Bring Him that lamb! Bring Him that lamb!"* Abel tossed and turned the rest of the night. His dreams were dark and violent, as if he wrestled against some malevolent force trying to destroy him. As he entered deeper sleep, the dark scenes changed. Now Abel journeyed up the river again and came to the place where Eden sat, hedged around by thick, high walls of sharp thorns and wild overgrowth. Abel could just see tiny gleams of light coming through as the sun shone down on the other side. His arms went out before him and carefully pushed through the foliage. But as he moved them apart to see beyond the walled veil and step through, a frightening whoosh passed over him. It was a wind like nothing he had ever experienced—powerful, awesome, fearful, and yet not malevolent. Then a bright fire flashed so hot on his skin that he felt it in his sleep. Abel woke up breathing rapidly.

Abel opened his eyes to find himself in his own home; his brother was fitfully tossing and mumbling, as was his habit of late. The oil lamp had gone out, and Abel glanced across at Cain, whose large arm was thrown over his dark face. Cain said something inaudible and lashed out. Then he turned his back to his brother, gasping for breath, and a loud snore escaped his throat. Abel swallowed the groan of pain he felt as he sat up. He carefully pushed the sleeping Bikkuwr aside. Then, quietly, he let himself up, burying the dozing animal under his coverlet.

While Adam and Cain had been focusing their thoughts on building the altar of sacrifice, Abel had been thinking other things. He brought several of his old toys from childhood out of a bag of hidden things he kept near his pillow. He smiled at the old bent figures, remembering happy days when he could only imagine possessing a real flock of his own. Abel dressed, and in the darkness he took the toy figures to the table. The drawing of the altar, its thick black lines ominous and unforgiving, was still scrawled on the table's surface. Abel carefully arranged the sheep on it. He put all but one of them near the end of the table in plain sight.

In the center of the table, he placed one sole figure under his own upturned bowl. Eve would understand that he had gone out in search of a missing lamb and all would be forgiven when he returned. He had dreamed the dream again, and it could no longer wait. With the message on the table, no one would be the wiser. If they asked, he had plenty of experience looking for lost sheep to make up a reasonable tale.

In the silence of the night, Abel took bread and a piece of Eve's curd cheese from the pantry. Staff and provisions in hand, he wrapped his vest around his still-bandaged waist. In the predawn dark, Abel slipped quietly out of the house, not realizing he was leaving the tiny figure of a sheep trapped under the upturned bowl directly in the center of the drawn altar.

✦

That morning marked the dawn of the eighth day after the harvest was finished. Adam was up before the rest and went out into the field. As he walked in the stillness, a cool, silvery mist and thick wet dew clung to his legs and feet. He took in all Jehovah had enabled them to accomplish. As he stood peacefully in the stillness of nature, hearing gently creaking insects in the distance and the frogs at the river croaking out an occasional note, a kind of comfort came to him. He sensed a hope of new beginnings for them all in the grace of Jehovah. As he contemplated the goodness they enjoyed, Eve called to him.

"Adam!" Her voice was anxious. "Abel!"

"Here, wife!" Adam shouted back. He started toward the house but then saw her coming through the field grass, a worried expression on her face.

"Is Abel with you?" She held up the figure she had taken from beneath the upturned bowl. "I found his old figures from childhood on the drawing of the altar."

Adam just shook his head. "The boy has become a good shepherd. Even a lion cannot stop him!"

"Should he be in the field so soon?" She wrung her hands around the toy.

Adam simply welcomed her under his arm in the cold air. Eve shivered. The smell of the field, alive and free, was in her face and hair. She looked this way and that across the countryside, though she knew Abel was not to be seen. Something inside told her where he had gone, but she dared not say it to Adam. They walked arm-in-arm back down the meadow to have breakfast.

As they sat down Cain asked, "Where is my brother?"

"He has gone after the flock," Eve said.

Cain muttered, and looked at Adam. "He cares nothing for your concerns, Abba." He looked at Eve. "He only thinks of himself."

She went to the door and looked out.

Cain saw her concern. "I don't know why you should let it bother you today any more than all the other days he's worried you." Cain scowled at his mother. Since the incident with the lion, she rarely let him out of her sight without fretting. "You've never worried over me like that," he heard himself say to her. Eve returned to the fire. She came behind her eldest and poured more tea into his bowl.

"That's because I have always been sure of where you were and exactly what you were doing," she said softly.

She hadn't whispered the words of the prophecy in his ear since Abel was attacked by the lion. These words were no consolation now.

"You are dependable, Cain. I can be sure you are attending to some sensible thing in the orchard or the vineyard," she said. The steam drifted up from the tea. "But him…" She watched the vapor dissipate and turn invisible before her eyes. "He is like a vapor sometimes, and I never know…"

I wish he were more so, Cain thought.

"You see to him first and last every day, fussing about this and that. 'Abel, lie down. Abel, drink this. Does that hurt? Let me see your wounds.'" His voice was singsong. "He doesn't even care that you worry so!"

A cold chill ran over Eve's shoulders. There was a tone in Cain's voice when he spoke those words that took her mind far away. It was an accusing tone; though all he said was true, the words sickened her.

Where It All Began

As the sun broke over the valley, Abel followed the river upstream towards the wilds beyond their valley, lands where he had never ventured before. He was following the path he had seen in his dreams. The headwaters were said to be within the Garden that God had planted for Adam in the beginning. Adam and Eve had been gone almost twenty years, leaving the garden untended. Judging by the way Cain meticulously fussed over the smallest details of his plantings, Abel wondered what he might find.

Abel climbed out of their valley onto the plateau. A single hawk followed him high above as if tracking his path. From time to time it cried out. Abel followed the riverbed, his feet often slipping into the wet, rich mud along its shore. The waters would take him back to the genesis.

By afternoon he had crossed the plateau and come to the gentle slope of terraced hills that flowed onto the Great Plain. Away in the distance, blue mountains with white caps of snow framed the horizon. Between those mountains and the place where he stood he would find the garden of Jehovah.

"Understand, son," Adam had said when Promise died. Perhaps his journey to where everything began would provide that knowledge.

Stretching out before him under the heat of the morning sun, the river looked like a murky leviathon moving steadily along. Its green and brown coils slithered across the plain to the mountains. In places it disappeared in dense green forest and reappeared again, with a few scales of glistening sunlight on its shimmering back. Abel rested where he was and ate some bread and curd. Then he went to the river and lay on his stomach to drink before going on. It took him until the afternoon to climb the terraced hills. The vegetation changed gradually from plains grass to more dense trees, the thick and verdant growth causing him eventually to keep right to the river's edge. He found himself often slipping in the yellow mud of the river to avoid cutting his way through the foliage. It was going to be a longer time than he first believed. Nevertheless, Abel knew there would be no going back until he had found what he was looking for.

The deepening undergrowth rose thicker and higher until it passed the height of his head and he was under the roof of trees and vines most of the time. The air was moist and fragrant with the smell of the river. Dragonflies and gnats swarmed around his head and stuck to his sweat in the heavy air. Strange foliage, unlike the kinds they cultivated or that grew wild in their valley, flourished everywhere. On several occasions, the trees grew right into the water, vines draping and catching Abel as he passed. Once or twice, their wet tendrils wrapped about his body. Their tiny burred ridges pulled at his clothes and hair, making them seem strangely alive, like the arms of lost persons clinging to him and begging him not to go on. Once Abel thought he heard the steps of someone, or something, heavy and stealthy, just beyond him in the undergrowth. His heart was pounding in his chest, not so much from the exertion of the journey and wrestling with the thick vines as from an eerie sense of being watched, Abel hurried on.

By late afternoon the sun was high, but in the woods where he walked the trees blocked out most of its light. Only in spots did shafts of light stream down to the center of the green river. The current flowed swiftly, but the water was not clear, as it was at the falls and beyond. It would be nightfall before long. Deeper and deeper he advanced into the forest. Occasional speckled patches of sun ceased and his breath echoed around him in the silence. The undergrowth spread down to the water and even grew over the surface, creating the illusion that a man could walk there. But if he put down a hand or stepped out on it he fell through the floating plant cover.

Abel forced himself onward. In places the path became so overgrown that the sun's light could not even speckle the forest floor. Low branches and impassable trees, gnarled roots and saw-edged grasses that sliced his skin as he passed, forced him down into the murky flowing water itself. The gentle brook had become a narrow deep channel. It was cold and dark and sometimes as deep as his chest. The swift current ran against him, forcing him to pull himself along on the rubbery slender branches of the trees overhead just to stay upright. At times he felt nameless *things* slide past his legs beneath the dark current.

Eventually, the river widened and the sky reappeared overhead. The sun hung low on the horizon as Abel emerged into a wide enclave. Strangely, as he climbed out of the water onto the riverbank, there were no sounds. There were no singing birds, buzzing insects, or other signs of animal life. The river turned around a sharp bend and, as he followed it, a new sight met him. Just ahead, less than a mile away, was a vast rectangular enclosure of high green vegetation that was obviously once cultivated by an ingenious hand. The vast hedge seemed to have no opening, and as the river moved toward the green wall it simply disappeared into it. The same river that watered their valley, gave life to Cain's fields, and watered Abel's flock began in this garden. Abel let out a low, long whistle.

"So this was home," he said softly. "Where it all began."

The hedge surrounding the long, straight plot had grown wild and appeared not to have been touched by human hands since Adam and Eve's expulsion. The ground between Abel and the Garden was wild, though not impassable. The current of the river flowed more gently and the water was warm. As he looked at himself in the evening light, Abel saw that he was covered with hundreds of paper-thin cuts and tiny scrapes, as well as mud and sludge. He decided to swim. Eyes on the mysterious enclave, Abel walked back into the pleasant current. He inhaled and dived beneath the water.

He swam a few hundred yards, happy to be in water that now seemed to be like any other peaceful river and the clear living water cleansing his body. Several species of fish frantically schooled away from the monster whose four limbs furled and unfurled as it cut a path upstream. Finally, when he had held his breath so long he thought his lungs would burst, he came to the surface in a splash of air and light. Excitement filled him. He floated and swam and eventually found he could dance along on the bottom, bobbing enough to keep his head above the water. As he approached the green wall, it was plain that the water he bathed in ran directly out from under the hedge surrounding the Garden.

As Abel surveyed the wall of green, he thought he saw something move from the corner of his eye, like an indistinct form or a flash of brilliant fire. But, when he turned, there was only the river, the hedge, and the landscape of green, silent except for the gentle murmur of running water. Abel took a deep breath and dove back under water, swimming just long enough to reach the shallows where he could easily walk.

He began to have the eerie sense of being watched again. It made him feel more secure to crouch and move, low, back into the tall grass along the bank, as he continued toward the hedge. He felt a distinct wariness of being out in the open or coming upon the enclave too boldly. He often stopped and looked around. He stooped lower and lower until he was creeping on his belly, the sticky river mud sucking and squishing where his arms and legs touched it. He felt as though his palms were glued to the mud. Abel came crawling to Eden. Every once in a while he stopped and sat up, head only visible above the grass, at the ancient Garden looming tall and wide before him.

At last he was within arm's reach. His heart beat faster as he reached toward the thick hedge. It was exactly as he had dreamed so many times. What lay just beyond? What mysteries would he find there? What knowledge would he gain? Was the Garden deserted now, or had someone else found it before him and settled down within its verdant borders?

As the tips of his fingers touched the shrubbery, the sound of a million fierce flapping wings and the thunder of a great and mighty hot wind overwhelmed him. It passed above and all around him in one movement. His very skin grew taut all over and his knees went weak. Something so huge, so raw, and so quick that it was impossible to catch with his eye went over him. Tree branches and tall grass lay flat in the presence of a great being.

For an instant Abel saw himself completely exposed. A wave of heat flashed before the mighty flying creature. It was so intense that, though momentary, it singed the hairs on his forearms and head and burned his skin. As quickly as it came it vanished, leaving his flesh scalded as red as if he had spent a day under the hot sun. Leaves and debris flew out of nowhere and ricocheted off the living wall of the Garden into his face and hair. Abel could barely see enough to escape as he scrambled away from the high hedge. Once back within the cover of the forest, Abel lay on his belly trembling with fright. Then he saw it. The most awesome, terrible, majestic apparition hovered just above the surface of the river at the spot where the water ran under the hedge.

A massive man-like creature with great wings and dual faces and eyes was casting its hot gaze all around, turning this way and that, all the while hovering just above the ground. The mighty being lingered, floating with energy, and it seemed to Abel that golden liquid was coursing over its mighty chest. The liquid flowed down the length of its man-like limbs to its feet and hands. With the same rushing sound of wings and whirlwind, as quickly as it had appeared it flew along the long terrace wall and around the end of it.

Following in the wake of the being came another strange sight. Great flashes of fire burst in the air at what appeared to have once been the very entrance to the Garden. A flaming sword, suspended in midair, turned as if it contained a life of its own. It moved in every direction, as if it contained the vigilance of a troop of watchmen. Its flames—blue, emerald, and red, all mixed with gold—appeared to burn, yet the mighty blade was not consumed.

The breath went out of Abel. Trembling uncontrollably, he slowly backed away, realizing that that the Garden was closed forever. His eyes on the hedge, he ran backwards until he was lost in the thick undergrowth again. Abel dove into the river, and, with the current at his back, fled for home.

Passing back through the thick dark jungle was terrifying. He bit into his own lip to keep himself from crying out many times, imagined or real terrors were all about him. It was well past midnight when Abel reached the falls.

Abel slept until evening the next day.

"Exiled from the Garden"

"We began work on the altar," Adam said, reviewing the sketch on the table during supper. "Since you are feeling better, we can use your help tomorrow to finish it."

Eve looked unhappy about it, but Cain grinned his thin-lipped smile.

"I'll dress those fresh cuts with oil first," Eve said.

Abel winced from time to time as she applied wet medicine to his arms and face. Cain moved away from the scene. He retreated to the shadows, his face out of the light and heat of the fire. He folded his arms and sat down with his back against the wall. After a while, Abel ventured to ask about the things he had longed to learn about the Garden.

"Abba?" he said.

"Speak, son," Adam said.

"Why were we kicked out of the Garden?"

Adam's eyes flashed as his gaze flew to Eve's face. He distinctly heard her curiosity in Abel's tone.

Eve's neck flushed hot. She avoided Adam's accusing glare and he knew it. Her face focused on the wool she was spinning; her fingers flew furiously in and out of the tufted strands.

"Why is there such enmity between us and the serpent?" Abel did not look at his father.

Adam had no choice but to answer his son. He saw a relieved look come over his wife as he began.

"The serpent is jealous. Jealous of Jehovah, and jealous of any man who serves Him."

The room was completely still.

"He desired to usurp the very One who gave him life."

Abel sat up, interested.

Cain's noticed Abel's intensity and frowned. "What is he up to?" Cain wondered. "He never cared about Abba's stories before!"

"Lucifer," Adam continued, "was called Shining One, and he was once a beautiful creature who was given great power and knowledge. He was created to be very close to the Most High. He ultimately led a war against Jehovah, seeking the throne for himself."

Abel immediately thought of the powerful being who guarded the entrance to Eden. "Was there a war fought with weapons and armies?"

"Yes," Adam replied.

But Abel was remembering the being at the hedge. There must be many more like it. Abel looked around the room wondering if creatures like the one at the Garden could make themselves invisible. He shivered. "How has the serpent's jealousy been the cause of our troubles?"

Eve caught Adam's eyes. She went back to spinning her wool.

"It was me," Eve said suddenly. "I listened to him." She stopped spinning. "And Abba listened to me."

Cain sucked in his breath. He had seen the wistful sadness in Adam's eyes a thousand times and known he was thinking of the past. This terrible knowledge was the reason.

"How could you let him use you, Eemah?" Cain blurted. He had been silent until now. They all turned and looked into the shadow where he sat.

"Jealousy is deceptive, Cain. It is the very nature of the serpent himself," Eve replied. "It strikes the heart with poison. Jealousy is his kiss. It starts a shiver, a silent bell tolling in the mind, a quiet alert that you are being left out when someone else is blessed." She shook her head and returned to her work. "I wish I had discerned it. Things would be very different now."

"Is there no undoing Eemah's mistake?" Abel asked.

Eve smiled, not looking up from her work. "You will undo it," she said. She worked again. "My seed will crush his head."

Cain nearly jumped into the center of the room. "You mean me, Eemah. *I* will crush his head!"

Eemah was startled by his sudden movement. "Goodness, Cain. What's come over you?"

Adam laughed out loud, and Cain, embarrassed, went bright red in the face, his heart beating rapidly in his chest.

"But I thought you said Jehovah sacrificed once to save you and Eemah when you should have died. So why can't we go back to the Garden?" Abel shuddered as his words left his tongue.

Cain spun around. "When did Abba tell him that?"

"Why is there a flaming sword that guards the entrance, preventing anyone from ever returning?" Abel asked before he caught himself.

Cain went white. His eyes narrowed and he rubbed a hand over his brow. "This crafty brother of mine is hiding more than one secret!" he thought.

The hair stood on the back of Adam's neck. He was too stunned to speak, but Abel knew he had crossed the line into difficult territory. Seeing the expression in Abel's eyes, Eve realized what all his questions meant. A sinking feeling overwhelmed her. But Cain's present state was a concern as well. He looked as if he might fall down at any moment.

"Cain," Eemah said softly. "Are you all right? Come here and let me see if you have started a fever."

Cain shook his head furiously. "I'm fine," he insisted.

"Where did you hear of this, Abel?" Adam looked at him soberly.

The room fell silent. All eyes went to the youngest son. Abel's face flushed hot. He glanced at Eve.

"I—I dreamed it once," he lied. He suddenly stretched, yawned a massive yawn and excused himself. "Well!" he said, and rose. "I guess if we are going to get an early start on that altar I better get some rest."

Building the Altar

The three men started early. Abel and Adam worked at the digging, and Cain carried boulders from the pile where they had heaped the rocks they dug out of the earth as they farmed. One by one, he hauled the stones to the altar site and heaved them to the ground. Each time, before he turned back to the pile of stones, he studied his father and brother working together, bending over their spades, talking, sometimes laughing, without him. Perhaps, he thought, they were laughing at him and talking about things Cain would never know.

"If my brother had been where he should have been yesterday, he, not I, would be hauling these stones. And I would be working there with Abba," Cain muttered resentfully. His anger drove him to finish his separate work quickly before Abel horned in on Abba's favor even more.

Once, after he had just let down one of the heavy stones, Cain studied his father's face, wet with sweat from the hot work. Adam looked serene, his face filled with hope in a way that Cain had never seen before.

Cain whistled to get Adam's attention. "It's a great day, Abba!" he called. Looking up, Adam smiled and straightened his back for a moment, briefly resting his arm on the handle of his spade.

Adam waved and bent to work. His form accented by the force of his breath as he drove the blade into the earth and lifted a heavy scoop of red clay into the cart they were filling. The altar site so far was just a growing mound of upturned earth.

Adam and Abel bent over their spades. Sweat glistened on their skin as they troweled up earth for the foundation for the great stones carried by Cain which in turn would form the table of the altar.

When Cain had hauled the last of the boulders, he paused for a drink. As he leaned his head back to pour the water from the waterskin into his thirsty mouth, he was momentarily blinded by the sun. Suddenly, Bikkuwr darted from out of nowhere. The lamb had grown rapidly, and its head was higher than Abel's knees by now. It knocked against Cain as it skidded to a halt, and almost took the startled man down by the ankles.

Cain choked, the water spewing from his mouth. "Get away from me!" He kicked at the lamb, catching it under the ribs with a swift foot. Abel dropped his shovel and came running.

Eyeing Cain furiously, but unwilling to start a fight with his already agitated brother in front of Adam, Abel led the lamb away.

"Come on, Bikkuwr." Abel looked back over his shoulder at angry Cain.

<hr />

By noon the altar was half-finished. Cain had brought over the many stones needed for the top, and the three of them were laying them one-by-one into the sides of the altar. Afterwards, they packed earth around them to keep them in place and make the altar permanent.

Eve brought lunch and made light conversation about the weather and the various projects she was working on. She fussed over the three men, filling and refilling their cups to be sure they had plenty to drink.

Abel thought that she didn't seem herself—she was nervous, perhaps.

"What will you bring Jehovah?" Cain asked Abel as he lay back in the grass, the sun high, and birds happily flitting here and there. A hawk screamed in the distance. Not receiving an answer, Cain turned on his side and propped his head on one elbow. "What have you prepared, little brother?" Cain asked again.

Abel's offering was none of Cain's concern. He finished his drink and set his cup down. "Thank you, Eemah," he said as he rose to his feet.

Cain sniffed. "It's a simple question!" he called after Abel. Cain lay back down contentedly and grinned.

A short ways away Abel heaved great scoops of earth onto the sides of the mound, beating them into the crevices between the stones with the back of his spade.

Adam watched him without speaking. He let Abel work while he and Cain rested, allowing their meal to settle in their stomachs.

They worked through the afternoon. All the while Bikkuwr gamboled about, often under their feet, getting in the way as they went to and fro. Occasionally, Cain kicked impatiently at it to get it out of his way.

Cain continued prodding his brother. "What are you going to offer?" As he spoke, he watched the lamb that followed Abel everywhere, like a shadow attached to his heels.

Abel stopped and stood upright. "I hadn't thought of it," he finally confessed.

"That's like you," Cain said as he put his shoulder against a boulder and struggled to move it onto the developing altar. Cain groaned as he pushed the boulder. When Abel also threw his weight into the task the huge flat rock budged and moved into place. "You only have a short time left to dream something up."

"Baah!" The lamb bounded suddenly between the two young men, its hooves dancing about on the granite slab. Abel quickly picked Bikkuwr up, nuzzling its woolly face.

"You are always underfoot!"

Cain eyed his brother and the lamb. "The perfect sacrifice," he said. "Isn't that right, Abba?" Cain directed his words at Adam.

Adam's head appeared from the opposite side of the altar, where he was carefully shoring up the foundation with dry mud. He continued packing the mud by hand into the largest gaps between the rocks.

"What is it?" Adam asked, not having heard Cain's question.

"Abel is still deciding on an offering for Jehovah," Cain said. "What would please Him?"

Adam lifted a mud-covered hand distractedly, his eyes still on his work. "Firstfruits," he said and disappeared again.

"You see?" Cain smiled.

Abel shut out the sound of Cain's voice.

By nightfall the altar had taken the form of the drawing on the table. Once Adam was satisfied, they all stepped back to survey what they had built.

"Well, Abba?" Abel asked. "What do you think?"

Adam took a drink from the waterskin they carried with them. He wiped the back of his hand across his wet mouth. "It is finished!" he announced firmly. He looked heavenwards once—almost cautiously. "May Jehovah be pleased."

"Amen!" Cain said heartily.

They stopped to wash in the river. The cool of it braced their sore necks and shoulders and cleansed their mud-crusted hands. As they continued on their way home, Abel stopped at the sheepfold. Cain strode on, eager for supper, while Abel meticulously inspected Bikkuwr for burrs or ticks or other things the lamb might have picked up as it gamboled about the fields that day. When he was satisfied Abel lifted the lamb over the rails into the pen where it joined some twenty other sheep huddled together there.

"Tonight you stay in the fold with the others," he said. The sheep looked up at the sound of the shepherd's voice.

"Baah!" the lamb replied.

The Day of Sacrifice

The sun rose white and hot on the day of the sacrifice. Adam longed for reunion with Jehovah. He inhaled deeply as he cast his eyes upward.

"May He hear us!"

The ache of longing to restore that first fellowship, to walk and talk with Him as a friend, to have the abiding manifest presence once again—Adam's emotions were too great for words. His deepest desire was that his sons might know Jehovah, too.

Adam shielded his eyes as he stepped out of the cover of forest immediately surrounding the house. Locusts, whose chorus of chirrups usually waited for the afternoon heat, trilled in a crescendo of sound all around him. In the distance, he saw Cain already making his preparations to worship. The bulky sun-darkened form of the muscular young man was bent beneath the weight of a high bundle of premium wheat as he marched toward the river. Adam smiled. His firstborn was everything a man could ask for in a son. The new altar stood at the top of the rise that ran like a spine down the center of Abel's field. As usual, Abel himself was nowhere to be seen.

Adam shouldered the vessels of flour and oil Eve had set aside. He lifted the handle of the firepan full of burning coals. Its smoke gently wafted on the morning air, carrying a comforting scent of the hearth. The coals would be nursed while they made everything ready, and then be used to ignite the fire beneath the sacrifice.

Adam followed Cain across the river. When he came up the rise he found the altar had already been neatly laid with firewood. Heaped on the wood were the abundant firstfruits of Cain's labor: every kind of produce from orchard and vine, the flowering plants and the grafts he had developed, fine grain and wheat from the fields.

Cain was just coming down the rise and expectantly met the eyes of his proud father.

"You do well, Cain!"

Cain turned around and crossed his thick arms over his chest in happy assurance. Excitement, mixed with strange curiosity from the stories Adam had finally been persuaded to tell of the terrible power Jehovah wielded, rushed through Cain's heart. He longed to see a display of the strength of the invisible God known to his father. Today God would approve of Cain for his faithfulness and great skill. And today, at last, his brother would learn an important lesson. Cain's offering covered the western side of the table, the side nearest his fields.

Opposite from his firstfruits, the altar was bare except for the firewood, waiting for whatever Abel found to bring. Eve's words—*"you shall crush his head"*—sounded in Cain's ear.

"Where is Abel?" Adam asked.

The smile faded from Cain's mouth. "Am I my brother's keeper?" Cain turned from the altar. "I'll wager Abel is off in the wilds, having forgotten all about this important day!"

Behind them Eemah was making her way through the field. She reached the altar and surveyed Cain's handiwork. Her eyes shone softly. Eve smiled.

Abel Offers His Firstfruits

Just then Abel appeared from beyond the rise. Cain could see him from where he stood. Face set like a flint, Abel marched toward the altar. Cain smiled his thin, cold smile. For there on his brother's shoulders was the lamb, Bikkuwr, Abel's firstfruits, its legs bound front and back.

Eve covered her mouth. She looked at Adam with pleading eyes and turned away, not wanting to see what would happen next.

"Here you are at last, little brother," Cain remarked as Abel came up.

The boy's knuckles were white and trembling where he held onto the legs of the lamb. "Here Abba"—Abel's voice cracked as if strained under the weight of the world—"are my firstfruits, as you have commanded." Abel looked at Cain's magnificently spread gift and at his own side of the altar, empty but for the stacked firewood. His single gift seemed insignificant by comparison.

Cain held his strong chin up proudly.

"All I have to offer is this lamb," Abel said humbly. His grief and sorrow were so painfully apparent that Eve hid her face from him. This one precious lamb, the only prize he possessed, was being handed over to death.

Adam put his hand on his youngest son. "Jehovah has provided a lamb. May He be pleased to accept it as sweet-smelling incense."

Abel trembled, restraining the sobs threatening his throat. He laid Bikkuwr on the altar and bound it to the tree. Bikkuwr's anxious eyes rolled up, searching the face of the shepherd. One final prayerful cry for deliverance rose from the lamb's mouth.

"Forgive me, Bikkuwr!" Abel whispered, the words full of sorrow. "You don't deserve this. You are innocent!" As his family all looked on, Abel pulled the knife from his belt and raised his arm over the sacrifice. Great tears fell from Abel's eyes.

But Adam was steadfast. He had disobeyed once and they had suffered because of it. *"Firstfruits,"* Jehovah had said. Adam nodded for Abel to go on.

Abel's heart beat against the walls of his chest like the drum of a madman, its deafening thump-thump overcoming even the sounds of his own weeping. His eyes tightly shut, Abel brought the blade down with all his might, determined that one stroke would do it once and for all. The razor edge slashed against Bikkuwr's throat. The blood of the lamb came pouring down over the tree and the altar.

The shepherd groaned. The blade fell from his trembling hand. He could not watch as the lamb died, his precious Bikkuwr, its life forever offered up, tied to the tree and freshly slain. As blood ran over the edge of the altar and down between the stones until covered the earth below, Abel turned from the sacrifice and rushed into his father's embrace.

Adam drew both sons to his side, trembling Abel and proud Cain. Together with his wife they presented themselves at the east end of the altar in front of their gifts. Adam lifted in his hands to heaven and prayed.

"Great Jehovah! Creator of heaven and earth, You alone are righteous. Hear our prayer! Receive these gifts and us with them. You who dwell in the dark cloud, be pleased to dwell with us. We have built You an altar and offered these firstfruits. Let Your eyes be open to the place of this sacrifice and Your ears open to our prayer. Do not turn Your face away from the work of Your hands. Remember Your mercy which endures forever. We offer the fruit of our labor and ourselves as Your servants!"

Then Adam held the handle of the firepan out to Cain.

"Put fire to the sacrifice," he told him.

Cain gladly took the handle in his hand. He had waited long enough and the interminable drama of Abel's sacrifice had tried the last of his patience. But as Cain took a step toward the altar, the sky turned black.

A great crack of lightening streaked out of the eastern sky. It crashed, a pointed finger touching earth, over the waterfall in the distance. The hair stood up on the back of Cain's neck. Thunder rolled all around them.

Abel felt the presence of life and death together in the air, just as he had when he had touched the wall of Eden. He looked at his father. Adam felt the presence, too. Eve cowered in the shadow of her husband, her hair over her face. Wind whipped around them and lifted their garments away from their bodies.

"Abba! Look!" Cain exclaimed. He dropped the firepan and pointed to the sky over the altar.

A wide shining stream of brilliant liquid fire came pouring out of the sky. The sound of its burning was like the sound of a rushing mighty wind. It pooled in living tongues above the altar over the sacrifice. Then, suddenly, it fell down upon the lamb. The fire licked up its flesh and head and entrails. Heat and smoke exploded and in seconds the sacrifice was completely consumed.

The first family fell on their faces. Smoke from the sacrifice rose thick and high. They remained on the ground while the fire raged. Then the column of molten liquid receded, disappearing into heaven exactly as it had come down. Adam and his family got up off their faces and stood watching it go.

When the rolling smoke had finally cleared, they saw that not all of the offering had been consumed by the living heavenly flame. To the chagrin of Adam's eldest son, only Abel's sacrifice had been received. The firstfruits offered by Cain lay untouched, cold, neatly arranged just as he had placed them.

Cain sucked in his breath. He blinked and opened his eyes again, thinking the storm had played some trick on his mind. But his sacrifice still lay there, rejected by Jehovah! Stars passed before his eyes. Cain felt his knees buckle and forced himself to stand tall. Aghast, he looked at Adam.

"What does it mean?" he cried. His face was contorted in disbelief. Humiliation and offense flooded his being. He thought of Eemah's promise. "Eemah?" Cain looked at his brother. "What did you ever do to deserve this?" Cain hissed. Then he turned on Adam. "You betrayed me! After all I've done! Why?" The sound of Cain's angry protest echoed over their valley.

But Adam did not answer. He remembered the coverings, Jehovah's gift, slain in Eden to save them, and he understood fully. He would explain it all to Cain later.

Jehovah Has Heard Us

"He has heard us!" Adam shouted. He grasped Eve. "His eye is on us!" Adam ran to Abel. He took hold of the boy by both arms. "Jehovah received the lamb!"

Abel saw the joy on Adam's face, but he didn't understand what he had seen on the altar any more than Cain did.

"You are worthy of all worship!" Adam threw his hands into the air, arms wide, back bowed, until it looked as if he would topple over. "Great Jehovah be praised!"

He embraced his wife again and danced around with her. "He has heard our prayer!" His words became a song of thanksgiving. Adam grabbed the sides of Cain's ashen face. "He has received us back!"

Cain and Abel only stood there, stricken dumb by the sight of the lamb consumed by the column of heaven's fire. Eve came and put an arm around Abel's waist.

"Bikkuwr," she whispered, "the lamb that was slain!" She looked at her youngest. "It was acceptable, Abel. Jehovah has received the lamb as a peace offering!" Eve hugged him tight. Tears of joy and gratitude rolled down her cheeks. *"The promise shall be fulfilled at last."*

As the words came from Eve's mouth, Cain's countenance fell. He stormed away in silence.

Heavy rain began to fall, instantly transforming the unburned offering into a soggy heap. The other three ran for shelter. Rain pelted them like millions of tiny stinging darts. Adam and his wife and son held their arms over their heads and bent down under the driving storm until they crossed the river and took cover in their dwelling.

Outside, the storm continued to rage. Inside, the awe of what they had witnessed settled on them. A weighty silence lay like a garment on each of them. Wonder mixed with fear and inexplicable relief produced no sure words for what they had seen.

Eemah prepared supper in methodical, quiet movements. Adam sat staring into the fire, his hand over his mouth and an elbow resting on his knee. Abel went straight to his room, and Cain sat on the floor in his usual place in the shadows against the wall.

"He accepted the lamb," Adam said over and over again.

"Come to supper," Eemah told them at last. She placed their food on the table. "Abel! Come to supper."

He appeared in the doorway.

"Why did He want Bikkuwr?" Abel asked. "Why was Bikkuwr accepted and Cain's produce rejected?"

Cain put his face down into his bowl and ate, tasting nothing. "Why indeed?" he thought. "Bushels of my best wheat, the stores of produce Eemah so carefully laid aside, all the attention I put into them, and an entire year of tedious labor rejected as a dry leaf in the winter wind."

While Cain talked to himself, Adam spoke.

"It is His salvation," Adam replied. "The life is in the blood. Don't you see? Jehovah received the lamb's life for ours."

"He has forgiven what happened in the Garden?" Abel asked. "Does that mean we can go back now?"

Adam looked at Abel. "There's no going back, only forward, son."

Cain looked up. The sound of Abel's voice stirred Cain and gripped his gut, but he didn't hear the words because of the loud thoughts raging in his mind.

"What, Abba?" he asked. "Did you say something to me?"

"I told Abel there is no going back."

Cain scowled across the table. It was settled, then. The right of b'kowr was forfeited to his little brother.

"Lost?" Cain thought, as he stared at him. Unconsciously Cain shoveled food into his mouth and swallowed it without chewing. "I will not rest until I have gotten back what is rightfully mine."

Cain did not sleep at all that night. His mind revisited the scenes of Abel offering the sacrificial lamb, Bikkuwr bound on the altar with its lifeblood flowing over the stones, the tears running down Abel's sick, white face, and the fire descending from heaven. It was a strange living fire, flaring up twice as high as a man. It pooled like liquid gold and fell upon Bikkuwr the moment Abel backed away.

Crouching at the Door

After what seemed an interminable length of time, a cold, irrevocable sweat of frustration finally forced Cain to sit up trembling. His burning eyes ached in their sockets. He finally fell asleep leaning against the wall. The last thing Cain saw before he slept was the dim outline of his younger brother sleeping peacefully across from him. Cain's own sleep was full of voices, fighting, and struggle. Just before dawn he heard what sounded like thunder and a crack of lightning in his mind. A man spoke out of the cloud.

"Cain!" A voice that seemed to come from above the roof of the house echoed throughout his being. "Sin crouches at the door. It desires to have you. Rule over it, Cain!"

He awoke wondering who was standing over him, not speaking softly as Eemah always had, but with loud words of warning. But he saw no one. As he arose, his head throbbed, his throat felt parched and burnt, and his skin felt feverish. Cain stood for a moment in the darkness over Abel, his eyes adjusting to the lack of light. His muscles tensed as he watched his vulnerable sibling sleep.

"That lamb was my idea," his whisper rasped. His fingers drummed slowly against his thigh. "You even used that to your advantage!" Cain turned from the bedside.

As Cain went out the door of the house, the words of his dream came back.

"Sin crouches at the door!"

Standing on the threshold, Cain looked around. "Sin indeed!"

Cain suddenly saw pitiful images of himself as a halfwit stumbling about, his clothing bedraggled and hanging from his body, spittle running down his chin, his hair wild and unkempt like Abel's. Abel was leading Cain by an arm as Cain played with shadows in the air. In the vision, Abel sat Cain obediently down, and then broke off bits of bread and put them into his brother's drooping mouth.

Cain fiercely rubbed his hands over his tired face, erasing the images.

"Am I losing my mind because of Abel?" he huffed. He stalked off into the forest, seeking solace in the thickest part of the grove. It was near the spot where he had once decided he would build a separate dwelling of his own to get away from the stink of Abel's lamb.

"At least there will be no more of that smell in the house!" Cain walked by the place where he had cut timber once with Abel.

Spiny, long fingers of sunrise shot between the trunks of the trees and shone along the misted ground, cutting yellow swaths over the thick calves of Cain's legs. Cain pulled his axe from his belt and began to wield it in heavy blows, hacking down limbs and biting into the bark of the trees around him. His mind was full of tormenting. It was a long time before he was winded and beads of sweat finally broke across his brow in release. He stopped, put the axe back in his belt, and sat down against the thick trunk of the tree.

Birds flitted through the underbrush, darting, chirping short trills of discussion and morning song between them. Cain did not notice that a serpent, wrapped in a chameleon's iridescent scales, was lying languid on the branch above. Its heavily looped coils silently waited. The head of the serpent, wide with a chiseled mouth, lay hidden in the shaded part of the grove. The serpent adjusted itself slightly and peered down on the eldest son of Adam, the *b'kowr* of the woman's seed.

Cain felt the heavy, dull pull of the sleep he had missed. Like a man with a millstone about his neck who had been cast into the sea, Cain's mind began to sink. Just before slumber overtook him, he heard the voice from his dream again. But this time it was not thunderous. This time it was only a voice, simple, no different than his own.

"Sin crouches at the door," the voice repeated. "Rule over it!" Cain wondered what it meant. He let out a deep sigh. His eyelids felt as heavy as the pressing weight on his heart. In a moment, gruff snoring gurgled up out of his broad chest.

"Cain!" Abel's distant voice fell on his ears. Eyes still closed, Cain sensed a shadow crossing his brow.

"Cain!" Abel called again. "Where are you?" At Eemah's insistence, Abel was searching the orchard for his troubled brother.

This time Cain woke up. Abel's footsteps came through the trees. At first Cain recoiled, thinking he would hide and avoid Abel's presence. But as the steps came closer, the anger of yesterday and the humiliating frustration of the past several days made him decide otherwise.

"I'll settle this fully before another hour passes," he promised himself.

"Here!" Cain called, forcing the sound of his voice to be welcoming. "I am here."

Abel found him at the site of a previous misunderstanding between them.

"Eemah was asking for you. I told her I would seek you out." Abel held out an earthen vessel of goat's milk and fresh bread from the hearth. "She sent you some food."

Cain accepted the offering but neither ate nor drank. He considered the words to express the hard feelings he now had for Abel.

Abel eyed the unused wood they had recently cut and the new mound of limbs that bled tiny crystal buds of sap from the open wounds where they had just been hewn. "There's no reason to move out of the house now."

Cain knew Abel was referring to Bikkuwr. He blew an insolent quick breath from his nostrils and smiled a thin cold smile at the remark. The irony of being pushed out by a lamb and then replaced by his sibling when the lamb died was more than he could fathom. He saw it all again. His own offering rejected while Jehovah manifested Himself in the firstfruits of Abel's flock. The injustice done to him rose in Cain's throat like black bile.

Abel sat beside him. After a few moments of edgy silence, he offered some words. "Have I offended you?"

Cain turned dark eyes upon him. In his look were a thousand blades, sharpened by envy and rage. Accusation shot from the very pores of Cain's countenance. His hands were clenched and the muscles in his neck thickened.

Unseen overhead, the constricted serpent waited.

"Offended, you say?" Cain muttered.

The tone of his voice sent a cold chill down Abel's spine. Abel stood up. "Where are you going?" Cain demanded. He also made a move to rise. "You're always slipping out to avoid every situation that makes you feel uncomfortable, still avoiding your responsibilities like a child. What are you really hiding from us all?"

Abel just put up his hands, realizing that an attempt to argue was useless with Cain's state of mind.

"Jehovah rejected my gift because of you!" Cain's face was unrecognizable, even to Abel, who had seen his darker side. "What do you have to say for yourself?" His eyes held Abel in their gaze. Those steely eyes had a cold light in them. Cain's lips were thinner and seemed more like a gray ashen line than a mouth.

Abel just ducked his head and took two steps back. "Never mind," he said tentatively. "Perhaps we can talk about it later." Abel turned to go.

Cain lunged. "We'll talk now!" He grabbed Abel by the back of his shirt.

But Abel had had enough. With one arm he threw off his brother's advance.

Cain fell back, almost losing his feet.

Abel kept walking, never even turning around.

Cain's lip curled in an angry snarl.

"Never mind?" he roared. "Is that all you have to say? Never mind?"

The sight of Abel turning his back to him as he simply walked away sent him into a fit of jealous rage. Cain sprang like a lion from his crouched position. A scream that sounded eerily like the wail of the lion that had killed Promise filled the forest. Cain's huge, strong hands clutched Abel's slender neck.

"No, little brother!" Cain said through clenched teeth. "You never mind! Never mind that you have been trying to steal my blessing from the day you came out of Eemah's belly! Never mind that you think to usurp me and become *b'kowr!*"

Abel was choking and unable to respond. His head felt as if it were swelling while his blood filled his veins under Cain's stranglehold.

"Never mind that that sacrifice of yours was my idea and now Abba thinks Jehovah has changed His mind about me and the promise He gave to Eemah!"

Cain fell on top of his brother. The whole world around him, earth, grass, sky, trees, their flesh and clothes, had all gone crimson. A river of raging passion swept up Cain; its rapid, unforgiving current dragging Abel in its flow.

Abel's head sounded a hard whack upon the earth as Cain came down on top of him. For a moment, Abel saw stars, and the pain was so great it seemed it would blow his ears right off the sides of his head. What he saw next was the black, jagged surface of a large stone, its rough granite surface dusted with tiny flecks of diamond light that caught the sun as Cain rose it high behind his shoulder.

Then down it came, flying toward Abel's face in a direct, unwavering arc. The thick, round ends of Cain's fingers gripped the great rock like five fat, brown knobs.

After long moments, the rhythmic sound of stone hitting smashed wet flesh crept into Cain's consciousness. He surfaced out of the red pool of anger like a swimmer coming up for air. When he broke back into the light of reason, Cain froze.

Sprawled beneath him was his brother. Abel's face and head were hardly recognizable. Cain turned his head sharply to see that his arm, like the handle of a smith's hammer, was still poised, ready to strike again. A bloody stone still was clutched in Cain's hand.

"Aagh!" Eyes wide, he grimaced, and the weapon fell from his open hand to the earth with a dull thud. Cain looked back at Abel's face. "Aaagh!" Cain scrambled backward off of the twisted body and slumped on all fours, breathing fast.

The warm, sickly, metallic smell of blood filled the air. Cain looked down at himself. His brother's blood covered his chest and hands and was smeared over the tops of his hairy knees where they had pinned Abel's shoulders to the ground.

"Aaagh!" Cain jumped to his feet, staring at the front of his own body, arms raised at his sides to keep from touching the blood that covered him. Cain looked back at the body.

"Abel?" he said in a soft questioning voice. He took a step forward. "Abel!"

Overhead the hawk that constantly circled the valley looked down and screamed. Its shadow passed over the corpse. The snake, still unseen, slithered back up the tree.

Summary

Cain "saw" that his offering was rejected and Abel's accepted. Cain's "countenance fell." Another spirit, or a literal change of nature, can take over when jealousy is aroused.

Know that when jealousy strikes, evil spirits are waiting to get involved. A spirit enters the jealous soul and brings a change in personality. Some indications that this has taken place are violent anger and obsessive accusations. An anxious spirit agitates and oppresses the jealous party. Every possible evil sweeps in to fill the void created, as communication breaks down and bonds of affection or respect are dissolved. Jealousy has begun to rage out of control. Nothing is too sacred to forestall it and no gift will satisfy its ire. Murder, by word or deed, lies at the door.

Heir

For three things the earth is perturbed, yes, four it cannot bear up: For a servant when he reigns, a fool when he is filled with food, a hateful woman when she is married, and a maidservant who succeeds her mistress.

—Proverbs 30:21-23, NKJV

Sarai settled back onto the bed of fresh straw newly strewn for her by Dinah. The familiar musky, metallic smell hung like a blanket in the thick air of the red tent. It had been ten years since they had come up from Egypt. One hundred and twenty weeks in this tent and still no heir.

Dinah gathered the used straw in a torn shawl and carried it out of the tent. Bright light shone in around the edges of the tent flap as the bent servant exited. In a moment she returned, shaking the water from her freshly washed hands. She approached the place where Sarai was resting.

Sarai took hold of one of Dinah's gnarled hands and pulled the woman towards her.

"Stay and sit with me a while, Dinah. Tell me the old stories again of when I was but a child...before Haran...before Egypt...before Canaan." Her voice sounded far away, dreamy, pining for her youth...and perhaps searching for a different beginning—one without this judgment against her body. A beginning that was fruitful, that allowed her the simple luxury of being like other women.

"All right, mistress," the old woman replied. She went to the corner of the tent and retrieved a large basket of uncombed wool and a half-wound spindle. She brought the work back to Sarai's side and folded her long, still limber legs across themselves as she lowered herself on the rug beside Sarai's bed. The hands of both women went automatically to work, carding, pulling, and spinning.

"Tell me of Terah and my mother from the first days as you remember, when she was so beautiful," Sarai begged.

"Their wedding was the grandest anywhere." Dinah's eyes sparkled. "She was a gift to your father when Bilhah ceased to bear." Dinah shook her head as she worked the wool. "The last child was difficult. They both nearly died."

"And my mother came to Terah," Sarai added softly.

"It was allowed with consent, then as now. And you were born within the year," Dinah said. The soft folds of the tired, thin skin beneath her chin went in and out like the pleats on a hand organ while she talked.

"Tirzah's girl," Sarai said.

"A companion for your brother," Dinah insisted. "From the very beginning you were Jehovah's gift."

Sarai and Abram worshiped the one true God: the invisible God, Jehovah. Their religion originated with Jehovah Himself when He made coverings for Adam and Eve as they were sent out of Eden. Abram's family had learned the blood sacrifice from their patriarchs. They were descendants of Noah through righteous Shem. Faith had saved Noah's family in the deluge.

But one of Noah's own sons had turned his back. The descendants of Canaan, following their father's apostasy, invented false gods and were banished. They had settled far from Ur, to the south of Haran. Their tribes were the inhabitants of the land where Abram and Sarai now sojourned. Abram had been nineteen and Sarai nine when Noah succumbed. Sarai barely remembered him. The patriarch was almost one thousand years old!

Abram's religion had become all the more resolute after Melchizedek, the mysterious king of Jeru-Salem, paid homage to Abram after he had rescued Lot from the kings of Canaan. It was then that Jehovah had spoken to him outside his tent and promised him heirs in numbers as the stars and sand. Jehovah had blessed Abram. His great wealth was the envy of all of Canaan. In addition to his flocks and herds, he had many servants and bondmen and much gold and silver. Even the Pharaoh of Egypt had been impressed, although he added to Abram's wealth according to the code when it was discovered Sarai was his wife as well as his sister!

"Terah loved your mother as a first, free wife," Dinah was saying.

Sarai recalled her father, Terah, a thinker and excellent herdsman. He was always protective of his household but also adventurous, a worshiper of Jehovah like her husband.

"And my mistress's beauty was legendary." The older woman paused with a twinkle in her eye. "Not unlike your own!"

Sarai sighed. "My beauty has been a blessing and a curse, I think. It is not the only trait my mother handed down to me."

"Shhh!" Dinah wagged her finger vigorously. "Don't say such things, lest it become more true than it is already!"

Sarai laughed at her.

"We are neither of us so young anymore, you and I. You shall surely outlive me, as you outlived her!"

"You should give me a child to care for first!" Dinah said, looking straight at the long spinning length of wool wrapping itself into a tight cord and turning around the flying spindle.

They sat for a moment.

"And what of Abram, then?" Sarai asked, as she always did. "Tall and straight and intelligent even before he was of reckoning age?"

"Yes. The patriarch's pride, for sure."

"And a master herdsman from his youth," Sarai said.

"And a stealthy hunter!" Dinah added.

"And handsome as a gazelle in the morning mists!" Sarai said.

"And brave as a lion!" Dinah replied.

They kept it up until they were both laughing foolishly. Sarai lay down on her side. In a moment her face returned to the serious expression that revealed the truth in her heart.

"I hate this tent, Dinah," she said. "It's as empty for me as my body."

Dinah's tongue clung to the roof of her mouth. Suffering through the long barren years of the only daughter of her first mistress was as painful as it had been to watch Sarai's mother suffer miscarriage after miscarriage. Dinah had spent years in the red tent, a silent companion searching for consolation to offer first mother and now daughter. But at least Sarai's mother had conceived. Her daughter suffered only shame. And time was running out.

"Your mother never ceased to hope," Dinah said. She looked at Sarai. "And pray." The old woman coughed. "Mistress," she ventured.

"Yes?"

"May I speak?"

"As if I am going to stop your mouth, Dinah, when something is on your mind. What is it?"

"It has been too long, and Abram is patient but already his head is filled with the sayings of his God. That his descendants will be…" Sarai cut Dinah off before she finished.

"…numerous as the stars. And like grains of sand on the seashore," Sarai snapped. "What is your point?"

Now the old woman spoke out of the confidence she had as the one nearest to the elder matriarch.

"But will these heirs come from you or will all this"—she threw up a hand, indicating the riches of Abram's sprawling household, then quickly caught her spinning again without missing a beat—"go to another?"

"And what else is on your mind?" Sarai asked tersely.

"The code allows him to send you away with no more than your dowry if you cannot give him his heir," Dinah stated.

Sarai laughed out loud, deep and melodious. But the sound of sadness was in her tone no matter how she appeared.

"I have no father's house to go back to," she said, "since our father is one and the same, and dead as well!" Sarai bent to rub a crook out of her neck. "Abram will never send me away, old woman!" But for all her brave words, within herself she admitted that the fear of her husband rejecting her, as Jehovah had when He made her a barren vine, was all too real.

Dinah was still unsatisfied. "I have lived long enough to witness more impossible things!" she insisted.

"You are a worrywart!" Sarai told her.

But something in Dinah's words lodged in Sarai's heart like a choking hand.

"Heirs means heirs. If not yours, than someone else's," Dinah said. "You know he trusts the word of his God more than any argument you can make. There is but one purpose that God gives to a woman: to make herself a mother in her husband's house!"

"And since I can't bring Abram this heir, what am I to do?" Sarai demanded.

Dinah stopped the spindle's dance with both hands. The woolen cord twirled into a knot over her great bony knuckles.

"Give him your bondwoman," she said.

Sarai shot her a fierce look.

"Hagar?"

Dinah did not need to answer now.

Sarai thought about the slave woman she had been given as part of her redemption price from Pharaoh during their long travels. "But that would make her his wife," she said.

"And her child your heir." Dinah's eyes gleamed as they always did when she knew her argument was right.

"No," Sarai said flatly. "God has said it. There will be heirs. Many of them." She ran dry hands over her even drier womb.

Dinah exhaled in a long impatient sigh.

"Time is running out, mistress. You have few seasons, perhaps two—God knows"—Dinah's old eyes flashed upwards—"left on that bed of straw."

Sarai's habitually quick tongue had no reply. She was conceding in spite of herself.

Dinah finished giving her advice. "Hagar shall bear on your knees! And pray she will be as fertile as the Nile she came out of."

A Wedding of Compromise

Wedding timbrels played their frenzied, boisterous jangle.

"Li-li-li-li-li!" trilled a dozen festively clad serving girls as they ran out of the women's tent to announce the approach of a bride. They flowed into a smiling line, bangles covering their arms, their black scarves wound with cords of gold coins, which hung over their eyes and were strung from ear to nose in rings. Stripes of bright earthen colors decorated their aprons and leggings. On their bare feet were drawn delicate henna designs in the fashion of the East.

One of the herdsmen beat melodically, expectantly, on the tightly drawn skin-covered drum. The tent flap opened and Hagar appeared, clothed, or rather bundled, in layer upon layer of festive attire, along with gold and silver bracelets, rings, and neck ropes. Holding out the bride's right hand, presenting her from behind, was Abram's first wife.

Dinah stood in the dark interior smiling, watching her mistress perform her duty.

"Now you shall have an heir at last!" she murmured to Sarai.

But Sarai did not hear. Despite her calm exterior, every fiber of her being was trembling. Not from joy, but from fear of the unknown realm that lay ahead as she gave her handmaid to Abram.

Hopefully, the slave would give Sarai an heir. She rationalized the plan to herself as the two women, one leading the other, passed through the gauntlet of household members toward the place where Abram sat at the door of his tent.

"If she does not conceive within the year," Sarai determined in her mind, "it will all be annulled." She looked sideways at the Egyptian woman. Hagar was silent and brooding by nature. She did her work and said little to anyone; she was willing to do little more than wait out her indenture, Sarai supposed.

According to code, Abram would have been within his rights to take a wife in addition to his barren one in any case. But Dinah was right, as usual, the cunning old crone. Had Abram taken a woman of his own possession, Sarai would have had no say in the terms of the contract. As it was, if Jehovah punished Hagar with the same curse He had laid on Sarai, Hagar would return to her former duties. On the other hand, if she produced an heir, she was still not permitted to threaten Sarai's position as mistress. If she attempted to supplant her mistress anyway—Sarai didn't know what she would do, but she planned to be vigilant and make sure it didn't happen.

Sarai held her head high, as though she were selling a ewe, as Abram rose from his pillow. Slowly, without trembling, Sarai put her servant's hand into her husband's. She focused her gaze on the hollow at the base of Abram's throat just above his shirt, saying nothing, and not allowing her eyes to meet his.

The women trilled again.

With no other ceremony, Abram's servant Eliezer pulled aside the tent flap and the master and his bride went inside.

Sarai did not wait for the flap to fall back into place before she turned.

"Go now! Dinah! Rud! Gezar!" She clapped her hands, ordering everyone to the open space in the center of the compound where they would eat.

Now that the newlyweds had gone into the tent, the rest of the household would celebrate the wedding with a feast. Everyone was expected to eat and drink to bless the marriage. Abram and his new wife would take their supper inside the tent; the servants would enter and exit the chamber backward so as to hide their eyes and leave the couple in private.

But Sarai wasn't hungry. She talked about the usual business and gossip of the camp casually but briefly while she pretended to eat. Then the mistress excused herself and retired to the tent of women for the night.

Trouble began the very next morning.

Sarai had arisen early that day, feeling excited, hopeful that a son had been conceived for them at last. She shooed

Dinah away and prepared breakfast for her husband and his new wife herself. She was walking between the tents with the bowls in her hands when Hagar stepped into her path.

"Good morning, Hagar!" Sarai said.

Hagar ran a hand over her hair as she stopped before Sarai.

"*Mistress,*" she replied. But the tone in her voice was almost taunting.

Sarai looked Hagar up and down. She had not noticed before that moment how appealing Hagar's form and exotic skin were to look at.

"I've prepared you some breakfast," Sarai said. She handed Hagar the dish and turned to take her husband's food to his tent.

As she started away, the bondwoman stuck a foot out and tripped Sarai, sending her and Abram's breakfast into the sand.

The bondwoman's eyes filled with disdain as she looked down on the sprawling woman. She passed a hand over her abdomen.

"I'm not hungry." She tossed her head and looked over her shoulder to Abram's tent. "I have other *food.*"

Before Sarai could recover, Hagar stepped over her and tossed her own bowl into the dust with Abram's and disappeared. Sarai went back to the fire for more food, and when she came into Abram's tent, he was sitting in silence with his head in his hands.

"What is it, husband?" she asked.

He shook his head and stared through the opening of the tent into the early light.

"What have *you* done?" he said.

Sarai came forward quickly and put his bowl before him.

"Surely Jehovah works in many ways to perform His wonders!" she reassured him. "Eat."

The Master Seeks Hagar

When Hagar appeared that evening the smell of perfume followed her around the fire. She lingered near Abram. Sarai dismissed it until after dinner, when Eliezer came to the door of the women's tent looking for the bondwoman.

"The master seeks Hagar," he told Sarai.

Hagar rose immediately. She paused just before the tent flap and shot her mistress a long glance. The whisper of a smile crossed her lips and she was gone.

Dinah sat up with Sarai well into the night. Hagar did not return to the women's tent, and Sarai paced and wrung her hands. Jackals ran near the encampment that night. Their eerie, laughing barks pierced the darkness.

Sarai finally lay down just before dawn.

Then Hagar returned. Dinah was snoring, and Sarai closed her eyes in imitation of sleep when she heard the tent flap come up. Hagar's bare feet padded past Sarai's pallet, stopping for an instant. Sarai waited for what seemed an interminable time until she was sure no sound but breathing came from Hagar's place. She left her own pallet and went to Abram's tent. He was asleep. She lay down beside him and he stirred, softly speaking in his sleep; he seemed like a drugged man. It was Hagar he asked for!

"Fair as the moon," he muttered. The smell of Hagar's perfume was still on him.

Lying asleep, Abram's words ignited a fire that raged—a rage that changed Sarai. A silent war began.

Jealousy Takes a Seat

Abram looked up at the sound of a commotion. The herdsman's intelligent gray eyes, chiseled nose and fine mouth were framed by a high forehead and angular chin. He adorned that regal chin with a meticulously manicured beard. Agile and commanding, Abram's entire appearance belied his eighty-five years. In the desert tribes known for their great longevity, he was not yet even middle aged.

A swift slap was immediately followed by a wail and shrill shouting. Servants exited the women's tent on the run. The shrieking from within was intense but short-lived. Standing in the tent was a sullen Egyptian woman, barely thirty years old, barefoot and clad in casual layers of light-weight garments that draped around her bronze-colored calves. Her dark, flashing almond-shaped eyes conveyed a look of triumph. Her long, slender limbs resembled a gazelle's, despite the weight of the child she carried in her very round belly.

Through strands of her obsidian-colored hair, which flowed over her shoulders and down past her buttocks, the woman stole a long glance at Abram. Touching the deep red mark on her cheek with her hand, she strolled across the compound to the cooking fire located safely within the circle of tents. There another woman ordered her to fetch firewood. The younger woman said something inaudible from where Abram sat watching. The words caused the older woman to rise and quickly chase the younger one, lashing at her with the stick she used to stir the fire. But the defiant woman only stepped just beyond convenient reach of the older woman and stopped in the shadow of the next tent, the cooking tent. Its long flaps were rolled up to allow any chance of a hot breeze to come and go under its covering.

Under its expanse, five middle-aged women and three small girls worked. The woman, sitting cross-legged in the midst of pots, utensils, and bundles—out of which came staples of wheat and spices and a few onions and roots— were occupied with routine matters of the encampment. They were preparing the day's main meal, which would be eaten by firelight after the sun had diminished enough for relief. The small girls were imitating the routine of their elders with smaller bowls of flour and water, receiving an occasional correction as they folded and rolled the flatbread.

At the northernmost edge of the sprawling tent enclave, wheat-colored sandstone cliffs rose and formed a windbreak. The great rocks cast a blue shadow over the dwellings during the hottest part of the day, when the glaring white sun was directly overhead. A sentinel was posted at the top of the cliff, but only had to act when travelers approached or a panther was spotted. In the center of the encampment, six lengths of a man from every tent stave, were six well placed fire pits. Those nearest the cooking tent supported cooking instruments. Two cooking fires smoked and generated heat within the wide mall where Sarai and Abram now stood.

Young lads squatted near each fire, tossing twigs into it. The boys were on duty to tend the fires throughout the afternoon in order to form a thick bed of cooking coals before it was time to put on the evening meal. From time to time the boys winced and covered their eyes with a hand when a changing wind sent smoke and sparks into their faces. They took turns tending the flames while groups of their skinny, half-clad smaller brothers darted and disappeared between the tents, heckling one another as they roved from the cliff base to the corrals below. Several small mongrel dogs barked at their heels. The young men and elders were all employed in the basin or further out on the plain tending the vast flocks Abram had acquired since receiving his inheritance and during his ten-year sojourn into Canaan.

The mistress of the household, Sarai, appeared from behind the flap of the women's tent, where the earlier fracas had occurred. Medium height and olive-skinned, more compact and muscled but decidedly lean from her life with the nomad shepherds, Sarai was more than twice the age of the servant she had corrected. Yet her whole appearance was ethereally timeless. She was untouched by the elements,

except for a ridge of slightly thickening skin where the soles
of her feet met her sandals. Her thick curly hair shone deep
mahogany in the sun. It escaped a single strand of graying
thusfar. Her face, like the rest of her body, was untouched by
the usual lining of the desert clime.

Sarai gathered her loose shawl around her head—not for
warmth, for the dry Mediterranean spring air was all the
clothing one needed in the daytime, but as a shield from the
dust and direct heat. It was also the custom that, in her sta-
tion as Abram's first wife, she should wear a veil except when
bathing. Behind her veil, Sarai had a fierce look of exasper-
ation on her face. She eyed the scene around her briefly,
sending a deadly glance after the servant she had just con-
fronted, and came resolutely to where Abram was sitting.

<hr />

"Insolent she-goat!" Sarai stopped before her husband,
hands clenched at the sides of her lean brown form, her
teeth tightly gritted together.

Abram waved off the Syrian bondsman sitting with him.
The young man obeyed the unspoken command as quickly
as if some specific task had been asked of him.

"She thinks because she conceived she's the Pharaoh's
daughter!" Sarai snapped. "She ignores my commands and
uses the fact that she is pregnant to undermine me in the
eyes of the household servants. Her spite has become
unbearable!" Sarai, whose peaceable and rational mind had
always made her fearless even in the face of foreign kings,
was in a rage.

"It is as though she is mistress of this house in my stead!
But she'll come down off that throne of hers once that child
has been born on *my* knees," Sarai swore, just loudly enough
for Abram to feel her resolve. "Hagar will find herself alongside the baggage in the next caravan from Haran."

Abram, Sarai's husband from her youth, didn't look directly up at her as she stood over him, waiting for some support. Also garbed with loose wraps of textured cloth hand-spun and woven by the women of his extended clan, Abram shifted on the rolled pillow where he had been conferring with Eliezer, the son of a Damascan-born widow. Abram had been placed in charge of Eliezer at the death of Abram's father Terah. The young man had been reared in his household and would be given the oversight and management of Abram's wealth and flocks in the event of Abram's demise. He was the constant shadow of the master of the household, and, being completely trustworthy, carried out Abram's will in everything.

The Semite patriarch looked out of soft brown eyes, flecked with gold and lined at the corners from the laughter and hardship of eighty-five years of desert life. "You should go easy, wife. She's far from her home and people," Abram said. "Your anger rages like a desert storm. Its sand is suffocating me, and just moments ago the air was clear."

Sarai shot her husband an angry look. Beneath her anger, the pain of his retort stabbed like a blade. How could a man understand the prison of shame that held captive a woman who had no children? And Sarai was tired of years of pretending it did not matter.

"You treat her as if *she* were your wife before me!" she said.

Abram stood, hoping to avoid any further conflict from Sarai's present distress over his second wife. His angular features retreated halfway into the veil of his headgear as he adjusted it. His rising unfolded his seasoned athletic body. Standing head and shoulders above Sarai, his garments fell around his calves as he turned to leave.

"Do not forget you sent her in to me," he said.

"*And mixed pulverized mandrake root in your food to assure the outcome*," Sarai confessed inwardly. Was this further punishment from God?

"I must speak with Eliezer about the herds before supper," Abram said, making his excuse to leave the scene.

Shall I Hold My Peace?

He walked away.

Hot tears flooded Sarai's face. She could feel the eyes of the servants gazing discreetly on her. Including Hagar's. Keeping her back to them, she stood and strolled after Abram out of the midst of the camp. She caught up to her husband just beyond the edge of the tent city and buried her face in her shawl.

"With the nature of turpentine and the tongue of an adder she daily provokes me since becoming pregnant. Shall I hold my peace?" Sarai spoke respectfully in her defense as she caught up with him.

Abram stopped and looked at his wife. This was not the same quiet nature he had always known and grown to expect from her.

"Perhaps you should have waited for Yahweh to fulfill His own promise," retorted Abram. "These passions you show in recent days were not in you before this."

Abram's voice sounded ambivalent. In his words and demeanor, she couldn't help discerning some advocacy of her bondwoman.

The donkeys brayed to one another from the corrals.

Sarai looked toward the wheezing sound of them. A wide alleyway out of the tent city led down the hill to the place where the land flattened into a half-circle basin before falling off onto the broad plain. Shrubs and gnarled, persistent trees clung to the landscape between clumps of coarse curling grasses and a scattering of rocks. Behind the master and mistress were a dozen or so sprawling tents, mostly long and black, squatted along the hillside. Each housed multiple men or women, with the genders always kept separate. The skeletal bones of the tent supports stuck up like crooked vertebrae along their centers and formed a linear enclave. Its four tilted acres housed some six hundred people, their ages spanning four generations, from suckling babes to old men and women.

"My wrong be upon you!" Sarai said defiantly. She pointed at the ever-increasing herds. "My *dowry* brought you the fertile herds from Pharaoh's best stock, and my bondwoman along with them!" Her voice was bitter and accusatory.

Sarai referred to the time they had sojourned together out of their famine-ravaged region and ventured into Egypt for respite for Abram's flocks. He had let the Pharaoh believe Sarai was his own sister because he feared for his life.

"The Lord judge between us!" she said.

Abram steadied his eyes on hers. "Careful wife," he warned.

Self-pity and torment burned within Sarai.

Why had she given the woman as a wife to her husband?

She had been thinking only of producing an heir. Before that Sarai had had no reason to envy Hagar so. Hagar was Sarai's junior by many years and was beautiful, but Sarai's own beauty was legendary; she had no reason to be jealous there. But a beautiful face was no consolation for an empty womb. She had never anticipated that the Egyptian would become her rival. And now she realized that Abram actually cared for the woman!

A Peculiar Uneasiness at Hagar's Presence

Sarai felt a peculiar uneasiness every time Hagar came into view. Uncomfortable passions pricked Sarai whenever Abram's eyes fell on the Egyptian woman. Her heart told her that Hagar now held the advantage, an advantage she desired for herself. Her husband was right. It was as though a terrible windstorm stirred within her, threatening to break out at any moment. Sarai had never known such feelings, feelings of insecurity and fear of something she could not put a name to.

She grew increasingly suspicious that she no longer retained the affections of Abram and the respect of the household. Every day that Hagar's figure grew larger the troublesome feelings increased. And with every day she found herself filled with more ill will for the pregnant woman.

Sarai searched the dry yellow sky. It, like the ears of God, seemed impervious brass in the face of her anguish. Her husband's heart seemed to be made of brass as well. She angrily felt that the two of them were one and the same against her. She shook her head in an attempt to clear it of her dark thoughts. She was still mistress of the household!

"The lazy, brazen glutton," Sarai reminded Abram, "doesn't even consider poor old Dinah! Again today she left her work to the other women. When I found her napping"—Sarai pointed back toward the tent from which she had come—"she threatened to slip poison roots into my supper!" She shot a determined gaze right at him. "So I slapped her." Sarai was unrepentant. "Am I not mistress? And she persecutes me at every turn!"

"Do with her what you will," Abram said, quietly resigned. But he added, "Remember she is also my wife...*now*." He walked on, leaving Sarai stopped in her tracks.

With each passing spring since Jehovah's first visit, her husband had become more devout. He performed regular animal sacrifices and had dark visions. The voice of God had promised descendants as numerous as the stars, and she was to become the mother of nations, according to Abram. Jehovah seemed to talk of things that were not as though they were, and now Abram had begun do to the same.

Sarai also observed their religion but suspected she had passed childbearing age despite Abram's faith, Dinah's potions, and the dark, painful spotting she experienced on occasion. It was the pain of that disappointment that had induced her to feed her husband the mandrakes and send Hagar to his tent.

Sarai now looked after Abram as he walked down the hill toward the corral, dust rising in the wake of each step.

"I should have sent Hoda or her sister to you instead," Sarai called after him. "At least they know their place!"

Abram stopped just where the hill met the floor of the plain. He turned again. As he looked at his distressed wife in the fading daylight the soft sounds of his herds came up to him.

"What good is all my wealth?" he said to her. "When I have a wife who has become as smoke in the eyes—contentious and bitter." He was silent for a moment, then finished, "Leaving me no peace and giving me no heir!"

His words stung deeply. Sarai looked at the livestock before them. Even Abram's cattle calved every spring! At the time of renewal each year, when singing birds returned to flit among the brush and every tree flowered, Sarai was still in winter. Waiting for the sap of life in the trunk of her body to put forth the bud of promise. She avoided the flocks so she that was not reminded that even the ewes had more life in them than she.

Sarai sat down where she was and wept.

"It's as much his fault as mine," moaned Sarai to herself. "If Abram had not lied, if he had not acted a coward, Hagar would still be in Egypt!" But, as she wrapped her arms tightly around her own empty waist, Sarai felt her barrenness and failure in contrast to Hagar's successful fertility. The Egyptian woman, who before this had been given no more thought than her orders for household duties, now seemed to possess Sarai. Thoughts of her dominated everything else.

Sarai sighed, recalling the despair of so many years of hoping. She prayed to conceive month after month, and still she was assaulted by her failure to produce an heir. Even now she still went to the red tent in seclusion, feigning continuance of her menses. She knew she was being whispered about among the servants. It was true that Sarai had given Abram the Egyptian to take into his tent. But now she wished with all her heart that she had not done it.

She felt as if she were losing her mind, as if everyone were against her, as if she were being laughed at behind her back. And she was certain that the bondwoman who carried Abram's heir was instigating all the scorn and trouble.

Sarai sorrowfully remembered her own laughing days, the days of adventure as they first journeyed from Ur and Terah, when her hope of producing a child was still alive. She continued to hope, even when they fled the famine in Canaan and sojourned in Egypt. That was when Sarai had been taken into the harem of the Pharaoh because Abram feared for their lives.

She remembered their clandestine rendezvous in the royal gardens where Abram would slip past the eunuchs to find her. She would wait for him, scented and bathed, with queen-of-the-night blossoms woven into her hair. God was with them in those days and part of the dowry paid to Abram for Sarai was the slave Hagar. Then God plagued the Egyptians. The Pharaoh, unable to sleep, came upon Sarai and Abram acting as husband and wife. It had been ten years since their return to Mamre's lands in Canaan.

The thought of Hagar sent daggers through Sarai. Abram's second wife, though Sarai's bondwoman still, had been belligerent and sharp-tongued towards her since the camp knew Hagar was pregnant. Daily she found ways to flaunt the pregnancy before Sarai in an effort to humiliate her. Still Sarai had held her peace...until today.

Sarai realized that she was no longer thinking rationally when she saw the woman or heard her voice. Sarai's imaginings ran wild. And each day of the pregnancy only made things worse. Sarai was beginning to resent the unborn child. Her dreams had become dark. Violent. She would wake in rivers of sweat, her hands cupped to her ears as if to shut out the resounding cries of infants.

Defiance drove away her piteous disposition.

Sarai wiped her face and stood up.

Mother of nations! If Abram believed it, why shouldn't she?

An Heir of Her Own

She remembered her stash of dried mandrakes. There had been no reason to use them after Hagar proved so receptive to Abram's seed—as Sarai had not been. But she had kept a few remaining mandrakes hidden in her belongings, despite their uselessness to her in the past. Their simple presence hinted at the remote possibility of fertility even now. There were very few of them left, and Sarai thought the likelihood of finding any more before the wheat harvest was very slight.

"No matter," she told herself, and swore, "By the new moon this time next year, I will have an heir of my own!" Under her breath, she whispered to the heavens, "If You listen, hear me now." She ran to retrieve the last of her coveted aphrodisiacs from their bundle and stole into the cooking tent where faithful old Dinah was overseeing the preparation of the evening meal.

Dinah had been servant to Sarai's mother and had been given to Sarai when she married Abram, an entire generation ago.

Coming up behind her, Sarai whispered. "Brew me some of your tea, Dinah. The more bitter the better."

Sarai pushed the mandrakes into the old woman's apron. "To sweeten my master's nature even more than it is," she said. "Use plenty of rendered butter."

Dinah chuckled and nodded knowingly. The tone in Sarai's voice was reminiscent of the early years, when this ritual between Dinah and her mistress had first begun. Sarai had not conceived in the first year of her marriage, so every new moon, Dinah would mix her potions. And every full moon, Sarai would lace her husband's food with the fragrant roots. On the fourteenth day of every month Sarai would sit in the red tent hoping for the sign. It never came.

It would surely take a miracle now. Dinah's eyes followed her mistress's exit. Sarai's barrenness was the worst of all curses that could fall upon a woman. Even Dinah had borne three sons of her own, though one had died at birth and the other two had been sent with the master's nephew to the south. They no longer lived with her, but she still saw them at the festivals and during the sheep shearing. Dinah looked down at the dried mandrakes. She put half of them out to use now and tucked the others away in her apron.

The entire camp knew when Sarai found Hagar that afternoon. The mistress's correction was severe, by the sounds of it. The other household servants stepped carefully for the rest of the day, and Hagar sniffled and nursed quiet tears when she at last appeared in their midst again. When evening came, everyone but Hagar had forgotten the incident. It was certainly not the first time Hagar's spitefulness had gotten her in trouble.

The sun hung huge and red in the thick haze of the atmosphere, lazing just above the skyline with two fingers of purple cloud across it. The scent of wild grasses flowering in the crevices of the cliff, where secret moisture miraculously sustained them, lent an ever-so-slight sweetness to the air. The sky turned orange in a blaze, dusting the tent tops and the earth itself with a pale pink glow as the red orb touched the horizon.

Bitten by a Serpent

Sarai came out from behind the bathing curtain refreshed and scented. She dressed herself in time to enter the color-splashed world moments before the painted sky faded into blue-black night.

She sat by Abram as they ate their supper and watched the rest of the household retell the day's events around the fires. Over the plain behind them, a star would shoot from time to time, its glittering tail trailing behind it, falling toward the earth.

When Abram had eaten his fill after supper, Sarai set a bowl of sweets before him.

"Forgive me, husband," she said softly, referring to their conflict earlier in the day. She motioned away the elder household members who sat with them.

Abram yawned as she crouched next to him and offered him the sweets from her hand.

"I'm already a fatted calf!" he laughed. He waved her offering away, putting his other hand to his stomach. Firelight glowed in his eyes and made his smile white.

"Just this one." Sarai held the sweet up to his lips. Its aroma was fragrant, laden with honey and cinnamon. "A peace offering."

"Peace, then," he said, and opened his mouth. Sarai's honey-covered fingertips brushed over Abram's lips as he accepted the gift to appease his wife. Then Abram grabbed her wrist before she could withdraw her hand. Sniffing the fingertips that had presented him with the sweet he said, "This perfume seems familiar to me." He gripped her firmly. "Does it not?"

She lowered her eyes in demure modesty.

"Cinnamon, husband, and whatever Dinah has devised. Wild roses perhaps." She pretended she had no other knowledge.

He chewed just twice and swallowed.

Sarai longed for the fragrant, yellow mandrake, *the cauldron* it was called, to do its work. In an hour she would be in his tent. For the millionth time, she forced the image of herself as pregnant as Hagar to come to her mind.

One of the herdsmen approached from the dim perimeter with an armload of crackling brush, quickly gathered on his way to camp as he returned from his duty at the watch post on the cliff. He piled the brush firmly atop the fire bed. Flames, orange and blue, immediately danced high, popping and trailing pleasantly into the sky like fainting fireflies. The man bowed slightly and touched his forehead in respect for the mistress and master as he retreated to the other fire for his supper.

Sarai gathered up the eating vessels around them and rose. She planned to go to her tent and wait for Abram to come for her. As she stepped away from the fire, a viper came sliding rapidly out of the heat into her path and stuck Sarai on the heel.

Sarai screamed out and convulsed in pain. Abram and the others came instantly to her.

"What is it, mistress?" The young man who had just been at the fire reached her at the same time as Abram.

"A serpent!" she cried. "There!" She pointed in the direction that the snake had slithered in.

While Abram helped Sarai to the tent, Dinah fetched medicine, a pungent liniment she drew from the base of the terebinths and used against poison and fever. Meanwhile, the elder men searched the encampment with torches looking for the snake. The additional noise and blazing fire alone would have made the unwelcome guest hide itself or slink away. Every carpet and pallet in every tent was shaken. After a full hour they came back to Abram with the word that no sign of the reptile had been found.

Sarai lay on her face in agony as her foot rested, hot and throbbing, in her maidservant's skillful hands. Dinah washed the wound and made small cuts around it to leech out the poison with her own mouth. She prepared to care for the fever that would soon come. The strong oily smell of Dinah's tincture filled the tent. Sarai's foot was swelling rapidly and turning black. Red streaking fingers ran up Sarai's leg ahead of the swelling. Droplets of sweat covered the mistress's neck and face. Her strength had gone out of her completely, and she felt as if the weight of a thousand millstones were pressing upon her.

"I'm thirsty," she managed before slipping into darkness.

At midnight Sarai was sleeping, however fitfully. Abram sat watching over her and at last dismissed Dinah.

"I'll send for you if she grows worse," he assured the old woman. "You've done all that can be done."

Reluctantly, Dinah obeyed and went to the tent of women. As soon as she lay down she was asleep.

She's Gone!

While Abram comforted his wife, Hagar waited for the rest of the servants to fall asleep. She heard Dinah's stirrings when she returned from Sarai's side and settled down. Then, amidst Dinah's snores and flatulence as the ancient crone turned over on her pallet, Hagar gathered her bundle of belongings together with a skin of wine, bread, and some curdled milk she had stolen. Hagar clutched them to her breast as she stepped over the sleeping bodies and into the chill night air.

She kept close to the tent curtains, crouching beneath the ropes to avoid the attention of the watchmen until she reached the edge of the camp. Then, without looking back, she ran into the desert. More than the wine and bread, she was taking with her the conceived seed of Abram and the only hope of a child her mistress would ever have. That knowledge was utter revenge. Hagar wrapped one arm under her bouncing belly as she ran. The viper had been a gift of the gods. Hagar looked up at the silver crescent moon overhead. It tilted languidly to one side, like a vessel tipped just enough to pour out its contents.

"Al-iLah," she said to the sliver of the moon, recalling the religion of her childhood and worshiping the god of her people. She called the name of the god, Zin, asking, "Judge my enemy and illumine my path!"

For the moment she was avenged, and that thought pushed any other concern far from her mind. She wanted to laugh, to shout, to pray out loud to Isis, thanking the goddess for this long-awaited victory over her rival, until a sharp stitch in her side brought her to a sudden halt. Hagar dropped to her knees in the sand. Great heaving breaths did little to relieve the pain. She put a hand to her face and was reminded again of the bruises from her mistress's heavy hand earlier. Hagar gritted her teeth and cast a curse on Abram's first wife.

But the pain in her side brought her to reality. Momentarily the coldness of the night desert assailed her. She tossed out her bundle and wrapped herself in her single cloak. It did little to protect her against the night air. And the moon in this phase gave little light of comfort. A panther screamed in the distance and fear settled upon the woman.

Back at Abram's encampment, Sarai struggled against the serpent's poison. At times her heart heaved with great sluggish thrusts that beat against her ribs as if it would break through them.

Abram watched her intently and prayed.

In her delirium Sarai was running—from what she was unsure. But in her dream she kept looking back over her shoulder, in terror of what was concealed in the darkness of the sandstorm that swirled out of the south and chased her. There was no sun. Only stinging choking sand.

She saw the form of Abram appear and disappear, an apparition in the sandstorm. He clutched Hagar in a passionate embrace. Turning once and seeing his other wife, he laughed at her and fell back to Hagar's smiling form. As she ran, Sarai's belly grew heavy with child. But the weight of it also carried the dreaded assurance that the son born was not her own. Did it die? Was it taken from her? Voices surrounded the delirious woman, taunting and abusing her.

As daybreak neared Sarai's strength was spent. The storm was overtaking her at last. It sucked at her clothes and licked viciously at her heels, a million knives of stinging sand striking every place where her skin was exposed. She looked behind her once more before she fell, succumbing to the rage. And then out of the cloud came the head of a huge black serpent, eyes red, mouth wide, fangs bared. It reared back and thrust itself downward to strike. With her last bit of strength she screamed out.

"Jehovah!"

Every ear heard. Every eye opened in the predawn at the eerie wail. Abram, who was dozing in spite of his own determination to stay alert by the side of his sick wife, started.

As he opened his eyes he saw Sarai suddenly sit upright, dripping with sweat as she screamed out the name of the God of their fathers. Her wet hair was matted against her face and neck. Breathing heavily, Sarai clutched at her body, as if looking for something that was not there.

"The child!" She looked at Abram wild eyed, not recognizing him. "My son!" she wailed, looking down at her body once more. Then she fell over as if dead and lay still in unconsciousness on the floor of the tent.

Dinah was in the tent in a moment, falling on her knees by Sarai's side.

"Mistress!" Dinah pulled Sarai into her arms and rocked her as if she were the child Dinah had nursed many years ago.

"Is she breathing?" Abram was on his knees with her as well.

Dinah was weeping silently, caressing Sarai's head and face.

"Dinah!" Abram said frantically.

Dinah shook her head from side to side as she rocked, holding Sarai's still form and touching her skin.

"No, no, master," she managed between her tears. "It is over now."

Abram's heart seized in his chest. "What do you mean?"

Old Dinah looked up at him. "The fever has broken at last! My mistress will live!"

Once Sarai's consciousness returned she lay weakly in her tent, assailed by the obsession with her enemy. Sarai was convinced that the serpent's bite had been an omen, an evil one sent by Hagar in some mystical way. An answer to the prayers Hagar prayed to the gods of Egypt. Sarai imagined that her slave and her slave's deities were pitched against her in battle. And Sarai was losing...

In the wilderness, Hagar was haggard by morning and grateful for the first hints of heat. Her stomach growled at her until she answered it with a breakfast of the curdled milk. As she sucked down the milk curd, Hagar hoped that Sarai was dead. Far behind her, her absence caused a stir in Abram's camp.

"Find her," Abram told Eliezer. "Look to the south, in the direction of her people."

The Damascan wrapped his face in the tail of his turban and nodded.

"Bring her back in safety." Abram touched the shoulder of his chief servant's camel with his baton and the camel lurched away.

By the time the camp discovered her absence, the sun was beating down upon Hagar's head as she put one angry foot in front of the other. The short shadows of the scrub brush offered little respite. Disregarding everything she had been taught about preserving her strength and provisions during daylight, Hagar defiantly marched in the direction of Shur.

Sarai, though weak, was fully conscious by afternoon, and furious. She was torn between fits of wishing wild animals would devour the bondwoman and vowing to recover the child in the woman's belly. It was as if Sarai had begun to feel the pressing weight of the unborn child within herself. She would bring back the heir if she had to go all the way down to Egypt herself to do so. Within three days, the swelling and discoloration were gone from Sarai's foot and leg. It was a miracle. Sarai was up and moving about the camp, using a walking stick for support.

In another day the Egyptian bondwoman came upon a spring. She was greedily sucking down handfuls of water when the voice of a stranger startled her.

"Hagar," a man said.

She choked and scrabbled for her belongings as she stood and prepared to run. She had heard stories of the terrible things that happened to women alone in the desert when men found them. She lunged away but the man, quick as a spirit, caught her by the arm. Screaming and kicking, pregnant Hagar resisted.

"Sarai's maid!" he said. "Do you think to return to your homeland? Egypt is many miles away."

Eyes wide, she stopped and looked up at the stranger.

"How do you know my name and my country?" she said.

"I will multiply your descendants through the child in your womb. No man shall be able to number them," the man said.

Hagar trembled in fear at this stranger and his words.

"Are you Horus? Of the gods of my father?" she asked, and covered her head with her cloak.

"The child shall grow wild. His hand shall be against every man," he continued.

The words comforted Hagar. She thought of the beatings she had received from Sarai.

My son will be slave to no one! the bondwoman swore.

"And every man's hand will be against him" the man said on.

Hagar's gaze shot upward at the stranger.

"He shall spread abroad and die in the midst of his own brethren. The Lord has heard your affliction," he told her. "Return to your mistress. Submit to the correction of her hand."

Return to Sarai? The words rankled her, but Hagar bit her tongue and kept silent. If the man was really a jinn he could strike her blind, or worse.

With that the man pointed into the distance. Two camels were visible through the waves of heat rising from the desert floor. Their riders bobbed up and down to the rapid trotting of the animals' huge padded feet as they came toward the spring. Hagar recognized the slender forms of Eliezer and one of the other herdsmen. When she turned back to the stranger, he had disappeared.

The God Who Has Seen Me

Was it a mirage? Or a spirit? Hagar piled several small stones together. She poured the remainder of her wine out upon them as an offering to one she called *The-God-Who-Has Seen-Me*. Then she made a vow before him that her descendants would be servants to no one. Afterward, Hagar sat down to wait for the men on the camels.

Without a word exchanged between them, Eliezer slipped agilely from his mount. His sandaled feet softly padded the earth as he came down. He took the waterskin from the back of his saddle and brought it to the slave. She stood up and waved the offering away, shaking her head in refusal. Without resistance, she followed the man back to the patient spindle-legged animals. The sour smell of sweat and urine surrounded them as Eliezer barked at the first camel and struck its shoulder with a baton. The camel groaned and grudgingly dropped to its knees. Eliezer waited while Hagar climbed onto the saddle.

"Hup! Hup!" Eliezer told the camel, tapping its underside with the baton. It rose and the men turned back in the direction they had come from.

To Hagar every step toward the camp felt like a defeat, a humbling, a submission. But with each plod of the camel's thick feet beneath her in the sand, she clenched her jaw and vowed she would never submit. Eventually she would have her son, her freedom, and Abram's riches as well. She would see to that.

⌦━━━━━⌫

Hagar's return was marked with absolute silence. No one spoke about her departure or return. Everyone went about his or her routine as though she had been neither missing nor present, away or returned. She grew heavier with child each passing day.

Dinah found her mistress silently weeping in her tent one afternoon.

"It's no use, Dinah!" Sarai told her, burying her face in her hands. "She has won! Hagar has won!"

The light in old Dinah's eyes snapped.

"Nonsense!"

But Sarai would hear none of it. She refused supper and stayed in the tent that night while the rest of the camp enjoyed their usual supper and exaggerated story-telling at day's end. Hagar was also confined to her pallet, but for other reasons. Her back and hips ached as the low, slow tremors of pre-labor pain began to overtake her swollen body. It would not be many days before the child would come.

Instead of Sarai, Dinah served Abram his food at the fire. She smiled as she came and went to retrieve the empty dish and hold the water bowl for him to wash in after he was finished.

"Thank you, Dinah," he said.

"Was the meal to your liking, my lord?" she asked.

"Delicious!" he replied. "But then, your craft is most practiced after all these years!"

The crone chuckled proudly and agreed. Then she wad-dled away, smiling not just from his compliment, but from her inner knowledge.

The mandrake-infused stew did its work. Sarai awoke to feel the kiss of her husband on her brow as he came to her in the dark. But despite Dinah's magic and Abram's cooper-ation, Sarai's womb remained shut up like a walled city before a siege. On the fourteenth day, Sarai lay in the red tent for what she was sure was the last time, praying to no avail. Dinah's tea was sent to her, hot and bitter. It made Sarai gag while her blood came and went uselessly. All the while Hagar grew more round.

An Heir Before Sunrise

Sarai stayed in seclusion. The Egyptian woman made sure to brush her thigh against Abram's arm as she went back and forth to the fire to serve him. Their eyes met, and Hagar could feel his gaze on her figure often.

Feigning the excuse of a needed rest, Hagar would steal away from the other women and servants in the midmorning when she knew Abram would be sitting at a vantage point in the basin above the corral. She would position herself in a place in the wind and sun where she was sure Abram could see her. She would stand on the brow of a hill or recline beside a rock at the foot of the crag, out of sight of the tents and those who might be watching.

She waited there for a breath from the desert floor to blow her clothes against her form in Abram's view. She would let down her hair to fly in the breeze and run her hands over the rotund fullness of her belly while he watched from a distance. And Hagar would turn toward him and recite the words of the man at the well, casting them on the wind as her vow against her mistress and her servitude.

At the end of the month, Dinah awoke Sarai just after midnight.

"Mistress," she said, "you will have an heir before sunrise."

Sarai sat up quickly. She went to the entrance of the tent, poured out a handful of water from the skin that hung there, and rubbed the sleep from her face.

"The child is early!" she told Dinah.

"It's a full moon," Dinah replied. Blue light from the gleaming white orb far above them in the night sky bathed the woman's wrinkled face.

Sarai's rival was in anguish, and in a few hours Sarai's greatest desire would be fulfilled. Hagar's wails could be heard coming from the red tent in the darkness.

Hagar was surrounded by the women of the household when Sarai came into the tent. Propped on pillows and covered by a woven cloth, Hagar's face contorted dramatically between tears and calls for her mother in her Egyptian tongue and prayers to her father's gods. Her knees made two sharp trembling hillocks under the blanket.

"Tell Eliezer to wake my lord," Sarai ordered one of the serving girls. The girl ran from the tent.

In another hour, Hagar was squatting on the midwife's bricks with Sarai supporting her. The posture made Sarai birth mother, and she molded herself into the birthing position, willing Hagar to disappear, as the long wet body of the newborn came forth onto Sarai's lap after one last great heave of anguish by her slave.

The shrill cries of the women, their tongues vibrating against the roofs of their mouths, announced that Abram's heir was born. Sarai had a son. The midwife took the baby to the basin and rubbed it briskly with oil and salt until a lusty cry opened its lungs and filled the night air.

Abram paced before the tent; young Eliezer sat helplessly by his master as the lamps passed to and fro with the activity within. Eliezer jumped to his feet and clasped Abram's hands at the women's trilling call and the baby's cry. A few moments later the midwife pulled back the tent flap for her mistress, and Sarai came out holding her son.

She presented the boy to Abram, smiling with satisfaction.

"I've gotten you an heir, my husband," she said. "God has heard at last!"

"Ishmael," Abram said softly as he took the wriggling bundle in his arms. "God has heard." He took the bundle carefully. "And Hagar?" he asked without looking up.

Ice stopped the blood in Sarai's veins.

"The child should go back to the midwife," she said. Holding the boy she disappeared into the tent again.

Abram left Eliezer to see after any needs in the camp and walked into the desert.

A son! A son! Abram laughed out loud and turned around, arms wide. Looking up into the night sky he shouted.

"Descendants as the stars in number!"

He felt suddenly years younger than eighty-six. It was not unusual among the desert people for men of his age to produce children. But he had lived more than half of his life out by now, and he had an heir from his own seed at last!

The bleating of sheep echoed his resounding shout to the heavens. He smiled and spoke out loud to them in the moonlight.

"You will produce great flocks for my son!" he commanded them.

In the birthing tent, Hagar collapsed into drugged sleep with the help of Dinah's medicines. Sarai ignored her completely as she held Ishmael to the breast of the wet nurse. The baby sucked and sputtered his first meal in the world.

"My son will sleep by me," Sarai told her. "Bring your things and make your pallet there for when he wakes."

The nurse nodded obediently.

At sunrise old Dinah squatted beside Hagar's bed attempting to attend her. Dinah tried to get the woman to take the bowl of porridge prepared for her, but Hagar refused.

"It will help you gain your strength back," Dinah said, trying to reason with her.

Hagar defiantly turned her head away.

"*I* should nurse him!" Hagar cried. Her engorged breasts dripped painfully.

Dinah put a hand to Hagar's skin. Fever had begun. The old woman refreshed the dressings, wetting and wringing them in a wash of diuretic roots and goat's milk to help dry up Hagar's milk.

"I curse the breast of any who nurses him but me! I want my son!" she wailed.

Hagar suddenly threw the covering off of her body and stood dizzily.

"What are you doing?" Dinah barked as she stood to restrain her.

Hagar wrapped herself in a shawl and pushed past the crone.

"I will see the master!" she said.

Abram was just finishing his breakfast when the sound of Hagar's shrill voice, arguing with Eliezer, reached him. In a moment, the half-clad woman was standing unsteadily before him.

"She has taken my son and put him on another's breast!" Hagar cried. Tears streamed down her face, wetting her tangled dark hair. "Master!" Hagar fell to her knees before him. "Husband!" she begged. "Please!"

Light broke behind her as the tent flap flew back and Sarai came in carrying Ishmael.

Hagar turned when Abram looked up.

"My son!" she wailed, reaching out.

The infant immediately began to cry plaintively.

Sarai held him tighter and gently bounced him in an attempt to console him. But he only cried louder, twisting his head about, eyes tightly shut, great tears sliding from the corners of his thick dark lashes. His tiny red mouth was open in distress.

Eliezer came in behind Sarai. He looked to Abram with a wide-eyed expression of helpless consternation and.

Sarai eyed the kneeling woman. Even in Hagar's distress, Sarai thought resentfully, the woman had seductive appearance as she sprawled before her husband.

She told Eliezer, "Take her back to her place."

At those words, Hagar swooned and fell over in Abram's lap. Eliezer came running but Abram waved him off.

"I'll take her," Abram said. He lifted Hagar, limp in his arms, and covered her with her shawl. Eliezer ran to open the tent flap for them. As they passed Sarai and the baby, Hagar opened one eye. She glared at her mistress and then resumed her faint.

Ishmael kicked his tiny legs furiously, beating himself with his own balled fists. He wailed louder and louder.

"Shhh! Shhh!" Sarai put her lips to his forehead and restrained his angry hands. "There, my son. Shhh!" But the baby would not be comforted.

When Abram returned Sarai was pacing up and down, fussing with as she tried to calm Ishmael.

She glanced at her husband helplessly.

"I don't know what to do for him," she said, her face distorted in empathy. "Will you have Eliezer bring the nurse?"

"No," Abram said.

"What?" Sarai looked up.

Abram took the boy from her.

"Hagar will nurse the child for us," he said.

The tone in his voice let Sarai know protest would be useless. Her temples throbbed, and she stood in the doorway with clenched fists as her husband took her son to her slave.

Hagar kissed Abram's hands and wept and smiled at him, her dark eyes shining gratefully. When she took her baby in her arms, he quieted instantly. She put her heavy breast to his mouth and he latched on lustily. With every draw of the tiny mouth, Hagar felt revived and unassailable. The baby was the testimony of her strength, of her womanhood towering over that of her mistress. The mother cooed and kissed her son, and after Abram had left her, she dedicated the boy to the gods of her people.

"I'll not be slave forever," she promised. "By the time you take a wife, my indenture will be up. We shall return to my people. To your people." Her milk flowed so abundantly that it ran out of Ishmael's mouth and caused him to choke and sputter as it covered his face.

Hagar smiled.

Sarai was still standing in the doorway of her tent when she heard the baby's wailing instantly stop as he came to Hagar's arms. She pulled the ropes from the tent flap and turned inward, letting the heavy flap shut out the light behind her.

That day a goat was taken from the flock. It was perfect, a yearling with good promise of producing many fine lambs. Abram slaughtered it and sacrificed it as a burnt offering to Jehovah in the presence of the whole household.

A calf was also killed for the feast in thanksgiving for his son. As the household ate that night, they took their food in honor of Abram and Sarai and in celebration of the arrival of an heir at last.

Hagar watched through lowered lids while the rest of the house rejoiced and feasted. But she only pretended to put the food to her mouth, and after a while excused herself as though needing privacy beyond the camp. By herself she spit the food out of her mouth and stuck her finger down her throat, forcing herself to regurgitate what little she had eaten in their presence.

She would not eat in honor of the woman who had stolen her son. If that offended Sarai's God, so be it. Hagar entrusted herself to her own gods!

For the next year, until the baby was weaned, Hagar had the bittersweet consolation of denying Sarai's demands. For

if the baby fussed, Hagar, not Sarai, could ultimately comfort him. If the child was sick, Hagar would be relieved of
her duties to tend him. While she held him, she constantly
whispered in his tiny ears, her voice softly and sweetly
imprinting in his heart that she, not Sarai, was the mother
who loved him and had given him life.

Prince of Canaan

Six more years passed. Every night Hagar whispered to
Ishmael just before he fell asleep. "You will be prince over all
of Canaan from here to the brook of Egypt! Prince Ishmael!
The whole land will submit to you, my son!" she sang.

Abram also doted on the dark-haired boy with round,
thick-lashed eyes. He often carried him around on his shoulders laughing, Ishmael screaming with excitement and
delighting the rest of the camp.

"Prince of Canaan!" they would shout and bow low in
playful obeisance. Ishmael was the darling of the entire
household. The master's heir would be their master as well
when he came of age.

During the day Sarai mothered the boy. She was determined that he would be the brightest lad in all of Canaan's
land. In addition to what Abram taught him, Sarai took special care to oversee his instruction herself.

"You must know how to number every head of your cattle," she told him. "And woolly sheep one by one!" She made
up a tune to fit the words.

Ishmael was hardly grasping what she was singing. He
squirmed impatiently and looked up eagerly when Hagar
came around the tent corner.

A gust of wind caught the woman's long black hair,
which she insisted on letting hang long and free, and, in
Sarai's opinion, seductive. No matter how many times she

ordered Hagar to bind up her hair, it was always free whenever she saw her. It was one of the many rebellions Hagar made against propriety to the continual distress of her mistress. Sarai imagined herself creeping upon Hagar while the woman was sleeping and cutting off her hair with shepherd's shears!

"Mother!" the small boy cried when he saw her. He twisted his hand from Sarai's and wriggled out of her lap. "Mother!" he cried again and ran to Hagar's open arms.

Sarai immediately stood up.

"No, Ishmael!" Sarai started after him "Come here!" She went after the child, catching him by the back of his clothes as he wrapped his arms around Hagar's legs.

"I want my mother," he insisted.

Sarai pulled at him.

"She is not your mother!" she replied through gritted teeth.

Hagar pulled back defiantly. The boy kicked between them and began to shriek, protesting Sarai's clutch. One arm around the boy's waist, Hagar clenched the fist of her other hand and swung at Sarai. Her action loosed a volcano of rage in her mistress. Sarai grabbed Hagar by her hair, twisted a long lock of it around her forearm, and yanked the woman toward the ground.

"Let go of my son!" Sarai ordered.

But Hagar clung all the more relentlessly. Ishmael shrieked at the top of his lungs.

Discord and Division

From a distance, Abram looked up at the sound of his son's distressed cry. He handed the lamb he was inspecting for parasites over to Eliezer and ran toward the sound, terrified that some awful harm had come to Ishmael. Sweating and panting, he came around the corner of the tent and found his wives locked in a furious wrestling match, his son caught between their struggling bodies. Dust flew as they rolled about.

"Stop it!" he shouted at the struggling women.

At that moment, Hagar lashed out with her fingernails and scraped them deeply across Sarai's face. Sarai wailed and grabbed her wounded cheek, and Ishmael tumbled free of both of them.

"Father!" The little boy scrambled up at the sound of Abram's voice and ran to him. Abram scooped his son up in his arms, and the boy's arms went tightly around Abram's neck. He hugged Abram, eyes closed, so tightly that Abram's air was cut off for a moment. He patted the boy's back. Then Ishmael looked at the women.

One arm still around his father's neck, Ishmael stuck out a stubby finger.

"She pulled my mother's hair!" he said. He pointed accusingly at Sarai.

Sarai stood up, still clutching her bleeding cheek, and dusted herself off. She grabbed Hagar's dress at the shoulder.

"You will be first up and last to bed after this!" Sarai swore. "I'll give you the duties of seven insolent slaves!"

"Enough, Sarai!" Abram shouted.

"Go away!" Sarai ordered Hagar as the woman got to her feet.

Hagar's eyes went directly to Abram and pierced his heart with an unspoken plea for kindness, mixed with accusations of Sarai's harshness. It pulled at him with the force of a millstone about his neck. Hagar's look, as always, evoked images of her soft body entwined with his. Abram's heart felt like it would burst. His veins bulged with the pounding pressure of the pulsating heartbeat in his neck. He hadn't brought her into his tent after the second night with her. It was as though God was speaking to his heart and requiring him to walk in a careful, restrained way before Him, especially in regard to his second wife.

"Do as your mistress says," he told her in a low voice.

"Not without my child," Hagar replied with a steely tone.

Abram put Ishmael down and nudged him toward her. The boy ran to Hagar and took her hand as she turned and left them.

Sarai thought she could not contain herself as she watched the woman walk away triumphantly, with Ishmael following at her heels.

"*Enough*, husband?" Sarai inspected the blood on her palm and pressed it to her face again. "We never should have gone after her when she ran away the first time!"

Abram heaved a great sigh.

"Entrust yourself to God, Sarai. You must submit to Him," he said.

"Is that your answer to a barren womb? *Enough?*" She struck herself on her own belly. "It is never enough!"

Sarai yearned for vengeance. She wanted to find something to validate herself in the face of the undeserving slave who had so easily produced a child. She pointed after Hagar, who was now out of sight around side of the tent.

"She prays to her foreign gods at night, you know. And teaches the boy their names as well!"

Then Sarai used her tongue to strike at Abram where it would sting most.

"A *pagan* has captured my husband and son!" Sarai turned on her heel and marched away in a fury.

Abram's heart ached. This war between his wives must end, but he knew neither of them would be the first to concede to the other.

Ishmael, still clutching Hagar's hand, scurried to keep up with her stride. Once they had turned the corner and were out of Abram's view, Hagar bent to pick the child up. But before she lifted him, she put her face solemnly into his innocent one and reminded him, "The Semite woman hates us, my son. You must keep your heart far from hers. Be careful of your words, even to Abram! For though he loves you, Sarai rules his affections." Hagar smoothed his hair ardently. "But she'll not rule us!"

The small boy looked back at Hagar wide-eyed, taking in these words he didn't understand. He would come to know their meaning in following years. But now he simply nodded and pressed himself into his mother's arms.

The boy grew into a lad, and all the while the enmity between barren Sarai and fertile Hagar simmered. From time to time the accusations and rebellion came to a boiling point.

Years passed.

Abram increased his herds, and his gold and silver grew along with his flocks, as well as the number of his servants. He was revered in all of Canaan.

During the day, Abram would take Ishmael with him to talk with the herdsmen and work with the livestock. Then father and son would go into the wilderness, where Abram was teaching the boy to hunt. Abram had fashioned Ishmael a bow and a quiver of arrows. He showed him the boundaries of the land that he had been promised. And he talked much of the Invisible God.

Ishmael grew confident and proud as a result of the attention paid him by Abram and their constant companionship. During the day, father and son were inseparable, and Abram allowed no one to correct the son on whom he doted so. The rest of the household gave Ishmael special respect and love as well. Old Dinah made him sweet treats to eat. The other boys in camp followed him and sought his favor, though he often played cruel practical jokes on them. Every day a different boy was excluded from the brotherhood of his clique.

In the evenings, he would sit with his father and the rest of the men and listen to their stories. And without fail, after the men had retired, Ishmael would return to bid his mother goodnight. His heart went out to her as he saw how she was always made secondary to Abram's other wife. Soon Ishmael showed the same disdain for Sarai as his mother did.

Hagar reminded Ishmael that he had two heritages. She talked to him of the great kings and mighty gods who defended the shining Nile. She sang him the songs of Egypt. And together they prayed the prayers of Egypt. All of it plucked at the strings of his heart. Her foreign tales and her untamed spirit made him feel wild and free!

As he grew, he began to feel something inside him whenever he heard Sarai spoken of. It was like a dissonant chord struck upon the lyre. An uneasy tremor seized his heart and made him inexplicably angry and suspicious. Because of it he came to see evil in everything that Sarai did. As he grew, he developed his mother's resentment. Ishmael often vented his unprovoked anger on the smaller boys or a hapless animal or bird. All the while he was careful to cunningly hide his defiance of Sarai from Abram. For he took his mother's warnings to heart and was careful not to give reason for offense and thereby risk his inheritance.

The Heir Comes of Age

When the day came, the smell of the stewing goat and the smoke of the stacks of flatbread being cooked filled the air in the midst of the compound. Everyone was preparing for the celebration. Today Abram's firstborn, young Ishmael,

handsome and tall, would be declared a man, and the heir
to all Abram possessed. The event, as all important passages
in this household, would be hailed with a sacrifice, a feast,
and singing and dancing to the sounds of tambourines and
drums well into the night. After this evening, Ishmael would
go permanently to sleep in the men's quarters, where he
would officially become prince among them.

Hagar smiled broadly. Her hands flew over the colorful
fabric of the vest she had made for her son as she fitted it to
his torso.

"Hold your head high. Proudly, my son!" She prodded
him playfully, tying the vest closed and straightening his
shirt beneath it. "There! The vesture of a king!" she said.
"Turn around so I can see you." She nodded approvingly.
"Thirteen summers!" Then Hagar's eyes flashed. "Today,
when he names you his son before the household, you
become heir! Everything will change for us!"

The boy smiled back at her.

"I love you, mother!" He hugged her and then straightened quickly. "But after today, I must act like a man. And
you must treat me so. No more holding my hand and kissing me in front of the others."

Hagar laughed. She bowed low, teasing.

"Yes, my prince!"

Then she stood before him and placed her hands on his
shoulders. A cloud crossed her face. Then, as if prophesying
about the storm to come, Hagar looked him sternly in the
eyes and spoke again.

"Never forget, Ishmael. You are Abram's heir! But beware
Sarai's influence on him. Feign respect of her if you must,
even love. But remember, she is your enemy. Your mother
who loves you has warned you. You are the rightful heir!"

"I am also your son, my mother," he reassured her. "And
when I come into my kingdom, you shall be queen, like the
Nile goddesses of old!"

Sarai stepped into the tent.

"Come, Ishmael," she said. "Abram is looking for you." She did not acknowledge Hagar, but warmly addressed Ishmael again as he turned to go with her. "How handsome you look!"

Ishmael looked at Hagar one last time and said nothing. He followed Sarai out of the tent.

"Here he is!" Sarai presented the boy to his father. "Doesn't he look proud? He reminds me of you when you were just a few years older than he is now."

Abram held his arms out to Ishmael. "Come, son. Men have things to say to one another that are not for women." His eyes twinkled at Sarai playfully. "What would you know of my appearance when I was his age? You were still being nursed by Dinah!"

"Shoo, then!" Sarai swatted at them both and sent them off laughing. But even as she watched her husband throw an arm over the shoulder of the handsome young lad, Sarai imagined the shadow of Hagar walking with them out of the compound.

After the sacrifice, there was dancing and telling of stories late into the night. It was all in honor of the prince in Abram's kingdom. At the midpoint of the festivities, Abram stood Ishmael before the household.

"This is the son of Abram. Receive your prince!"

The women trilled their tongues against the roofs of their mouths and everyone clapped and shouted. Then the dancing and eating resumed. When the festival was finished and Ishmael had gone into the tent of men, Abram and Sarai retired to their own private quarters.

That night Hagar slept soundly, as did Sarai.

But Abram had just fallen into a deep sleep when a voice startled him.

"Abram!"

Abram sat up and looked at where Sarai slept soundly.

"Abram!"

He rubbed his eyes in the darkness and looked up as he scrambled for his dagger. But he could see no one. He sensed only the voice and the nearness of an invisible Person, great and holy.

Abram dared not move for fear of what might happen next.

"Do not fear," the voice told him. "Walk before Me and be blameless."

Abram fell on his face.

"Lord?" Immediately Abram thought this must be God's way of sealing the events of the day and Ishmael's becoming a man and his heir.

"I am Jehovah, all-sufficient for you. My covenant is with you and your children forever," the voice told him.

A wind, like the very breath of God, passed through the air.

"From today you shall be called Abraham, father of many nations."

Abraham. Exalted father.

Abraham could feel a strange change happening within him. It was as if with the sound of the name a new identity was taking hold inside and lifting him up to a higher plane.

"This land in which you sojourn shall be your everlasting possession."

With those words Abraham knew that he had come home forever. This was the place of which God had spoken when He called him out of Haran.

"This shall be the sign of My covenant with you, you shall circumcise the flesh of the foreskin of every male who is come into your house."

Abraham listened, trembling, his face pressed into the carpets that covered the floor of his tent.

"To you and your heirs I am giving all the land which Canaan settled before, from the brook of Egypt to the great river Euphrates."

As for Your Wife, Sarah

Sarai stirred and turned over in her sleep. An unconscious sigh escaped her lips and she curled into a fetal position, holding her empty womb with both arms, dreaming.

"As for your wife, Sarah shall be her name."

Again the sound of the wind pronounced the new name. *Sarah.*

"Sarah!" Abraham whispered.

Noblewoman.

Abraham thought of Sarah's undaunted courage in the face of any adversity.

"She will bear a son," the voice said. "Nations and kings shall come from her. Have I not told you before?"

Abraham started. A son besides Ishmael? He thought of the trouble it had been to conceive one son, the constant bickering and jealousy between Sarah and Hagar. Would it start all over again?

In his heart Abraham considered his age, and Sarai's.

Eighty-nine and one hundred!

He laughed out loud! He opened and closed his eyes several times and shook his head as if to remove water from his ears. Perhaps he had drunk too much sweet wine during

Ishmael's coming of age feast. Perhaps this voice was a product of Abraham's imagination.

"Shall I break the law?" Abraham reasoned with the voice. "I have just tonight made Ishmael my heir." He stopped for a moment, testing the atmosphere. "May Ishmael live before You! May Ishmael arise to inherit all my possession!"

At that moment Hagar's bare feet silently trod along the side of the tent. On the way to the desert for her ritual nocturnal rendezvous with the moon, she overheard Abram's voice. Hagar sucked in her breath.

"Ishmael my heir! May Ishmael inherit all my possession!"

The woman smiled. From the mouth of Abram himself, on the day he called Ishmael his son. So much for the hand of Sarai! Triumphant, Hagar hurried on.

The atmosphere around Abraham froze as if suspended in time. Fear spread through the tent. Abraham felt as though his very breath had been sucked out of him. He struggled to catch enough air to fill his lungs. He put a hand to his throat.

"No," came the reply. "Ishmael is the son of Abram and the bondwoman. But Isaac your seed shall be called. The son of Abraham, and the son of Sarah."

Abraham's heart sank. He was tired of trouble and only wanted a corner of a tent where there was no contention.

But the voice spoke on.

"Sarah shall conceive. At this same time next year she shall bear a son! His name shall be laughter. My covenant shall not depart from him or his heirs."

Abraham was silent. Ishmael, his firstborn, was almost a man. According to custom, the boy had become Abraham's heir this very night. Abraham tried to picture the likeness of a new boy in Ishmael's stead, but images of Ishmael were all he saw. There was Ishmael together with Abraham tending the sheep, learning to hunt, driving the cattle to water.

Laughing, handsome, inquisitive, and sometimes fierce, his son was a quick learner, devoted to his father.

It was as if the voice had heard Abraham's thoughts.

"And I will bless Ishmael," the voice said. "Twelve princes shall arise from him. His descendants will spread out to the right and to the left."

"To whom are you talking?"

It was the sleepy voice of his wife.

Abraham crawled back onto their bed to quiet her in the presence the messenger in their tent. He pulled her close and put a hand over her mouth.

"Shhh!" he whispered. "Careful, Sarah!"

She pulled away from him.

"Have you gone mad?" she pulled his hand away from her mouth. "Who are you talking to? Who is Sarah?"

"He has come to us again!" he told his wife.

As their voices sounded in the darkness the sense of that Presence departed from them. Abraham pulled Sarah close. She looked up at him in the dim light, trying to see his face and understand his mood. Then she shrugged and dozed again, her breath softly touching the skin of his neck.

Sarah.

Abraham held onto her. Her fearlessness and spirit made her a mother of kings! He would tell her in the morning. Abraham thought of the last time she had believed this promise. Abraham sighed.

When Spring had fully come and the trees were in bud, and the herdsmen were busy with the new lambs, Abraham returned to his tent one afternoon for his customary rest until the heat of the sun lessened. As he sat in the shade of his tent front, he looked up to see three men passing across the desert floor. The men were headed south, striding quickly as if intent on some specific business. Abraham quickly got to his feet. Their appearance drew him in, and he thought their form was worthy of closer inspection. He reasoned that if their business had concerned him they would have come straight into his camp.

Grabbing his cloak and staff, he called for Eliezer and went out to intercept them.

Abraham squinted his eyes at them and had a strange sense of recognition, as he had when God had visited him. A sense of holy awe and of being removed from time came over him. As he drew closer to the visitors' tracks, he made out their shining visages, particularly that of the man in the center, who was taller than the others and seemed to be flanked by them. Abraham recognized Him from before.

The three men did not acknowledge Abraham and his servant. Neither speaking nor uttering any sound, they had the countenance of kings. They stood a head taller even than Abraham. Their garments, unlike Abraham's shepherd's garb, fell around their ankles and flowed out from their sandaled feet as though they hardly touched them.

Abraham told Eliezer, "These are no ordinary men. See how they turn up no dust in spite of the wind around them!"

Eliezer answered, "And no sweat clings to their robes!" His own garment hung damply under his arms.

The only sound made by the men was the sound of their staffs striking the ground every few steps and the sharp snap of the cloth of their garments, like the sound of tent flaps in a gale. As they neared, Abraham rapped Eliezer firmly on his shoulder and the two of them bowed themselves low to the ground. When Abraham thought they would pass him by, he shouted.

"My Lord!"

Eliezer thought Abraham addressed the man in the middle as if he were speaking to God Himself.

Still not looking up but with intense zeal Abraham said loudly, "If I have found favor in your sight, turn in here! Take rest here if it please you," he pleaded. He and his servant stayed still, bowed down to the ground in the noonday sun. "Here is water. Let us refresh you. Allow your servants to prepare a meal for you."

Eliezer waited with his master. His breath stirred the dust before his face, the smell of sand was in his nostrils, and his heart beat wildly. This was the first time he had been with the master when God had visited him!

The men stopped a short distance from the prostrate shepherds.

"As you have said," they replied. The sound of their voices was as one together and in it was the sound of the air itself. In it was also the voice Abraham had heard in the tent when his and his wife's names were changed. The voice that had said Sarah would give birth to kings.

Abraham touched Eliezer.

"We have persuaded them," he whispered. "Come!" As he rose up, Abraham stole a glance from beneath his brow at the tallest man. He sucked in his breath and clutched Eliezer's garb. "It is the Lord!" he said with certainty.

They scrambled to their feet and hurried back toward the camp. The three visitors followed them, seeming to take fewer steps to cover the same distance. They came to the terebinth grove just beyond the tents. The men sat down in the thick shade of the tall trees.

As he came into the compound Abraham shouted.

"Sarah!" Abraham ran under the roof of a tent whose sides were rolled up for air and light. His wife sat there. "Sarah!" he called.

She looked up from the bundle of wool she was carding.

"We have guests. Quickly! Prepare portions for three," he said. "Use the fine meal, and tell Dinah to bring out some fresh butter and yogurt for them. Have the lads get the fire ready. We shall bring a calf immediately!"

Sarah raised her brows. A calf meant these were special guests indeed. Her husband's countenance was rapt with light from a source not of earth. It was the same light she had seen upon him when God spoke to him. It was the same look Sarah remembered from the dramatic time that God had addressed him many seasons ago when they camped in this same place before Ishmael was conceived. It was the same look Abraham had had after eating with the priest Melchizedek from Jeru-Salem.

Abram, as he had called himself then, had returned from recovering Lot's family. God's voice came to Abram, promising him an heir from his own body. In obedience, Abram prepared a great sacrifice according to the instructions in the vision: a heifer, a goat, a ram, and birds. In the heat of the day, he had fended of the persistent vultures that circled overhead and descended in twos and threes to the animal carcasses.

The herdsmen and women had retreated, not wishing to watch the strange behavior of their master as he shouted and flapped his arms at the birds, driving them away from the sacrifices he had carefully arranged on the ground. It continued all day and into nightfall. Abram watched the pieces of the carcasses and then looked skyward. Only Eliezer stayed nearby.

Now, as the strangers entered the camp, Abraham addressed his servant who followed him.

"Take water! Wash their feet. Once they have been refreshed, come to the corral." He looked at Eliezer steadily.

"Be careful," he cautioned. "Say nothing unless they speak to you first."

Eliezer bowed and went to do as he was told.

Ishmael came back from roaming the cliffs while the other men of the camp took their noonday rest. He came to Abraham's tent to see what the commotion was about. He eyed the three men under the trees as he passed Eliezer and came into the tent.

"What's going on, father?" the lad asked. "Who are those men?"

"Visitors, son." Abraham smiled excitedly at the young man. "Special guests!" He pulled his knife from his belt and fingered its blade.

"But who are they?" Ishmael asked.

"No less than the Lord!" Abraham said. His eyes were wide with exhilaration as he started for the corral.

Ishmael glanced toward the shade of the trees. The men lounged peacefully, like any visitors awaiting hospitality.

"The Lord, father?" the lad asked. He ran after Abraham's quick strides.

This was the first time Ishmael had seen God with his own eyes! The gods his mother told him about were strange and frightening. And Abraham's God was called "the Invisible God" by the local people. How was it that these three strange men were the One Invisible God?

Abraham brought another of the herdsmen with him as he went out of the compound to select the best calf. Ishmael followed Abraham. He stayed close by his father without asking too many questions. But occasionally he looked back beneath the terebinth trees.

Sarah glanced at their guests as she hurried to the cooking tent. Her eyes widened and she pulled her covering close over her head when she saw their visages. They appeared to be as she remembered the men of old—the celestial messengers who used to come to observe the affairs of those who kept the way of the fathers! It was more common in those days to hear of angels, and even of God Himself, coming down to walk and talk with men. Some mortals, like Enoch, had even gone up to God, having passed over death completely. But such things were now heard of less and less.

God Was in the Camp

Sarah shivered with excitement.

God was in her camp! And in daylight, where everyone could see! Her heart beat as fast as her steps touched the hot sand.

Sarah clapped her hands quickly, calling the household servants to attention, as she came into the circle of the cooking fire.

"The master has guests," she said. Sarah barked out the orders of the meal to be prepared. Men and women darted away to obey.

"And me, mistress?"

Sarah turned. It was Hagar standing in the shade of the tent.

"Help Dinah," Sarah said coldly. She marched past the Egyptian. "And stay in the servants' quarters."

Abraham selected a young calf, well-fed with a good form to its hindquarters. He and the herdsmen had slit the animal's throat and were hoisting it to drain its blood and skin it in preparation for cooking when Eliezer joined them. He reported on the preparations and told them that the visitors still reclined, without words, where they had first stopped under the trees.

"They seem content there, my lord," Eliezer said. "And in no hurry."

"Go on back to the camp," Abraham told Eliezer. "See that the fire and the spit are ready for us."

Eliezer obediently went off again.

After two hours, the meal was ready. Sarah and two of the other women brought it to the men and served them. Sarah dismissed the younger women and retreated within the tent for modesty's sake, leaving the strangers to talk with her husband as was customary when men visited the camp. But she lingered just behind the curtain flap, straining to hear what they said. After the women had gone, Abraham dismissed Ishmael and his servants.

After the men had eaten, they asked for Sarah! The hair on the back of her neck stood up when she heard them say her name.

"She is there." Abraham indicated the tent next to the place where they reclined. "In the tent." He rose to call her but the tallest man stopped him.

"In the spring as now." The sound of the air was in the voice. "At next year's calving time, I shall return," he said to Abraham. "At the time that I visit you Sarah shall bear you the son I have promised."

In the shadow of the tent, unbeknownst to the visitors, Abraham, or Sarah, Hagar crouched listening. Her countenance fell.

An heir besides Ishmael!

A child! Hagar wrung her hands. Was it possible? What would happen to Ishmael if Sarah bore Abraham a son? She hurried away.

Abraham was stunned and silent at the announcement.

But even as he sat speechless, he heard laughter coming from the tent.

Inside the tent, Sarah's thoughts had turned unruly as she eavesdropped on the conversation outside. But she caught herself too late.

Me? Pregnant with the ewes? Shall my husband and I become like young lovers again after so many years? Even Dinah's potions had long been abandoned. Sarah's body had finished its season long ago! Abraham's wife of his youth held her sides and laughed out loud.

You Shall Bear a Son

The men turned in the direction of the sound of laughter. Abraham could picture her in his mind's eye.

"Your wife is laughing," the first man told Abraham. "Is anything too hard for the Lord?"

Abraham flushed with embarrassment. "No!" he said adamantly. "Forgive her. She is a silly woman sometimes!"

But the men seemed not to be put off by his wife's bad manners.

"Bring her out," they said.

Abraham hurried to the tent and opened it.

The light found his wife just as he had imagined. Hands tightly over her own mouth, she had a wild wide-eyed expression of delight and disbelief on her face.

"Stop it!" he whispered harshly. "They want to talk to you!"

Sarah straightened her face and clothes and quickly followed Abraham outside to the terebinth trees.

When Sarah's eyes met the men's one of them asked her, "Why did you laugh?"

Blood drained from her face and her knees suddenly went weak.

The locusts sang loudly in the heat beyond the shade.

"I didn't laugh," she lied. "Whatever you may have heard, it wasn't me!"

Abraham's throat went dry. First she laughed and now she lied!

"No," the second man said, "but you did! We heard you."

The other two agreed.

Sarah thought to answer them again, but the first man spoke before she could.

"As you have said," he told her, "life is renewed at the same time as the lambs."

Sarah flushed brilliant red. She pulled her shawl around her face.

They had heard her very thoughts!

The middle man went on.

"You shall bear your husband a son."

Sarah instantly knew that God saw all her ways as well as heard her thoughts.

With that the men gathered their cloaks and took their staffs in their hands and stood to leave.

As they left the grove and Sarah went to tell Dinah the story of the strange visit, none of them knew that the Egyptian bondwoman had sneaked to the master's tent and overheard the entire exchange.

As much as they made Sarah laugh, the words of the visitors also renewed her youth. She couldn't help it! A son! The thought caught her up like a sweet rushing river. But she would tell no one this time; she would wait to see the words fulfilled in her own body. It would be only a year in any case, and what was that compared to the decades she had already waited?

And this time not even Dinah shall me persuade me otherwise!

That night Abraham returned very late. When he came into the tent and lay down, Sarah was still thinking of the events of the day and all the men had said. When Abraham pulled his coverings over himself, his wife reached out.

Her heart was suddenly filled with a grand mixture of wonder and new love for this man—this man of faith in

their God. She smiled in the darkness as Abraham took her
into his arms and comforted her.

⟨~⟩

The heat of summer approached, and Abraham's vast
herds quickly consumed the grasses. He was compelled to
move them often to preserve the land itself. And so they
migrated again, this time towards Kadesh. The king of the
place where they were going was a Philistine from the coast-
land, and a descendant of Canaan's brother Mizraim. As
their great entourage came into Gerar, King Abimelech sent
men out to investigate the new arrivals and see if they had
come in peace.

They returned to Abimelech with news that the master
of the household was called Abraham, and he was peaceful
and very wealthy in gold as well as animals and servants.
Abimelech had heard of the Semite and of his God. But he
had also heard of the beauty of the Semite women. His messengers had reported that among the women in Abraham's
house was one who was particularly beautiful. She was the
man's sister, a woman called Sarah. When Abimelech heard
how desirable she was, he sent gifts to Abraham and asked
to have her as a gift for his harem!

Abraham dared not refuse and offend Abimelech. That
could result in an attack on the entire camp. He had thought
the same thing as a young man before they left their homeland. Sarah's beauty was a blessing and a curse!

Abraham told her the shameful news.

"How many times will you pretend I am not your wife?"
she demanded. "You have flocks and gold enough for seven!"

"All the more reason," he said. "I will do so as many
times as necessary to save us from men who do not fear God.
You swore when we began to sojourn from Haran, before

our father died, to say you were my sister to the kings of this strange land. Abimelech's men could easily have overpowered our house and taken you and the rest away! Ishmael, myself, and most likely Eliezer would have been left as food for the vultures. This act has bought us protection for the time being while I discover what I can do against this king. If he desires to make you his wife, it will be days before a wedding occurs. In the meantime, I will decide what to tell him when I come."

He paused. "Besides, in truth you are my sister. Terah was father to both of us."

Sarah resigned herself to his argument and prepared to go with Abimelech's men, just as she had gone to the Pharaoh in Egypt. She fearlessly steeled herself with the knowledge that God had promised an heir to Abraham from her own body. Until God's promise was fulfilled, she needn't fear for her own life or that of her husband! Despite how the situation appeared right now, she was confident that she would return and the king's hand would not touch her.

Abraham and Eliezer stood on the brow of the hill beyond the newly pitched tent city as Sarah was placed upon a camel to be taken to the king. She gave her "brother" one last look and covered her face against the desert wind. Then the men of Abimelech took up her camel's rein and turned to lead her away.

It would be many days before Sarah would see her house again.

❦

Hagar laughed out loud when she heard of Sarah's departure. She bathed herself in secret and made herself very attractive. That evening she stopped Eliezer at the door of the cooking tent and took the master's supper from his hands. Flashing a defiant look at him she said, "I must go to him and comfort him for the loss of his sister!" She strode away between the tents. Perfume lingered in her wake.

When Hagar came to the tent flap she called softly, "My lord?"

"Enter," Abraham's voice answered distractedly.

As Hagar appeared, Abraham started to rise.

"Where is Eliezer?" he said.

"One of the watchmen sent for him. He went to attend something at the corrals," Hagar lied. She bent before him, and the fragrance of her perfume washed over him. "Shall I feed you your supper tonight, my lord?" Hagar asked sweetly. Her dark eyes beckoned him.

Before he could catch himself, the moment he saw Hagar, Abraham's body reacted. Hot waves of desire rushed through him. Hagar's appearance and manners still tempted him. But he knew that Jehovah would not be pleased if he had relations with her, though she was his wife by Sarah's own hand and the birth mother of his only child thus far. The visitors had made it clear that God intended to fulfill His promise that Abraham and Sarah would have a son. Abraham refused to allow a second intervention in the divine plan, as had already occurred with Hagar and Ishmael.

He made an excuse. "I must wake early."

"Shall I wash your feet then? And anoint your head. Let me prepare you for your rest." She began to move about the tent, pouring water into a basin.

"No!" he said, suddenly impassioned.

Hagar turned. "What is it, lord? How have I distressed you? You are not pleased with the supper?"

"It is fine," he said. "Excuse me now. Eliezer will attend me. I am weary from the events of the day."

On this night, as on many before, Hagar was rejected by Abraham. He had not received her since the second night she had gone to him, the night after she had conceived Ishmael. Hagar knew it was because of Sarah's actions, and Abraham's faith in his God. Still, Hagar never ceased to take every opportunity to persuade Abraham to return to her arms. Another child by him would surely push Hagar into his affections again and drive Sarah into a secondary place in the eyes of the household. But alas, not on this night! Even though Sarah was nowhere in the encampment, Hagar had been rejected. She left the tent in humiliation.

Eliezer met her beside the door.

"Has my master retired?" he asked her.

Hagar shot him a spiteful look and did not answer him as she strode past him into the night.

When Ishmael came to say good night she was not beside her pallet. The boy went and stood outside Abraham's tent listening for some sound of her within. When he heard only Abraham's snores Ishmael walked out to the dunes beyond the encampment.

Ishmael found Hagar, sullen and thoughtful.

"What is it, my mother?" he asked.

The desert moon shown silver down on them.

"She controls my every breath even when she is absent!" Hagar told him. She turned to her son. "I swear by this moon that you shall have a wife from *my* people in Egypt, not one of these Semite women!"

Ishmael threw his cloak around her shoulders.

"I will have the wife that Abraham finds for me," he said in a very grown-up manner. "And as wedding gift, I will ask that you be given as nurse to my children." He chose words that he hoped would comfort her. "Now come out of the night air. There are wild beasts out here!"

They returned to camp.

When Hagar lay down, her last thoughts before she drifted off were images of Sarah in the harem of the king of

Gerar. Sarah might never return to her husband. Hagar rolled over and smiled in her sleep.

Escape from Abimelech

But it was not to be.

Before the week was out, messengers from Abimelech arrived at the camp announcing the preparations for the king's wedding to Abraham's *sister*. An entourage from Abraham's house was invited to come and celebrate the event. There would be days of feasting and convivial fellowship in honor of the wedding. Then, as soon as the time of ritual purification of the bride had passed, Abraham, as guest in the royal house in Gerar, would give his sister in marriage. King Abimelech would become Abraham's brother-in-law!

As Abimelech's servants retired to the men's quarters after supper, Abraham went to his tent in distress. He paced back and forth and finally lay down. He tossed and turned upon his bed.

"Jehovah," he prayed, "You have heard me before this! Remember the covenant with me and my house. Deliver me from this king and his strength!"

All night Abraham tossed and turned and talked to his God.

Night became day. Abraham feigned the happiness of a brother for his sister's marriage as he and several members of the household loaded gifts for Abimelech on camels.

Ishmael was disappointed when his father told him the boy would stay behind with the camp.

"But father," Ishmael pleaded, "I have not been to a city such as this, or an event such as a king's marriage, in my life so far!"

Abraham shot him a stern look.

"You know your mother Sarah is in danger!" he said under his breath. "Indeed, our entire household could yet lose our lives!" Abraham continued tying the bundled gifts onto the kneeling camels. "I'll not have my blood and that of my son wash the streets of pagans in a single night. Stay here and be a man. In case I do not return you must see to the flocks and the women. Flee further to the east. Cross the brook of Egypt and dwell there until you see how it goes. If you do not see me within four days, flee. The experienced herdsmen will be with you to help you."

"Yes, father," the boy said.

He stopped and took Ishmael in his arms and kissed him.

Abraham looked up. "We depart!" he announced.

The women who were staying behind came running out alongside the caravan. They ran the first short length of the journey trilling their tongues in celebration of the wedding in Gerar.

Eliezer rode at his master's side as they departed for the city. He glanced at Abraham's countenance behind the covering wrapped over his face to keep the dust out of his mouth. When they were riding far enough behind Abimelech's men that they wouldn't be overheard by them, Eliezer spoke.

"How shall we do with this king, my lord?" he asked. "What shall become of my mistress, Sarah?"

"Trust in Jehovah," Abraham replied. "I have prayed. The answer will come from Him."

After they had gone Hagar came looking for Ishmael.

"You will be the wealthiest son in Canaan if he does not return!" Hagar told him wistfully. "Perhaps this is the fulfillment of the man at the well! Abraham's riches will provide a good dowry to get you a wife from Egypt."

Ishmael listened to her words.

As it turned out, while Abraham had been tossing and turning in his tent all night praying, God had visited Abimelech. By the time the caravan reached the king's city, Abimelech himself was waiting at the gates. The king had Sarah in tow.

"Here is your *sister*, prophet!" he exclaimed to Abraham as they came down from their camels. "Take her and leave me a blessing! Why did you deceive me so that such a great evil as defiling another man's wife should come on my household?"

Abraham came down from his camel and bowed sincerely before Abimelech.

"I thought there was no fear of my God in Gerar," Abraham explained. "But in truth she is my sister, only not the daughter of my mother!" Abraham motioned to Eliezer to bring forth the camels carrying gifts for Abimelech.

However, in the manner of Pharaoh, Abimelech compensated Abraham with sheep, oxen, and servants, both men and women, that he had prepared for him to redeem Sarah according to the law of the land.

"Your sister, perhaps. But she is also your wife! Your God terrified me in a dream and warned me not to commit the sin of touching this woman," the king said. "He made me understand that every womb in my house has been closed because of her."

As the king's herdsmen drove the new flocks out of the city gates past them, the sheep bleated plaintively.

"Bless me now, Semite! And pray to your God on my behalf," Abimelech said. "For since the day Sarah has come under my roof the women and the livestock have ceased to bear. Who is this great God who calls you His friend and commands kings for your sake?"

"Jehovah, the Almighty!" Abraham told the king. A shiver ran over Abraham's neck beneath his clothing. God had answered in a miraculous way once again! And He did so despite the deception he kept concerning Sarah. It was pure mercy!

"There is no God besides Him in Heaven or on earth!" Abraham testified to the king.

"Take her back," Abimelech said. He brought Sarah forward to her husband. Abimelech also motioned to a steward standing in his entourage. The man ran forward, bringing two pages with him, and spread a lamb's skin on the ground. The lads each carried a heavy bag of coins. The silver made a fine ringing sound as the bags were untied and emptied onto the skin. The king spoke as the servants gathered the bundle around the money and took it to Eliezer to secure for Abraham.

"A thousand pieces of silver!" the king said. He spoke in the hearing of all who were gathered. "You are my witnesses that I have not taken another man's wife to defile her! According to our law she is redeemed." Abimelech turned to Sarah. "You are justified in the eyes of my house and yours. Go back to your husband."

Sarah quickly crossed to where Eliezer had prepared the camel to carry her home. She said nothing, and kept her eyes averted and her face covered. Quickly putting her leg over the camel's back she mounted upon it, and Eliezer urged the animal up. Sarah's silver compensation was tied behind her on the saddle.

Beneath her veil, Sarah smiled and thanked God for the return she had been sure would happen.

"Peace between us!" Abimelech said to Abraham.

"Peace!" Abraham replied. Then he stretched his hands toward heaven. "Almighty God! Maker of heaven and earth, open the wombs of Abimelech's house, I pray! And make all of his livestock bear double for his righteousness towards me!"

To the awe of those in attendance the sky suddenly thundered and a wind swept past their legs, kicking up the dust and blowing the hems of their robes across the men's faces.

So Abraham and Sarah took the riches given them by the king and returned to their land. Once again, in spite of his folly and fear of an earthly king, God had blessed Abraham and increased his wealth. And God heeded Abraham's prayer for the king's house, which gave Abraham and his God much reverence in the eyes of the king of Gerar and his people.

Hagar Has Poisoned Me!

When Abraham and Sarah had come back to their camp there was much relief in every heart.

Except Hagar's.

"I would rather have died at the hand of marauders than see that woman returning here with my lord," she said to herself when it was announced that Abraham's entourage was in view and Sarah was with them.

That night, and every night afterward, Abraham took Sarah into his arms and his bed. The visitors had been right after all.

And Hagar slept only in the tent of women. In the eyes of all the household, she was wife to Abraham in name only. And she was still subservient to Sarah. Hagar had hoped against hope. But her heart remained stubborn and sullen. If she could not be mistress in Sarah's stead, she might as well return to her own people. Any respect she held now was only because of the son she had born for Abraham's name's sake. The fact that she would be provided for all her days unless they sent her away was little consolation. She had never been able to win Abraham's affections away from Sarah. But for Ishmael, Hagar would have run away again long ago, in spite of the words of the man at the well.

Four months after the visit of the three men, after her return from Abimelech, Sarah awoke with a dizzying upset in her stomach and head. Before she could escape the tent, she was retching miserably and feeling every bit of her age. The first images to run through Sarah's mind were of Hagar bending over the cooking fire the previous day mixing spices into the preparations for the evening meal.

She has poisoned me at last! Sarah thought.

"Send me Dinah!" she said to Abraham, clutching her head and stomach at once. Then Sarah remembered the cycle of the moon, now well behind her. She felt the same slight tenderness in her breasts, and the tingling sensation that turned into dull rhythmic pains in her womb. Jehovah and her body were in some conspiracy against her, punishing her. Now, having gone beyond all possibility of childbearing, her body was feigning.

Sarah retched again. Only bitter bile came up. She groaned and lay down again, a hand to her brow searching for sign of fever.

When Dinah came to her she inspected Sarah's eyes and the inside of her mouth. Then she abruptly stuck her gnarled hands beneath Sarah's garments.

"Ouch!" Sarah swatted at the impertinent old crone and pulled away, wrapping her arms over her tender breasts.

Dinah's eyes brightened and she chuckled, shaking her head incredulously.

"Oh, mistress!" The old woman wagged a crooked finger at Sarah knowingly.

"What is it?" Sarah demanded.

"The promise," Dinah said.

"Promise?" Sarah replied. "You crazy old crone! What are you talking about?"

"The promise," Dinah said. "The promise of God!"

Sarah's feeling of sickness was immediately overcome when she finally understood the meaning of the old woman's words. She sucked in her breath. Her hands went to her stomach as she lay back on her pallet.

"Call my husband!" she said.

Dinah rose and moved as fast as her old legs could carry her to find Abraham and tell him the news. As Dinah exited the tent, she listened to her mistress. In between the attempts of her stomach to turn itself inside out with morning sickness, Sarah was laughing.

Filled with Laughter

"Everywhere this story is told," Dinah heard Sarah saying, "all who hear it will laugh as I do now!"

In her eighty-ninth year, Sarah grew round with the promised pregnancy.

The caravans that traversed Canaan heard the incredible tale. From the firelight of desert camps men boasted of Abraham's strength as they repeated the amazing story, including the part of the three mysterious visitors.

They talked of Abraham's faith and of his Invisible God. Fear and respect of Him grew throughout the regions where Abraham migrated to pasture his growing herds. Some who had been in Abraham's encampments testified to seeing his wife. Still attractive enough to draw a man's interest in spite of her age, but even more amazing, heavy with child!

The story became a legend in those days. And wherever it was told, just as Sarah had predicted, people laughed at its incredulity and its wonder.

But Hagar did not laugh, except in her heart at the sight of the ridiculous aging woman fat with child waddling back and forth from her pallet.

As if changing her name would change her spoiled nature, Hagar thought. *Wishful thinking on her husband's part!*

The child in Sarah's womb posed a threat to Ishmael's future. And a child by Sarah meant further insignificance for Hagar in the household. Sarah had won again! Every time it happened, Hagar remembered the words of the man at the well.

Submit to your mistress.

Those words plagued Hagar and filled her with dark, churning resentment. She had returned to the camp from the well that day more than a dozen years ago, but she would never submit her heart to Sarah. Hagar would never allow the Semite woman the satisfaction of feeling she had gained an upper hand. Jealous Hagar would resist Sarah with her very last breath! And she detested the unborn child as much as she did its mother.

But Hagar clung to the other words the man had said—the words about Ishmael. Hagar comforted herself with them.

He shall be a wild man. His hand against every man!

Hagar smiled in satisfaction. Words of prophecy, she hoped.

In the second half of that year Sarah's condition caused her to become more demanding than ever. With Dinah also growing older, Hagar's responsibilities increased. She fetched and carried for the mistress, turned out the carpets and coverlets of Sarah's tent and pallet, and directed the other household servants. She even rubbed olive oil into Sarah's tired back and feet in the evenings.

Hagar marked every task in an account in her head, determined to someday extract payment for each one. All the while, Hagar bit her tongue before Abraham and inwardly plotted. Her revenge would come through the next generations of her offspring if necessary. Future generations would break free of the bonds that kept Hagar a servant to Sarah.

Ishmael would have many sons. Hagar would see to that. Since Abraham would only give her one, she would find that son many fruitful wives. Beginning with women from her people. Her grandchildren would become so numerous, as the man had said, that they would drive any children this Isaac produced right out of the land!

Hagar prayed often these days, but not to the God who had made the promise to Sarah.

All the while Hagar continued to acknowledge Abraham as her husband. In spite of Sarah, Hagar took special care of Abraham's food and clothing, behaving not so much as Sarah's bondwoman as Abraham's wife.

Hagar's attentions served as painful reminders to Sarah of her rash, skeptical act of giving her slave as her husband's second wife. She had tried to make God's promise come to pass according to the customs of the land where they sojourned.

Abraham felt compassion for Hagar. Whenever he looked long at her, he remembered the cool touch of her slender fingers on his sun-baked skin the night she conceived Ishmael in his embrace.

Devoted to Strange Gods

Ishmael came to his mother most nights before he retired. They would sneak away from the camp, being careful to avoid the notice of the watch posted each night. Under the bright silver light of the desert moon, Hagar would entertain him with magical tales. She described events of her childhood and the great days of the Nile empire. Its rulers were richer and wiser even than Abraham, she said.

There were tales of caravans of other kingdoms that came down to pay homage and tribute to the Pharaohs, bringing gifts of all kinds, including strange animals never before seen in Egypt. Ishmael's favorite was the description

of creatures that walked upright on two legs like great hairy
men with huge feet, long arms, and drooping faces. Ishmael
held his sides and laughed until he cried whenever Hagar
imitated the creatures called apes, scratching herself under
her arms and lumbering about on the dunes, imitating their
sounds and throwing handfuls of sand over her own head.
He longed to go to the places his mother spoke of and see
these things for himself. When he was grown and had
become heir he would do just that. The next son could stay
home and look after the sheep!

Hagar would retell the prophecy of the jinn-spirit at the
well. Ishmael would imagine himself as the stallion at the
head of a herd, like the wild onagers whose hooves thundered on the earth when they stampeded. At the same time,
a strange sensation came alive in the boy during those nights
in the desert when his mother spoke and his imagination ran
wild. It began as a tiny vibration, urging him to become as
suspicious as Hagar was of all that Sarah and Isaac intended
for them. It made Ishmael anxious.

As the vibration stirred up Ishmael's mind and tore at his
heart, he found himself plotting ways to keep Isaac from
robbing him of his rightful place in Abraham's heart. After
all, Ishmael, by right, by birth, was still the first son in
Abraham's house. That inward vibration intensified, growing like a bitter vine, until it seemed to spread throughout
his entire being.

"No one will tame me!" he would shout to Hagar as he
ran in wide circles under the moon, bucking and braying
like the small wild desert horses.

Isaac Is Born

By lambing time next spring, just as the visitors had predicted, Sarah's time to deliver had arrived.

The entire camp waited out the hours in anticipation. The sun was setting and the desert sky was ablaze with brilliant reds and oranges when the cry of a newborn boy resounded in Abraham's camp. As soon as they heard the child's cry the women trilled their tongues in the traditional celebration of his birth.

"Isaac!" Sarah said. She cradled the child in her arms. "I'll name you Isaac, for you have made me and my husband laugh! Blessed be the God of Abraham, the God of Isaac! The God who keeps His covenant to the third and fourth generations!" For now she knew she would have grandsons and great-grandsons and daughters by wives fruitful and numerous as the stars and the sand. She had waited long, and the answer to all her heart's desires had arrived at last.

Abraham hugged Eliezer and bowed down to the ground in thanksgiving.

"Blessed be the God of Heaven, Who keeps His promises just as He has said!" he prayed.

Eliezer also bowed and worshiped.

"Blessed be the God of Abraham!" he agreed.

"My son, firstborn of Sarah, has come to me at the time of sacrifice," he told Eliezer. "Even this must be a sign of Jehovah's covenant with him. Tomorrow we will prepare the offering—a thank-offering for this son!"

Sarah held the miracle child to her breast as soon as he was laid on her stomach and the cord to her womb was tied off with string. She thought of herself and of the baby newly emerged from her body. She looked at Dinah, who stood by smiling widely, eyes flashing with glee and mischief. The two women laughed at the mistress's happy and amazing miracle.

Abraham heard them from outside the tent as he waited to see the new child. He threw up his hands in happy frustration.

Finally Abraham could wait no longer. He opened the tent. The women gasped and looked at one another wide-eyed.

"Where is my son?" he bellowed happily. "Am I the last to see him?"

"Take him then, husband." Sarah handed the child to the midwife and settled back onto her bed to rest in peaceful contentment.

The woman carried the baby to Abraham and laid him in his father's arms.

"I have named him Isaac!" Sarah said.

"And Isaac you are!" Abraham told the baby boy. "Laughter!" He put a thick, hard worn finger to the soft new flesh of Isaac. "Born to me in my old age!"

"And don't forget, born of an old woman!" Sarah laughed. "Isaac. He is a miracle of God!"

She closed her eyes, remembering the feel of Isaac cuddled in her arms. Sarah smiled. "Surely there is no God like our Jehovah!" She turned over and slept.

<hr />

But the next day, as word of Isaac's arrival spread throughout the camp and Ishmael came with the others to see the new son, Sarah's laughter ceased. Unhappy foreboding settled on her at the sight of the elder boy. Her first thought as he came near to peer at the newborn was fear. Would Ishmael stand in the way of Isaac's blessing somehow? The thought troubled her from that day on. And she prepared herself to make sure Isaac would surpass him in everything.

In another eight days Sarah had recovered. According to the command of God, Abraham took the child and circumcised him. Isaac was the very first male born to Abraham after God had made His covenant with him.

Abraham continued to love his first son Ishmael, whom he had doted on proudly since the day of his birth. But the very nature of this new son was different. Isaac drew him with a sweetness that he had not shared in the son before him. And Isaac was the direct fulfillment of the word that God had spoken. He was a miracle, for he was the son promised years earlier, when Abraham had first heard the voice of God.

Since that time Abraham had become very dependent upon his God, and very obedient. God had delivered him from pharaohs and kings and had given him the power to get wealth as a testimony before the whole land of God's covenant with him.

Ishmael, in the meantime, was receiving less and less of his father's affection, or so it seemed. He deeply resented Sarah as the reason behind it. Since becoming pregnant with a son of her own, Sarah had become the fulfillment of all that Ishmael's mother had warned him of. Sarah ignored him once she had Isaac. Ishmael was no longer her son, as she had always before insisted that he was. Before she had attempted to win him over, but now she snapped at Ishmael, if she paid him any attention at all. In his mind, Sarah deserved all the ill will that he and Hagar ever wished upon her!

And Abraham—in fact, the entire household with the exception of Hagar—talked of nothing but Isaac. Ishmael's hatred for the squalling baby grew by the day. It humiliated him that a helpless infant with fat hands and big ugly feet had more influence on Abraham than Ishmael. He was now almost a man, excellent as a hunter and learner of the ways of the desert.

Ishmael comforted himself and ran alone into the wilderness to work on his archery. He practiced all his knowledge of the livestock and still sought to perform well before his father. But when he showed off some skill or some bit of knowledge before Abraham these days, his father seemed less attentive than before. He often just smiled distractedly. The doting and the insistence that the other herdsmen stop to watch and admire him were gone. Ishmael imagined that Abraham was thinking of the time when Sarah's son would replace him. And Hagar continued to remind him that Sarah would do everything in her power to push him out of his father's heart completely, leaving room for only one son. It seemed to be working. Abraham even seemed impatient with him.

On one occasion, during a very hectic washing of the flocks before the summer heat fully set in, Abraham lost his temper and rapped Ishmael sharply on the back of the head in sight of all the herdsmen. It was a rebuke for letting a pregnant ewe slip past and into the dipping pool.

"You are no better than a woman today," Abraham shouted at the lad while he and another herdsmen dove for the ewe, soaking themselves with the sheep dip. Abraham shook out his garments. "You may as well join them in the tents! Go!"

<hr>

Abraham turned back to his sweaty work, and the rest of the men laughed at the boy. They jeered and made kissing noises after him as he ran from the corral in disgrace and frustration. Abraham did nothing to stop them!

Hagar saw him come into the camp and went to see what had happened.

"It's her influence on him, my son! Just as I have said," Hagar told him. "She will make him hate you to ensure that Isaac inherits!"

"What am I to do, mother?" he cried.

"Never submit to her!" Hagar told him. "I may have been sold, but you are not her slave! You possess your pride. No one can take that from you!"

"But what of the promise and the words of his God?" the boy replied. "What of Him?"

Hagar flashed an angry expression at him.

"Worship the gods of my fathers, then!" she snapped. "They will not forget you! We will see whose god is great!"

But sadly, the answer for Hagar was the very one she rejected: the words of the man at the well. *Submit to Sarah as your mistress.*

Obeying those words would have ensured that Hagar would have been included together with her son safely into Abraham's covenant with his God and his family forever.

From the day of his rebuke Ishmael became increasingly insolent. Envy of his half-brother and hatred for him was conceived that day. Ishmael vowed in his heart that if he was to be usurped in the eyes of his father, at least he would win the affections of the herdsmen and the other servants. Then in the end, when Abraham died, Ishmael would have their favor rather than Isaac. His silent vow caused him to imitate every wild thing the men ever did and conceive new antics of his own to get their attention.

And in response to his insolence Sarah became more and more resentful and suspicious of the son of her slave. She even imaged that Hagar and Ishmael conspired for ill against the baby Isaac!

Ishmael's behavior erected a wall of miscommunication and alienation between himself and his father. Though Abraham cared deeply for the child who had been his chief joy for the thirteen years preceding the birth of Isaac, his feelings were changing. Ishmael's eyes were often on the wide expanse of wilderness waste beyond the flocks and tents of Abraham's house.

Jealousy Begets Jealousy

In the first year of Isaac's life the baby became the unsuspecting enemy of his half-brother as jealousy begat jealousy. Ishmael made Isaac the butt of insults and caused the other children in the camp to mock him. And he himself taunted him, keeping playthings just out of his reach. He would wait for the baby to doze off to sleep, then sneak up and frighten the child into a scream. Then Ishmael would hide to watch as Sarah came running.

When Isaac was weaned, Abraham held a great feast to honor the day. As expected, Abraham began with a sacrifice in the morning. For several days the preparations of special savory foods, festive attire, and plans for a great bonfire turned the camp into a beehive of activity. Amidst the excitement, Ishmael was reminded of the last feast like this they had celebrated. Little more than a year ago they had honored him.

The joy and dancing and music would last well into the early hours of the desert night.

Everyone was filled with joviality. Everyone except Hagar and Abraham's first son, who were weary of the continual fuss that was made over the new heir.

When the time of the feast finally arrived, the people ate their fill of roast goat stuffed with figs and dates and sopped up oil laced with salt and spices with pieces of bread made from freshly-ground roasted wheat. They drank down great bowls of sweetened milk and wine bought from the caravans or made with wild honey. Afterwards Abraham took Isaac up on his shoulders as he once had done with Ishmael.

Abraham danced Isaac around the fire. Everyone clapped. But the adulation fell short of being appreciated by the sleepy toddler. He squirmed and fussed until his discomfort gave way to an open-mouthed squall with tears streaming down his pudgy face.

Ishmael looked on in gleeful disdain. His heart burned at the sight of Abraham cherishing and cradling Isaac. His father's smiling eyes were full of love and devotion, as if he had only one son now.

Doting Sarah urged Abraham to let the unhappy Isaac down. The baby, who had just begun taking his first steps, sat where he was placed when Abraham finally gave in to the fussing. Sarah stretched out her hands to Isaac and called to him, cooing and urging him to stand and toddle to her open arms.

Abraham also tried to encourage Isaac to take the four or five steps to his mother on his own two feet. Unhappily, Isaac struggled to stand upright, leaning toward Sarah's outstretched arms a few feet away. As he did, Ishmael was reminded of his mother's stories of the apes brought down to Egypt. He made a long face and grimaced, parodying baby Isaac. The lads around him saw it and snickered, putting a hand to their mouths lest the master rebuke them. Ishmael glanced sideways at his mother, who was watching his mimicry. She covered her smile with both hands as well. It encouraged Ishmael. He rocked back and forth on his haunches, imitating a clumsy ape.

Isaac struggled up to his unsteady feet and started towards his mother. But Ishmael stuck out the tip of his archer's bow, which he almost always had with him, just beyond the circle of the seated household members. He caught his half-brother's already unsteady foot and tripped him, quickly pulling back his bow and looking innocently into the night sky, lips pursed as if whistling. The shepherds sitting around Ishmael saw it. They guffawed at his unruly antics, further encouraging him. Ishmael basked in their attention.

When Sarah turned to see Ishmael mocking her son, she went black with rage.

Ishmael's trick had made the baby fall forward into the dirt. He came up filthy-faced and bawling loudly. Sarah leapt to her feet and rushed to keep Isaac away from the fire. When she had retrieved her child, her gaze shot across the leaping fingers of the blaze between them to where Hagar sat. Sarah was met with an equally defiant stare. Her baby in her arms, Sarah marched out of the circle of celebrants towards her tent. Abraham saw the spectacle and rebuked the herdsmen and Ishmael. They instantly quieted. After an uncomfortable moment, the festivities slowly resumed their happy din.

He Shall Not Inherit

When Sarah brought Abraham his breakfast the next morning he knew she had an agenda in mind. Sarah placed his plate solidly before her husband and announced her business without hesitation.

"Isaac could have fallen into the fire. The slave's son has become just like his mother!" Sarah warned. "Impudent and rebellious. Ishmael grows more wicked by the day." Sarah's uneasy passions were stirred up again. She pictured scenes of Hagar and Ishmael plotting evil against Isaac in the future. "Husband, now it is enough! Ishmael rejects correction and makes a mockery of you and your true heir before your entire household!"

Sarah's words pierced Abraham to the core. But he too realized that Ishmael had grown increasingly difficult and stubborn—and dangerously influenced by his mother's words.

"He is a lad," Abraham offered in Ishmael's defense. "Be patient."

But Sarah would not. "Ishmael is your son only in the flesh. His heart is joined neither to you nor to this house, any more than his mother's is. Hagar serves you only because she has been sold here in payment of a debt. She will return to her people the very day she is freed. Then what? Shall Ishmael take your inheritance with him?"

Her tirade was like a torrent that could not be stopped. Abraham wanted to put his hands on his ears as she raged on.

"Isaac is an innocent baby now. But what about when he is grown? You may ignore it, but I'll not sit by while they threaten to do something dreadful when no one is watching!" Sarah looked at her husband with a steely countenance.

Her words assailed him as she marched around the inside of their tent, arms flailing as she spoke. Sarah suddenly stopped and looked at him with clenched fists.

"I am fully within my rights, as you know!" Sarah announced. "She is mine to do with as I please under the law. She and her son will leave this house forever." Sarah put her hands firmly on her hips. "Divorce her—I demand it! Ishmael will not become heir together with Isaac."

Abraham choked on the hot tea he had just sipped, spilling the burning liquid down his front. Dropping the cup, he pulled the hot, wet garment clear of his lap. Ishmael had been his only son for all the years before Isaac's birth! He had watched him grow and change. Like any father, Abraham was devoted to both of his sons. The rivalry born in their mothers was splitting Abraham's heart in two, like the pieces of the sacrifice he had made when God first promised him an heir from his body. It seemed that the same vultures circled overhead to devour him. The reality of that knowledge, along with the tea in his lap, added distress to Sarah's offensive demands. He stood up and kicked the breakfast away.

"Demand, wife?" he roared, stepping close to her. He pointed a finger in Sarah's face. His voice was low and threatening. "It is you who are enough! I will have no more mention of this imagined conspiracy against Isaac! You have become crazy, always suspecting them of evil. Ishmael is my son as well as Isaac. Leave the management of him to me and do not speak of it again. Not now, not ever!" He stormed out of their tent.

Abraham stayed away all that day, nursing his anger and waiting for it to subside before returning to his household.

Ishmael searched until he found him.

"What is it, my father?" he said humbly. "Send me to deal with whomever has troubled you!" He had some fear that he was in ill favor from the night before and was seeking to repair Abraham's feelings for him.

Abraham clasped Ishmael's hand.

Finally he said, "Your mother Sarah is angered by your taunting of Isaac."

Ishmael instantly replied in a low tone, "She is not my mother!"

Abraham was silent and in a little while sent the young man back to camp alone.

⚜

Thirty

It was past midnight when Abraham finally lay down on the pallet in his tent. Sarah had taken Isaac and gone to the tent of women, her own pallet separated from Hagar's by a distance of three curtained partitions.

Abraham had barely closed his eyes when he heard the voice of Jehovah.

"Abraham, do not let this thing displease you. Listen to Sarah your wife, for what she has said is true. Though you have regard for the bondwoman and her son, it is in Isaac that I have called your heritage. Yet, I will do this for your sake: because you care for Ishmael I will make a nation of him."

Abraham had dreaded that it would come to this. He turned his face into his blankets and let them drink in his tears. The next morning Abraham roused Ishmael in the predawn darkness.

"Arise, my son," Ishmael heard his father say as he awoke from sleep.

"Go and bring your mother to me," Abraham said.

Ishmael sat up, rubbing the sleep from his eyes.

"What is it, father?" he asked. "Has something happened?"

"Get up, lad. Bring Hagar to me. Tell her to bring her belongings."

Ishmael didn't question him. He simply rose and went swiftly through the cold morning air to the tent of women. Eliezer met him.

"What is it?" the man asked.

"Abraham has sent for my mother," Ishmael replied.

"Go then," said Eliezer.

Ishmael imagined that Hagar's prayers had been answered at last. Abraham's heart had turned back to Ishmael's mother. When the boy and his mother came back Abraham met them at the entrance to the camp. He had with him Ishmael's cloak and bow. Ishmael was confused.

Without a word, an ashen-faced Abraham took Hagar's hand and pushed provisions of bread into it. He placed the cloak and bow upon Ishmael's back.

Hagar's heart sank as she looked at the loaves. It was bread for a few days' journey. After that they would die in the wilderness! An angry fire burned in Hagar's mind, for this was Sarah's doing. Hagar knew what this meant. Abraham was divorcing her, and sending Ishmael away as well. The humiliation and rejection burned like acid. Bitter hatred filled her heart.

She searched Abraham's face with imploring eyes, waiting for him to speak.

He avoided her gaze and hoisted a skin of water from beside his feet. Putting it on her shoulder, he hung his head, resting a hand tentatively on her shoulder as he did so. She reached for it, but he drew back before she could touch him. Then Abraham walked away from them. He could not look at them as he cast them out according to the word of his wife and his God.

With the desert before them and Abraham's back turned to them, Hagar and Ishmael clung to one another. After his first confusion, anger came over Ishmael with the bitter recognition that Sarah had gotten her way. Ishmael was being expelled from his birthright by the Semite and her clumsy baby! He started to speak, to run to Abraham, but Hagar restrained him, putting her hand on his arm and signaling him to be silent. The knowing look on his mother's face was more than he could bear.

Abraham waited. Tears brimmed over his eyes and splashed down his face.

Ishmael and Hagar said nothing to one another as the young man threw his cloak over his mother to fend off the chill air. Taking the skin of water from her onto his own shoulder, Ishmael supported Hagar as they walked into the desert.

The soft sounds of their feet upon the earth grew more and more faint. At last silence tore at Abraham's soul. He spun around and stared into the darkness.

"Watch over them since I cannot," he pleaded in a whisper that reached the heavens.

Eliezer silently witnessed the departure in secret. He ducked away when Abraham turned back to the camp and returned to his tent.

The sleep of exhaustion came at last for the master.

"Look Up, Hagar"

Hagar and Ishmael wandered in the wilderness for three days. At first they were distressed that they had been rejected and sent away. Then defiant...and then desperate, when their bread and water ran out. At last weariness and thirst overtook even the hunger pangs in their stomachs. Not knowing what else to do, Hagar made Ishmael sit down in the shade of a shrub. After a time the lad fell asleep. When his mother saw that he was sleeping she quietly got up and went a distance away from him. She fell down wailing.

She tore at her clothes and hair and could not be consoled.

When Ishmael woke and saw that his mother had disappeared he began to frantically run to and fro, the hot sand flying up his legs off the backs of his sandals. His thirst and panic were dizzying.

"Mother!" he cried. "Mother! Where are you?"

He strained his eyes as far as he could see in every direction but Hagar's form was nowhere to be found. Ishmael's cries reached her ears but she kept herself hidden from him. When he sat down on the ground at last, hot and thirsty and sobbing, Hagar could bear it no longer. Ishmael cried out.

"God of my father, help us!"

Then he fainted from the heat and from his anguish.

Hagar uncovered her head, hoping to swoon in the heat as well. However, the voice of the same man who had found her when she first ran away from Sarah spoke out loud. Hagar turned around in place, but this time there was no figure standing by her, only the voice. She thought that the heat was overwhelming her, and she prepared herself for death. But the voice sounded comforting.

"What ails you, Hagar?" the voice said.

"My son and I are as good as dead!" she replied.

"Don't be afraid. God has heard the lad. Go and take his hand. Remember what I said to you in days past: Ishmael will become a numerous people!"

Locusts sang and the sun beat down upon Hagar. Her head hurt and her mouth was as dry as the dust beneath her. Bright fingers of light passed before her eyes.

"Look up, Hagar," the voice insisted.

But she shook her head, wailing, and covered her face with her hands.

"Look up!" the voice said again. "There is water!"

At that Hagar took her hands away from her face and looked up. She stood, and there in the distance before her she saw what appeared to be a well stone. Hagar shielded her vision from the sun with her hands. It was a well!

She picked up the empty waterskin and ran in the direction of the stone. When she came to it, to her amazement it was not a mirage!

Water!

She dropped the skin into the well and drew it up again, full, wet, and dripping. She rubbed a bit of the water over her lips. Then she ran back to where Ishmael had fainted.

As she lifted his head onto her lap and poured water into his mouth, the lad sputtered and came around.

"Drink, son," she said. "The god of the desert has saved you for a great purpose!"

He drank, and then Hagar drank after him. Revived by the water, the two of them went back to the well. They poured water over one another, laughing, as hope returned and the water cooled their brows.

When their spirits had recovered from the heat and their thirst was quenched, they reappraised their circumstances and retraced their steps to find Ishmael's bow.

"I can hunt food for us!" he said firmly. "Why should I sit down like a coward?" He looked out across the landscape. "This wilderness will submit to me!" he shouted and beat upon his chest with a fist.

Hagar, wrapping her dampened hair into her covering, affirmed his words.

"Yes!" she said. "The prince of Canaan's land has come to his kingdom!" Hagar shouted at the wilderness.

When the moon had come up and its silver light bathed the land, Hagar looked into the face of the white orb and swore by an oath in her mother tongue.

"What are you doing, Mother?" Ishmael asked when he saw her face and heard her prayerful words going up.

"When I was a girl in Egypt, my father showed me the face of the moon god in the river. Look at his light, my son." She pointed up. "He has saved us. As long as we must dwell in this desert he will not fail to show us his face and give us his light night after night!"

Ishmael looked up at the moon as Hagar prayed.

"God of my fathers, god of this desert moon over us, make us as great as the God of Abraham has made Isaac live before Him!" said Hagar avidly. "Strengthen Ishmael's hand against every man according to the word of the man who saw me at the well!"

"What is our god's name, mother?" her son asked her.

She didn't look at him, but kept gazing upward.

"The Sumerians call him al-iLah," she said wistfully. "Some of the nomads call him Zin. This wilderness belongs to him!"

"Is al-iLah the One Abraham worships?" he asked.

Now Hagar looked at him.

"Abraham has rejected us," she said coldly. "Al-iLah is the supreme judge of all. Now he will judge us"—she paused—"and our enemies as well."

Ishmael said nothing. He simply shut his eyes tightly and agreed in earnest with his mother's words. When she was finished the boy opened his eyes and stared up at the moon again.

"Al-iLah," he whispered.

Mother and son rested by the well for the next two days. As he had promised, Ishmael hunted small animals for them to eat. In the afternoon of the third day, they spotted a caravan coming across the landscape towards them. Hagar and Ishmael ran to hide themselves from the strangers.

The caravan came noisily to the well and settled for a day-long respite. In the predawn, the food of the merchants stirred the hunger of Ishmael and his mother. The lad sneaked past the noses of the watchmen and was rifling through a food supply when a strong hand grabbed him by the neck.

The tall watchman's voice spoke. "Well, thief!" the man said. "Let us find what the boss has to say about you."

But instead of delivering retribution, the caravan boss found the brazen boy intriguing. In fact, he laughed when Ishmael was brought before him. Once the travelers learned that the boy was the exiled son of the great Abraham, they thought to hold him and his mother for a ransom from the wealthy man.

"Take us with you!" Ishmael insisted. "I am strong! I will hunt fresh game for the camp! Besides, we do not wish to return to my father's house, nor will he receive us."

The boss laughed at him and sent them away to sleep.

As they lay down among the baggage unloaded from the camels, Hagar pulled her cloak over her head. She smiled to herself.

"Sleep now, Ishmael. Tomorrow we start south toward home. We are free at last!"

In the morning the caravan rose up. Just as Hagar had said, the caravan boss humored the cunning boy. With Ishmael and his mother loaded into the baggage, the caravan traveled towards the cities to the south. Every night of the journey, Hagar pointed at the crescent moon and reminded Ishmael of the deliverance al-iLah had brought them.

Peace at Last

In Hagar's absence, Sarah regained her former spirit. Quietness and contentment returned to reign again in Abraham's wife and in his house. They delighted continually in Isaac as he grew before them. His happy countenance and faithful spirit were a balm to Abraham's heart after his loss of Ishmael. Occasionally, Sarah remembered the stormy days when she had resented Hagar so, constantly fearing that the slave's son would usurp her own.

But ultimately Sarah had submitted herself to Jehovah, as Abraham had once told her she must. When she had, all the troubles of those former days melted behind her. In her repentance, Sarah even prayed that God would bless the bondwoman and her son. She was glad to hear that Ishmael had gotten a wife who bore him sons, for she well understood the pain of barrenness. Sarah consoled herself with the knowledge that Hagar had grandchildren to renew her youth and finally make her happy.

Hagar and Ishmael never returned to Abraham. Instead, they came to dwell in the wilderness of Paran Arabah next to Egypt. Though Hagar was no longer a bondslave, she never found freedom from her hatred of Sarah. As she had sworn, Hagar took a wife for her son from her own land.

While his contemporaries were merchants and shepherds, Ishmael became a famed hunter with his skills of the bow and arrow and spear. He cared little for the domesticities of pastoral life. Instead he trained his sons to raise livestock and increase herds according to the knowledge he had learned early from his father.

News of Ishmael eventually came to Abraham. Tales of his son's great prowess as a hunter and word that his clans grew in strength reached his ears through traders. So Abraham remembered Ishmael and gathered together a great gift for him.

When Abraham's gift arrived, loaded on a great caravan of camels, Hagar looked at Ishmael bitterly. Then the woman gathered spittle in her mouth and spat into the dust at her feet.

"There is my reply to this gift!" she said. "You should have been his heir. All of Canaan was to belong to you!" She turned her back in disgust and walked away.

Jealousy's Bitter Legacy

Bitter jealousy, like a cancer that would not die, continued to beget jealousy.

Even when Hagar was greatly advanced in years and Ishmael was past fifty summers, word came to her that Sarah had died and been buried in Hebron to the north. For Hagar it was one more reason for triumph. And she thanked her gods. Not only had she escaped Sarah before her bond was fulfilled, but she had outlived her. Hagar was proud that her son was like a spreading vine, though her bitter spirit found little joy in anything.

"May Isaac's wife, if he ever finds one," Hagar often repeated, "be as barren as his mother!" The poisonous laugh that followed these caustic words grew increasingly brittle each time she spoke them.

Hagar longed to see her beloved Egypt to the south once more before she died. Ishmael made arrangements, but she never went. Instead, she fell deathly ill. Ishmael threw himself down at her bedside and wept. She came out of her fever long enough to acknowledge him. Her eyes like glass, she smiled dryly; her joyless grimace lacked several teeth by now. She tried to speak, but then returned to the images of her delirium. Figures from the past marched her back through the mists of time. There she revisited and drank once more from the bitter pool of envy that had poisoned her soul and stagnated within her heart year after year.

As Ishmael crouched by her side, the last words he could make out were of Hagar's old rival, Sarah. Fevered and out of her mind, Hagar rasped her grating whisper into Ishmael's ear. Her gnarled fingers and coarse nails bit into his skin as she clutched him, wild-eyed.

"She could never rule me!" Her breath was foul with sickness and death. "Never submit to her! If any submit, let it be to you!" she told him for the final time. "Now al-iLah and death have won."

She slumped down and Ishmael supported her weight on his arms.

"No, Mother!" Ishmael cried. "You will recover to see still more grandchildren!"

But Hagar could not hear him. For Sarah was there before her—as beautiful as she had been, pregnant and laughing. Laughing, it seemed, at Hagar. Hagar lashed out to wound Sarah once more, but the image eluded the shriveled, angry hand. And Sarah seemed to smile back peacefully. Then the apparition disappeared into the mist and Hagar's breath went out of her for the last time.

"Mother!" Ishmael wept. He shook her.

One hand still clutched him; the other was frozen in midair like the barren limb of a winter tree. The dead woman's crooked fingers still grasped for something that was beyond her reach. That grasping had begun between two jealous women in the desert of Canaan over half a century before. It had continued to grow, generation after generation, as a poisonous vine whose wild thorns would eventually prick the entire world.

Hagar's eyes glazed in death, with the name of her former mistress Sarah the last bitter word on her tongue.

Summary

Hagar shows us how jealousy begets jealousy. Jealousy creates an unholy influence that reproduces itself in those who come under the influence of the jealous party. It infects in much the same way as one prong of a tuning fork passes along its nervous vibrations to the other prongs until all vibrations are in unison with the first.

When ancient priests began to worship idols and drew those evil images on the walls of the temple, God became "jealous." Whenever He drew near to the temple, those images inspired His wrath and destruction. Unholy jealousy works the same way. The appearance, traits, resemblance, or reminder of the object of jealousy become reason to reject or attack any representative. Hagar perpetuated her offense, legal arguments, and plots to usurp the blessing ordained for Sarah and Isaac. She passed her jealous spirit to her son. Ishmael passed it to his sons, and it has continued to reproduce for thousands of years. Hagar's jealousy has reproduced to infect millions with the "ethnos rising against ethnos", racism rampant in acts of international terrorism which threatens today.

Familiar Friend

Jealousy is as cruel as the grave; its flames are flames of fire, a most vehement flame.

—Song of Songs 8:6, NKJV

The ancient trees gestured, their bony, crooked fingers pointing as he entered the garden. They seemed to whisper to one another, recognizing him. He stooped and passed beneath the branches. Their dust-skinned leaves brushed the hair of his head, making him itch and adding to his urge to run. Like sentinels, watchers, their eyes were on him all around. He swallowed. Thick saliva stuck against the sides of his dry throat, tasted bitter. He rubbed his aching face on the sleeve of the outer garment he carried, hoping to awaken, longing for the free feeling of lucidity instead of this thick confusion. The acrid bite of his own dried perspiration met his nostrils.

In spite of the fresh morning chill of spring, his clothes to his unwashed body stuck between his shoulders. Any other day he would have washed at least his head and beard by now. He longed for the comfort and lingering fresh scent of soap and oil to anoint his head. Any other day he would have finished his prayers by now. But he wouldn't pray today. Who would listen?

Through the branches he could see the light blue sky of Palestine. It was cloudless and clear, except for two swallows that cut across the open places like dark arrows hurled from a hunter's bow. Their wings curved and fixed between intervals of furious flapping, they shot across the valley. They flew over the brook and disappeared into the camouflage of mottled sandstone houses stacked one upon the other behind the great wall, eventually giving way to the grandest edifice on the face of the earth. That place was the center of the entire universe.

Like a tower, tall, straight, golden in hue when the sun fell on it, open toward heaven, its high walls of massive stones hewn from the nation's quarries formed a chimney to direct the smoke of its incense and burnt offerings upward. The altar there ran red with the blood of sacrifices. They were offered up again and again as devoted pilgrims presented themselves before the Lord, according to the command. A myriad pressed into the area around altar, while waves of worshippers stood shoulder-to-shoulder pressing forward. They waited in line to give an accounting to the priests and make confession of sin, or give thanks, or appeal for help in time of need. No man considered himself above the next here. All were the same. Sinners every one, they came. A lamb for every house was brought for Passover. They were keeping the commandment and applying afresh the blood that once long ago had delivered them from the hand of the destroyer.

The sounds of the temple filled the air. Singers in perfectly formed ranks, voices raised in songs of reconciliation and promise, held their instruments just so as they stepped in cadence to their songs up the Ascendant Plain. The low breathy voice of the shofar, like the sound of a great bull trudging toward battle, pierced the atmosphere. It's shrill blast signaled the culmination of the festival, reminding the nation to be watchful and circumspect, until they returned, house by house, with their firstfruits.

Just then the sun broke between the trunks and branches of the grove as it made its steady climb into the sky. Yellow shafts of light shimmered where they cut through the fading haze of the lingering morning dew. Tiny moving rainbows drifted down on the sunrays.

The rains were over. Winter was past. Spring had come. Tiny flowers of pastel blues and yellows were nestled between high golden grasses whose long thin necks held erect tiny red-and-white petaled heads. The sweet bouquets graced the base of every rock. They were also sprinkled down the terraced hillsides and they spilled out onto the open fields. The tinkling of a sheep's bell, from a stray animal loose somewhere on the hillside, sounded softly through the gray morning mist. Then the lowing of cattle from the valley below mixed with the shouts of commerce as it awakened the city. The ebb of the first wave of pilgrims was beginning to make its way onto the bustling roads.

He paused.

They were going home. The thoroughfares leading out of the city were already packed when first light came. Extended families, mothers with their babes in arms, the old carried on litters by the young, children in instant happy ranks of new friendships with those next to them on the road, all patiently surged out. Many of them had a week's travel back to their homes and villages ahead. The beginning of their journey today was a commemoration of the day their forefathers had gone out of the cities of Pharaoh laden with gold and silver. Free from the lash of taskmasters, bondage forever behind them, the wilderness and Promised Land loomed large before them.

It was a costly pilgrimage. But then redemption never came without a price.

"Betrayer!"

His temples throbbed as if a drumbeat pounded against the sides of his head. His red eyes burned. Dark circles made his already sunken eye sockets look like the holes in a skull. Death stared out.

The trees, first one and then another, hissed at him, accusing him.

"Betrayer!"

He stumbled over the flapping sole of his sandal. A strap had come loose the night before in the melee of burning torches, frightful shouting, and the slice of a sword. The broken strap no longer held the shoe to the bottom of his foot.

"Murderer!"

Backing up, he straightened, trying to discern which of the trees had spoken.

"Fiend!"

"Son of perdition!"

Whirling around, he knocked his head hard on a branch behind him. All were witnesses against him all; their voices grew louder. One after the other hurled accusations at him.

Stumbling recklessly over the spiny roots circling the base of a tree, he fell hard on both knees. The edge of his garment caught the point of a low branch. The weight of him broke it and ripped his shirt as he went down. The sound was abrupt, and the rest of the fabric pulled tightly around him, holding him firmly in place, half suspended. He reached back to wrench the snag free and cursed as the limb broke and the sharp point raked his palm, drawing blood.

"He is innocent!" the branch whispered.

They continued to assail him.

"Traitor!"

"I didn't think they would go so far as to kill Him!" he whined, and rolled himself into a ball. His face screwed up, and none of its customary congenial good looks were visible anymore. He put the cut hand to his mouth. "They weren't supposed to kill Him! They tricked me!" Tasting his own blood before he realized what he had done, he spat. Unclean! "They promised me a place! Something for me at last!"

Face wet with anguish, the salt of his tears in his mouth, he fell hard against the trunk of the olive tree. "It's not what they said!" His fingers curled, digging into the skin of the tree. Frustration, anger towards everyone and everything in his life, screamed up from within. But he knew there was no relief.

"He trusted you!" the trees insisted.

"You were His close friend!"

"His blood on your hands!" one shouted.

"His close friend?" he screeched back, voice as wet as his face. "His close friend? He never took me into His confidence the way He did them! I gave up everything for Him! I endured humiliation every day for three years to prove myself! And He still preferred the fishermen," he argued miserably. "I healed as many, didn't I? I was the one who always made sure there was food and a place to sleep!" His voice broke. "I was the one who kept Him informed of his enemies' plans!"

Earth and heaven glowered at him as the witnesses leaned towards him. He continued his complaint almost inaudibly. "I was never more than a beast of burden—someone to carry bundles from place to place."

He had betrayed perfect love. He had set himself proudly against perfect innocence. Even the men he had sold himself out to laughed now. There was no place he would not be recognized and hated—or ridiculed and ostracized. The hateful doom of judgment ran at him from the ancients.

"Strike the shepherd!" one of them barked at him.

"Thirty pieces! Thirty pieces of silver!" several hissed. Their voices blended. "Wounded in the house of His friends!"

"Awake, sword!"

The din overwhelmed him. He pressed his palms to his ears to shut out their voices.

"Stop it!" he shouted. "Stop it!" His voice cracked.

Dizzy stars of mounting turmoil passed before his eyes, for a moment blinding his vision entirely. His nose, swollen from weeping, stopped his air. His heavy head ached. His own voice sounded distant. He retched. Bile and saliva came up from his nervous stomach and poured onto the tree roots between his knees.

"I didn't think they would go so far as to hand Him over!" he protested.

Once the disciples escaped the city, every village would know who had done it. There would be a mob looking for him anywhere he tried to hide. He could not lie to himself and pretend that he would not answer for it with his life. And once they had killed his body, he would meet the true judgment.

He knew better than to even consider any one of *them* would overlook his offense. Peter had chopped off the ear of the soldier. He was sure to avenge Him. Judas could not let the sound of the Name pass through his mind. The fishermen would surely track him down, and not them alone. He had destroyed the hope of Israel.

He was marked, as Cain had been—an outcast. He could never go home again. Pain tightened the skin of his face. He could not contain the weight and scope of his sin. Misery plagued every fiber of his being. Black fear of what would come hung by its jagged claws on every breath. He imagined the abyss, ridicule, certain poverty, humiliation.

If only he had left before Bethany. If only he had gone away. He had considered it. But he had let his disdain for John anger him once again. He should have turned back long ago, as had the affluent young ruler from the synagogue in Capernaum. That man was surely happy now, and free of trouble.

"I should have left them the minute I realized He would never receive me as He did that dreamer John," he berated himself angrily. "They were too much alike!" His empty stomach growled noisily and painfully. He groaned and sat down, leaning his back against the olive trunk. Pulling up his knees, he hid his sad face in his arms. Thoughts of the beginning of banishment, like shards of a broken vessel, pierced him through.

Words from the prophets drifted up from the pit of his soul.

"They weighed out for me my wages...that princely price!" another shouted from the edge of the grove. "Throw it to the potter! His arm shall wither...his right eye be blinded!"

Judas imagined himself.

"You made it too hard!" Judas screamed. He hoped and feared that his voice was being heard. He resented being cut off. "It's unfair to test mortal men so! You were against me from the beginning! Why am I the only guilty one?"

Then he heard something from the city. A slamming door? The turn of the key in a stone hall? They would have Him in the prison by now, the Romans.

It had begun.

The image of Jesus the last time he saw Him here in the garden suddenly loomed before him. The sign, the kiss—he watched as they embraced in his vision, dancing hideously between the trees. He touched his lips with his fingers and began rubbing them furiously on the back of his hand until they were hot trying to erase what those lips had done. Remorse suffocated him.

His bowels felt like water, and every joint of his body was rubber instead of bone. He was tired—tired to death of the words in his head, the arguments, the attempts at justification, and the final, utter condemnation. He had no skin anymore. Repugnant truth oozed like acid out of every pore of his being until he felt as though he were dissolving into nothingness.

"Master, who is the greatest?" he could hear Peter and John arguing.

"The one who makes himself the slave of everyone else," Jesus had said, laughing. His bright, shining eyes quickly glanced in Judas's direction…as if He knew…as if He were warning him in advance.

"There is no love greater than this, that a man lay down His life for His friends."

"Why did You keep me at arm's length?" Judas shouted at Him. "I would have followed You to the end if only You had received me as You did them!" He sobbed again with no one to hear. "I put myself on the line for You time after time." His voice faded and the image of Jesus disappeared.

Judas's dry lids, full of sand, dragged on his pupils. His eyes were drawn to the multitude of confused footprints from the scuffle that had taken place on the previous night. He frowned and squinted. A piece of flesh lay turned up in a soft place on the path. A chill passed through him. It was the severed ear.

The soldier had gone away with a new one.

He pulled his crumpled outer garment over his bent body. The faint smell of the oil press, woody, familiar, reached him. Here, beneath this very tree… he glanced away with swollen eyes. There, against that one…they had often spent the night in delighted musing and intense discussion and prayer to God. Three years of visions and miracles, of expectations and disappointments, of love and hatred, of notoriety and infamy—all of it had crashed to a fruitless end.

From where he was, the entrance to the garden seemed like a corridor of unending darkness bending through the trees. It was the corridor he had chosen to walk the night before. He wished he could go back, back before the bonds were broken, back into the light. But, while the whole world beyond was starting afresh, hope fled and he was left behind. Judas was alone in the garden looking down on Jerusalem.

An Encounter with Destiny

The fire crackled. Sparks exploded and danced into the blue-black night sky. In the circle of the heavens over the camp in the foothills of Tabor, a million glittering diamonds shone down on twelve men who had left everything to follow an encounter with destiny. The smell of the air was clean, from the baking blast of the desert sun that day, and woodsy, from the dense cedars that grew around them and thickened into great forests farther north. The glow of firelight illumined three faces. Two of them were men who were sitting, intently facing one another, engaged in a testy conversation. The third man lay in peaceful repose, eyes closed. He appeared to be asleep.

Locked in discussion was a stocky, bearded, fisherman whose thick curly hair and unshaven face matched the dark carpet that covered his neck, as well as his torso and his arms and legs. With a trim waist but legs like two hairy tree trunks and arms to match, Peter leaned forward, resting one elbow on his thick muscled thigh. His fingers unconsciously stroked the overgrowth that covered his entire face from just beneath his eyes to his shirt collar.

The man talking now, taller than Peter, had none of Peter's bulk and even less of his hair, except for the usual covering on his head and dark brows that formed a continuous line across the top of his dreamy eyes. The apostle John always had his head in the clouds, or at least on things beyond the sight of a natural man's eye and mind. He was concerned, no, obsessed with heavenly things, and he didn't mind letting his brethren know the impressions the Spirit brought to him at every turn.

Jews and Galileans both, and fishermen from families that had worked side by side on the sea for four generations, Peter and John were more like cousins than friends. Both of them had brothers who accompanied them, leaving the family fishing business to their fathers and siblings on the day that Jesus had invited them to come with Him. They joined Him as He began teaching and traveling from place to place.

Peter's eyes, deep brown but strangely flecked with gold, flashed in the glint of the fire. He listened defiantly to John's argument.

"But I found Him first!" John boasted. "And told you He was the One. I saw it in a vision while He was in the Jordan with His cousin. I told you how the dove of God came down on Him! Don't you remember? That was long before He called us to come with Him!"

"What are you talking about?" Peter shot back. "Andrew found Him with the Baptist!" Peter put both hands on his knees, almost rising. "And who's to say you don't invent half of the visions you're always reporting?" Peter spoke in jest about the visions, but he was fully standing his ground in the argument over who had had been with Jesus longer.

Just then two more disciples came into the circle of firelight. One of them spoke as he unloaded his burdens near the fire.

"The synagogue is in an uproar," the eldest, tanned and leathery from years of fishing, announced in the direction of the reposed man.

Jesus opened one eye and looked up. His head rested peacefully in the cradle of His arms as He stretched out on the pallet of His own outer garment. It had been a costly gift from Joanna, Chuza's wife, one of the rich women. She generously supplied the treasury of the traveling company of ministers who followed the Nazarene.

"Your saying that the ruling Pharisees are nothing more than grave markers has set them on their ear," Andrew reported. "They claim it was just one more of Your strikes at them as rulers in Israel!"

The more slightly built and lighter complexioned of the two arrivals, a young, handsome fellow of less than thirty years with deeply set eyes, a clean-shaven face, neatly trimmed hair and a soft wide mouth, added, "It has made their critics happy. The whole city is in debate about You, Master." The messenger's garments were clean and smooth, and fitted neatly on his frame. They certainly were not what one might expect of a man who had spent as many nights on the open ground as he had. "They claim people are neglecting the synagogue because of it."

"Nonsense!" Peter bellowed. "Hypocrites and fools they are!"

"The treasuries are surely suffering because of us," the young, neat fellow added.

"I don't care what they say about Me, Judas," Jesus responded kindly. "But when they start saying the miracles of the Spirit are from Beelzebub they go too far!" Jesus' eyes flashed. In a moment of thundering silence, every man at the fire felt the force of His words and trembled.

"The Rabbi was exactly right, as usual," John said smugly, looking at Jesus with reverent eyes. "Like the bones the prophet saw. But when it comes to these Pharisees, I already know God's answer to that great question!"

"Answer?" Andrew asked.

"Can these bones live?" John spread out his arms as if he were Ezekiel standing in the ancient vision.

Across from him Peter cupped his great hands to his hairy face.

"Nooo!" he thundered theatrically.

They all laughed. Except Judas. He resented John's constantly making himself out to be more spiritual than the rest of them. He was weary of hearing John expound upon everything Jesus said, adding his own confirmation by using dreams or visions he'd had to back up Jesus. Judas couldn't imagine that anyone with a sound mind could have as many revelations as John claimed.

"I wondered if we would escape with our skins had they recognized us!" Judas said as he unloaded his burden beside Andrew's. He forced himself to maintain a placid expression while he loosed the purse from his belt and fussed with untying the cords of the moneybox. Already his soul frothed at hearing John's arrogant voice spewing out what he seemed to think was useful instruction for the rest of them. Judas was losing the ability to even be within the sound of the man's voice without wanting to rush at him and put him in his place. Still, the fisherman hung on Jesus like a disease!

"Their house is divided." Jesus stretched His legs, turning His sandaled ankles around in circles several times to relieve the ache of hours of ministering to the sick who had been brought to them that day. Jesus lay over on His side facing the fire. He smiled carefully looking into the flames. "It will fall eventually."

Who Is Greatest?

"Can you believe it, Andrew?" Peter cut in. He gestured to his brother and pointed at John. "Their mother asked the

Lord to give him and his brother first place in the new government!" Peter grinned broadly, confident. "Ha!" His sudden exertion of sentiment also inspired a bit of flatulence.

The circle of men broke into laughter when they heard it. The hairy fisherman laughed at himself and waved the rest of them off.

"And that's exactly what you are, Simon!" John said. "A bunch of hot air!" John leaned close to Jesus. His look was one of absolute solidarity and expectancy. "Who is more qualified for the chief seats, Rabbi? Who should have the right hand? Those who found You first and believed, or the ones who joined You later?"

Jesus sat up, yawning unconsciously. He rubbed the early sleep from His eyes and reached for the bags of fresh provision that Judas and Andrew delivered.

Judas retrieved the sicarri blade from his belt. His former weapon, the trademark of the most radical wing of the new revolutionaries rising in the land, was now no more than a tool for opening things like the tightly tied bag. Jesus took the knife, deftly cut the bindings, and handed the blade back to Judas.

"You mean who is the greatest?" Jesus asked John as He opened the first bundle.

The hair on the back of Judas's neck stood slightly on end. He felt it move like the hair raised along the spine of a cat, uneasy, suspicious. The fishermen, two sets of brothers whose fathers still worked together on the Gennesaret, had been in Jesus' company longer than himself. In Judas's mind they were low-class by comparison. He secretly feared the fishermen would ultimately influence the Rabbi's thinking in such a way as to keep him from promotion in their midst. The threat nagged him. It was insulting, as if his very presence were being privately ridiculed. His efforts could all turn out be a humiliating waste of time.

Judas's eyes were locked on the face of the Rabbi as the Master took provisions from the bag.

"There's a roasted shank and handful of fresh figs given by a widow You prayed for two days ago," Judas offered, attentive. "Her granddaughter was delivered of a demon that made the girl rant violently."

Jesus was interested.

Judas smiled proudly.

"The child is completely in her right mind now. The family is very grateful."

"You were there and helped pray for her, if I am recalling the one." Jesus reached around in the bag and brought out a warm, aromatic package. He put it to His nose and inhaled.

Judas looked down humbly. "It was You who healed her, Rabbi. I was just standing by."

"Umm! Feasting fare!" Peter, smelling the aroma of roasted meat, grabbed the satchel and pulled it to himself. Feeling through it, he said, "What else is in there?" He brought out first one thing and then the next, unwrapping and inspecting or sniffing.

Jesus laid the wrapped shank aside and started to get up.

"What would you like, Master?" Judas quickly asked.

"I'll just wash My hands," Jesus replied.

Judas stopped Him. "Please, Lord, it's been a long day. Sit. I'll bring it to You." He went off immediately.

Peter was suddenly uncomfortable. He took his hands out of the satchel. His eyes followed Judas's back as he went to retrieve the waterskin from the branch of a nearby tree.

"Is there anything else, Rabbi?" Peter asked. "Can I get You something?"

Jesus sat back down.

"Thank you, Simon, no."

John remained completely distracted, his attention entirely focused on waiting for the answer to his question.

"I clearly remember the dove," he was still saying. "White and shining, it descended as the voice spoke to me."

Judas smartly returned with the water and a towel. He unstopped the neck of the vessel and poured some over Jesus' hands, then handed Him the towel. Judas stood by waiting while Jesus dried His hands and face.

"We should have had you with us all along, Judas. We would have eaten better and rested well!" Jesus looked up into the night sky briefly, raising the food. "Father, we thank You for this provision! Bless that widow again and show Your power in Israel!" Jesus began unwrapping the meat. "Remind Me to let you have the money box for good, Judas. I'm sure Matthew wouldn't mind being relieved of the accounting." He bit into the meat shank. The firelight flickered warm and golden on His features.

"The last will be first," John remarked, suddenly coming to the exchange at hand. He smiled a quick smile.

"Insincere," Judas thought. His hands formed fists at his sides, and his jaw tightened. Judas was the only non-Galilean among them, and John was referring to the fact that Judas had been the last to be chosen. He ground his teeth together, and the muscles in his jaw tensed in anger. Judas resented constantly feeling that he was outside the comfortable bonds shared between the others, especially the companions sitting here. His eyes drifted back to the Rabbi. *And perhaps I'm not even accepted by Him, as yet.* He revisited the thought that had been plaguing him for weeks. It constantly drove the last apostle to look for ways to ingratiate himself to the rest. He sought their favor through self-abasing little gestures, like raps upon a door in hope that it would open wide and let him into the inner circle.

Andrew's quick senses noticed Judas's reaction to John's gibe. He caught Judas's eyes and offered a consolation.

"Iscariot sold his second cloak and paid for our supper with it."

Judas returned a silent "thank you" for the compliment, but a searing, sinking feeling dropped through the bottom of his stomach as he realized that Andrew recognized his insecurity. Judas raised the waterskin and poured some water over himself to try to take his mind off those thoughts while he washed the sweat of the day from his head. The wet flow of cool liquid tingled as it ran over the crown of his head and behind his ears. It made a delicious wet sound as it splashed in tiny pools on the ground.

Andrew watched the eager disciple. "He put the rest of his money into the box."

Judas shrugged as one by one the men acknowledged his selfless act.

"Speaking of Matthew," Peter said, "shouldn't they be here by now?"

"By daybreak perhaps," Jesus answered. "Those mobs following us for food all are still hungry, I suppose, if they've kept them this long."

John glanced sideways at Judas, still bathing his face. The puddle between Judas's sandals was growing.

"We may need that water for drinking," John reminded him.

Judas froze. It was obvious that John considered Judas a novice at being on the road. The water ran into his collar as he stood upright. He quickly shook out his hair, patted his face with his cloak, and recapped the waterskin.

John was a Galilee bumpkin, uncouth in speech and manners. It was the pure mercy of God that they had the opportunity to advance themselves under Jesus' instruction and influence. Judas wondered if Jesus handpicked him. Judas was the only man besides Jesus who came from the region around Jerusalem. He was educated, capable, and certainly more presentable in appearance, and not lazy like John, who preferred talking to working. It made perfect sense that God had sent Judas to help.

"I hope that's all that is keeping them," Judas said, sounding concerned.

Jesus tossed the bag of provisions across the fire. John caught it directly.

"You'd better have your supper if you plan to spend the night with Me on the mountain," Jesus told him.

Judas's attention shot across the fire after the bag. Mountain? As John rifled through the bag, Judas suddenly imagined John eating his second cloak—the one Judas had sold to pay for their meat and contribute to the box. For a moment the fisherman sat there, cross-legged before the fire, stuffing Judas's thick, woolen garment into his mouth fist over fist, chewing it and swallowing in great difficult gulps.

"I'll drink some of that," Jesus said to the staring Judas. But the disciple seemed not to hear. Jesus reached a hand toward him as Judas stood holding the waterskin, his gaze transfixed on John. The distracted man still did not respond. "May I have a drink, Judas?" Jesus said more loudly.

Judas came to himself and thrust the skin into Jesus' outstretched hand. "I should speak to you in private, Rabbi," he said. He shook his head sharply and glanced once more at John as he spoke. "I have other news from the synagogue."

Jesus' face became serious at the Judean's tone.

John was inquisitive. He looked from the Rabbi to Judas and back.

"What news?" he asked. But his question went unanswered.

"After supper," Jesus said to Judas. The fire's glow flickered, emphasizing the carved shapes of their features as they ate. Then Jesus called into the darkness. "James!"

"James!" John shouted immediately after the Rabbi. John put his fingers to his mouth and whistled a sharp summons for his brother.

There was scuffling from the dark in the hedge of trees that ringed the camp beyond the firelight. Jesus' band of fellows always had someone posted as lookout whenever they were in the open. These were hard times in Israel. Dangerous times. Times when peace fled and men were not safe in their own beds, much less when they were spending the night in the open with a moneybox. It was necessary to keep a lookout in case of marauders. The man who had been keeping watch, John's brother, appeared in the firelight.

"Lord?"

"Eat something," Jesus said without looking up. He studied His own food, turning it over in His hand. His words were slightly muffled as He pulled off another portion of the shank with His teeth. "We're spending the night on the mountain."

John cleared his throat and went back to the earlier discussion.

"Who will it be, Lord? My brother and I?" John threw a gesture in the direction of Peter and grinned. "Or these second-rate fishers of men?"

Jesus laughed out loud. "I thought you had forgotten the argument!"

They were still obviously waiting for Jesus to answer.

"You should already know the answer," he told them cheerfully.

John jabbed Peter and roughly chafed his shoulder.

"What did I tell you?" he said.

"The one who becomes the slave of everyone else," Jesus said. His bright eyes shining, he glanced in Judas's direction. "There is no love greater than this, that a man lay down his life for his friends."

Judas's expression softened. He ducked his head humbly.

The rest of the men were silent.

When they had finished eating Jesus rose and called Judas into the dimness beyond the circle of light.

"What are they saying?" Jesus asked as they walked to the brow of the hill.

"The synagogue rulers are growing ever more zealous, Lord. This time they were devising ways to have You arrested. The chief priests sent men from Jerusalem to bring back reports about our work, particularly concerning Your teachings, which they claim insult the law and prophets. They fear You are gaining the hearts of the people. It's why they always show up among the crowds. It's growing more dangerous, I think," Judas told him. "They believe You intend to undo their hierarchy."

Judas could hear Jesus chuckle softly.

"Keep going to them, Judas. Keep putting yourself into their midst while they don't recognize you as one of mine," Jesus replied. "We should keep our enemies as close as our friends for the time being." He put His hand firmly on Judas's shoulder. "I sleep easier because of you."

Judas cleared his throat.

"Is there something else?" Jesus asked.

"The mountain, Rabbi," Judas blurted. "Shouldn't I come with you?"

Judas was certain from remarks at the fire that Jesus had discussed the particulars of the excursion with John and Peter earlier, while Andrew and Judas had been in the town buying food.

Jesus didn't hesitate to answer. "Who else would I leave in charge of things? John?"

While He chuckled, a cold chill stabbed Judas's heart. He had been set aside in favor of the fisherman again.

"I need you here if I want fire and food when I get back," he said. "Andrew will stay behind and keep you company." Jesus made a sucking sound with his tongue against his teeth, cleaning the meat from between them. "Matthew and the rest will depend on a good signal fire to show the way. And they'll be hungry, I'm sure! If the crowds find you before we return, take care to minister to them as before." Jesus turned to go back into the circle of the campfire. "We should be back by tomorrow evening."

Judas forced a smile, wondering why he bothered when he realized Jesus could not see his response in the dark.

"Happily, Lord," he lied and followed Jesus back to the fire.

That night, as the last of the scarlet embers of the campfire died out, Judas lay in his one remaining outer garment wishing he were with the Rabbi and the three fishermen instead of here. He groaned to think of John coming back tomorrow and telling them tales of some awesome occurrence, describing a detailed canvas of sights and sounds, and adding his own revelations regarding the unique significance of whatever happened.

Anyone else witnessing the same moment was sure to have less to report. Judas tossed and turned uncomfortably, his thoughts racing and refusing to let him alone long enough to drift off. The longer he lay there, the more frustrated and anxious he became.

After a long time Judas sat up, miserably unhappy. The night overhead was clear, and the moon washed its silver light over the clearing. Matthew and the others had returned, exhausted but talkative. After supper they had rolled out their beds, and by now they were all sleeping noisily around him. Andrew had taken the first watch. He was still out there on the point just beyond the tall, black cedars that surrounded the enclave. The wind swept through the high wall of limbs and branches, making an intermittent rushing sound. It should have been comforting.

The Moneybox

As Judas twisted around to rearrange his cloak under his head, his fingers stumbled upon the moneybox. He thought of his second cloak and his mental image of John eating it. Then he remembered the money he had added to the box after selling his second cloak. He looked around carefully to make sure no eyes were on him and quietly opened the treasure box.

Feeling the surface of each coin on his fingertips in the darkness, its weight and the texture of the stamp on its face declaring the value of each coin, Judas counted out the sum of the contribution he had made in his earlier benevolence. He quietly returned the money to his private purse. Before he closed the box, he also weighed out the cost of his cloak. Then, subtracting what he imagined to be the cost of his individual supper, he returned that amount to his personal cache as well.

The coins made a muffled clink together as he fastened his own purse tightly in his belt and lay down again. Now he felt less exploited. When Judas finally slept, he dreamed of Moses on the day that he took Joshua with him into Sinai. But in the dream, John was Joshua and Judas was the priest Aaron, who was left behind at the camp. Most of Judas's dream was a hateful vision of scores of Israelites persuading Aaron to fashion an image they could worship. It went on and on, shouting, scuffling, angry, and confused. Judas awoke in the predawn cold in a sweat, breaking through the images of raucous gyrations to wild music. The scenes of golden earrings and heavily jeweled Egyptian bracelets tossed at his feet unnerved him.

Judas got up and went to relieve whoever had taken the last watch.

The Moneyman

The point of the scribe's pen scratched dryly on the parchment as he tallied the temple contributions. Leaning poker-straight over the counting table, his fingernails made rapid clicking noises on the surface while he added on one hand and recorded with the other. Checking and rechecking his figures, he spoke flatly.

"The offerings decrease with every festival," the treasurer told the priest who was pacing the room around him, deep in his own thoughts. "The vendors sell little more than turtledoves and barley for the altar. There is not much profit in that." The treasurer put aside one set of figures and the tallied chests of money that corresponded. He then feverishly started a new batch.

Caiaphus lifted his hands and looked up to Heaven with a pious pleading face. "Shall we bring forth payment from wind?" The priest had an odd tic to his expression. He always held one hand to his face because of a tooth that grew in the very center of his mouth. When he developed facial hair he arranged his moustache behind his studiously perched hand to hide the dental defect, which otherwise made him look pitifully foolish. "You," he spoke heavenward, "You make bones to grow in the womb." He put manicured hands on himself. "But we are mere men!"

The moneyman was frowning at the next set of figures and rechecking his work. He shook his head with concern. "Even the sin tax has dropped off. That means fewer are coming to the temple daily."

The priest turned. "It's that heretic," he spat. Caiaphus stood momentarily in one spot, speaking to the treasurer as if to a confidante. "Mark you, He is preaching somewhere outside the city." He rested his pointed chin in one hand, as was his custom, propping his elbow in the crook of his opposite arm, which crossed his chest. His prematurely gray hair, already turned white at his temples, was set in stark contrast to the long, dark mustache that curled smugly over his mouth. "That won't keep Pilate's outstretched palm from extracting the taxes from us!"

The high priest's robes, straight and impeccable, made a swishing sound around him as he arrived at the opposite wall and turned to cross the room again. The accountant murmured something as the priest passed his table.

"What is it, Joses? Make yourself plain, for God's sake!" Caiaphus ordered.

The treasurer looked sheepish. "In Capernaum, He produced the sin tax for himself and His men with gold from a fish's mouth."

The high priest wheeled around. "Legends! Beelzebub's trickery!" Caiaphus looked out from under his bushy brows and muttered, "If only Herod's first solution had kept this fish from slipping through the nets we would not have this problem now!"

The treasurer looked around the royal room. The flicker of light from the oil lamps in the shadows, like figures conspiring one with another, danced on the high, cool stone walls.

"Carefully, lord," he said in a low voice. "The walls have eager ears."

The aging treasurer, and one of the dozens of minions who hurriedly went about the temple in silent duties, shivered. Thankfully the treasurer had been old enough to escape the king's insane purges three decades earlier, when the eastern kings claimed a new ruler had been born in Jerusalem. Herod was still paranoid.

The priest's brow furrowed. Caiaphus pointed at the counting table and the coinage stacked around it. "Restrict your counsel to things you know." He started to pace again. His talked to himself, but from time to time directed his remarks to the moneyman with his dark eyes.

"Miracles! Double-edged sayings! It all has the commoners doubting us! If we leave Him as He is, that illegitimate son of a quarry hand threatens to deceive the whole nation into worshiping him!"

The scribe went on poring over his account books, fingertips tapping as he prepared his report. The priest continued to pronounce his thoughts.

"He is set on bringing us down! Nothing would satisfy Him more than to see us run out of our houses, left to beg on the street corners. He'll make a laughingstock of us all!" Caiaphus's eyes narrowed. Wheels turning in his head, he mumbled, "As if His cousin wasn't headache enough. At least the Baptist kept to the wilderness!"

The treasurer snickered. "A headache is exactly what he got from Herod's wife!"

Then he remembered himself and sobered his countenance once more.

"You know they hailed Him as king and tried to anoint Him when He came to the city this time!" The priest stopped. "Now He's got them believing He's God's ..." It seemed the word was stuck in his throat. "Son!" he choked hoarsely.

The treasurer nodded grimly, not taking his eyes off of his accounting. "They followed him into the portico. There was almost a riot. The Nazarene had thrown down the moneychangers' stalls before the temple guard could get to Him. The chief priests were barely able to persuade the Roman detachment that we had things in hand." The treasurer's fingers tapped furiously. "Since then attendance has fallen off."

"As if Pilate isn't problem enough, the Nazarene's motley sect is gaining notoriety." Caiaphus let out a sigh of weary frustration. "I'm like Moses between the sea and Pharaoh's armies." He began to pace again.

"We need a lamb," the treasurer said, referring to the approaching festival. "A lamb like the first one but this time to make Caesar's hand pass over us!" His fingernails clicked away.

❦

Caiaphus whirled around.

"That's it, Joses!" he whispered excitedly. "Ho-ho!" the priest half-laughed, his eyes gleaming at the man's remark. He pointed at him. "And that is precisely why you keep your job! Efficient! Very efficient!"

The treasurer looked up, confused, and lost his place. He started all over again with the batch in front of him.

"They always make a show of their control during the festivals." He began to pace again. "As our token of submission, we will give them their man this year—one to die for the nation as our token of good faith." The priest laughed with happy relief and walked back by the table. "The Romans will have their spectacle, and our hands will be clean!" He clapped his accountant on the shoulders with both hands. "Two birds. One stone. It's brilliant. We will give them the Nazarene!"

The treasurer stopped, but not before recording where he was in the counting process. "We don't even know where to find him. He's like a ghost."

Caiaphus swung around and pointed a long, manicured finger at the treasurer. It's jeweled ring flashed. "Increase the reward money!"

The treasurer's mouth dropped open.

"Begging your pardon, sire, but the sum is already nearly a quarter year's wage!"

The treasurer sat up straight, recalling the multiple interviews he had recorded while the priests interrogated of men from all walks of life who had come forward when the temple rulers announced a reward for knowledge leading to Jesus' arrest. The ransom had produced nothing but a long line of false men and scoundrels with made-up tales that led to dead ends. "A bigger prize would only bring more rats to the cheese."

Caiaphus grasped the table edge with both hands. Leaning over, he stared into the face of the treasurer. "Have any of these so-called informants had an actual history in the man's close company?"

The treasurer laughed as he finished the sums. He closed his accounting books and tightly secured them with cords.

"You mean finding a man from His company to betray Him for money?" He looked incredulous. "His disciples are no less zealous than the Maccabees and the priests of Modin." The ancient Zealot uprising was still the light of inspiration for every oppressed soul. Mothers named their sons Judas, for the Hammer who had routed the foreign conquerors and reclaimed the temple.

"Every man has something in here." Caiaphus touched his heart with a delicate finger. "A stomach that digests a different food than what goes into the mouth. Power and position give men cravings that nothing else will satisfy."

"Not the Nazarene. Or His men," the treasurer insisted. "Their solidarity is impenetrable."

"You just haven't found the right food." Caiaphus's voice went low. "We need a man..." His hand hid his dental defect. "A dissatisfied soul." The priest made a play of putting an invisible glove on one of his hands and moved his fingers inside it. "A perfect fit." His voice whined melodically, as if sirens were in it. He suddenly grasped at the air as if capturing something by the neck.

The treasurer jumped, spilling a stack of coins onto the floor. The noise brought the priest's attention to him with a frown. The accountant immediately groped around on his knees to collect the fallen treasure.

Just then the servant entered the room, floating like a ghost.

"My lord?" the tall turban-topped man interrupted.

Caiaphus turned.

˙"What is it?"

"There is a man at the gate. He is insistent that he speak with you personally," said the servant in a monotone just above a whisper.

"An audience at this hour?" Caiaphus was impatient. He waved the man away. "Tell him to come back at a more courteous time!"

"Excuse me, sire." The Ethiopian cleared his throat as he spoke. "You may want to receive him."

Caiaphus stiffened and shot the servant an arrogant glare. "Now you've become my counselor also?"

The servant lowered his eyes.

"He is one of the Nazarene's, sire. I recognize him myself."

Caiaphus's expression completely changed. "Are you sure?"

The servant nodded. "I'm certain I have seen him among His bodyguards in the city."

Caiaphus narrowed his eyes slyly. "I should see to it that you get out more often." The priest rubbed his hands together with relish and said to the servant, "Don't just stand there. Let him in!"

A Dissatisfied Soul

As the man exited, seeming to float just as he had when he entered, Caiaphus exclaimed gleefully, "God is with us, Joses!" The priest looked at the groveling treasurer. "Well, what are you waiting for? I have an important audience to attend! Away! Away!" He pulled the man to his feet and helped him gather up his reports before ushering him from the room.

As the accountant disappeared, Caiaphus grabbed one of the gold coins from a stack on the table. He tossed it into the air and deftly caught it.

"A gold coin in the fish's mouth, eh?" Caiaphus covered his own mouth as he smiled.

❧

At the gate Judas was stolid, intent. His jaw tightened in tiny determined spasms as he waited to see if the high priest would receive him. If the man was serious about putting a stop to Jesus' influence, as the price on his head indicated, Judas was their man. The rebuke at table in front of all the prominent men of Bethany had been the last straw.

It capped three years of humiliating, patient attendance, and it lay in the pit of his stomach like a poisoned stew, slowly being absorbed into his system. He wished he could vomit up the whole thing. Once again the memories returned: John's look of disgust, Jesus' unyielding tone, and the fierce look in His eyes as He dismissed Judas from supper, topped off by the audacity of the others, some of them sniggering as he stormed out. And all because of a woman's foolish display of emotions! The fever of his anger, together with the loose ends of Judas's frustrated intentions, knotted together irreconcilably while he sought balm elsewhere.

It was plain that Jesus was content with being nothing more than a country preacher who appealed to the emotions of the poor. He sounded just like John, keeping his head in the clouds, while the opportunity to seize a moment in history slipped away. That was all well and good, except for the fact that those starry-eyed masses would continue to follow Jesus from place to place. And no one, not even one of His own disciples who possessed the same power to heal, was going to win their affections as long as Jesus was still on the scene. Without their support, there could be no revolt, no new regime, no new hero.

The walk from Bethany had cleared his head a little and had steeled his resolve. Whatever bonds he had shared with the Galileans were frayed beyond repair. In the meantime he sought balm elsewhere. Judas had always been a practical man, a man of action. He would take what action he could to set things right for himself. Starting tonight he would forge a new alliance with men who could offer him something in exchange for the information he could provide about their enemy. At least he wouldn't go away empty-handed.

Judas had set his face like a flint. After all, he possessed the same miraculous power to heal. He had a similar persuasive way with words. He had studied Jesus and learned how to sway the hearts of a mob when it was convenient. For the past three nights he had dreamed a dream. It was clear and powerful, and strangely like the ones John always described. But Judas had dreamed of the ancient hero for whom he had been named, Judas Maccabee, the Hammer. This man had led Israel to freedom and established a new dynasty. The dream had been filled with fantastic images of the other Judas a century and a half before receiving the mantle when Eleazar's time was finished. The rest was glorious history.

Since the dream, Judas could envision himself marching into Jerusalem by year's end, at the Festival of Lights, with the populace fully behind him. He remembered how Jesus frequently told his disciples, "You'll do greater works than I've done!" Judas smiled.

"Indeed!" Judas whispered. It was interesting symmetry. The last apostle straightened his apparel and touched the trimmed edges of his beard to make sure his appearance was at its best.

"Perhaps this is the way things were meant to be," he told himself. "One door closes, but elsewhere another window opens."

Judas had been in an audience with Caiaphus before, but had never spoken to him face to face. He knew well that Caiaphus had watched Jesus' every move for the past two years. Judas had witnessed many of their heated discussions about the Nazarene problem. In fact, Judas secretly had been the man Jesus relied on to keep the apostles out of the traps of the jealous Pharisees.

***

The sound of iron scraping against the latch within the recesses of the courtyard was followed by quick footsteps across the stone paving. Judas stood up straight as the dark face of Caiaphus's servant, torch in hand, appeared between the bars of the outer gate.

The servant swung the gate wide, entreating the visitor to enter.

"This way," he said. The man in the turban disappeared down the stone corridor between lit torches that hissed and spit from their wall sconces. Judas followed him into a compact labyrinth of passages leading to the inner chambers of the high priest's palace. Judas was led into a room with a few grand furnishings. A crimson carpet intricately filigreed in Persian design with silk tassels covered the stone floor. Several brass oil lamps sat on clay plates on tabletops and lit the room. Their yellow flames, like flags waving from a windy parapet, sent up intermittent black wisps of smoke and filled the space with the warm fragrance of scented oil. Costly vases sat in two of the corners.

The high priest Caiaphus sat at the center of the room upon a throne, fashioned in the manner of the one occupied by Herod himself but an obviously smaller, plainer version. Opposite his seat was a second chair for receiving guests. A low table had been placed between them. Beyond it, nearer the wall, stood another table stacked with gold and silver coins. Judas checked his facial expression to make sure it didn't change as he surveyed the treasure.

"Welcome, Judas." The priest's voice was calm and accepting. Caiaphus stayed in his chair but opened his arms to receive the visitor.

"You know who I am?" Judas asked. A strange prickling, like a premonition, went up Judas's spine. He had thought that he had kept his identity concealed from them.

"I know," the priest returned. "Iscariot. A Judean as I am."

Judas appreciated the priest's recognition that he was not from Galilee.

"Then you know whom I follow," Judas said.

"Few in Israel are unaware of the Nazarene and His men." The priest motioned Judas into the chair in front of him. "May I offer you some food or drink?"

Judas shook his head. "I've just come from supper." Judas sat up straight, a hand to his stomach. "I've had my fill." His eyes darted around the room as he settled himself down. Now face-to-face with Caiaphus, Judas felt a sense of awe towards the man. He held the second position in the temple. He had the king's ear, and he controlled the great treasury. Moreover, he was poised to play politics with the Romans.

"I apologize if I have inconvenienced you," Judas said. He looked Caiaphus directly in the eyes, feeling the presence of lawfully pristine authority. The whispers of solemn words spoken in this chamber in the past, of lofty ideals and guiding hands that ministered at the temple altars, spiced the atmosphere. Great decisions had been made here. A thrill went through him. It was heady as wine.

"I am your servant," Caiaphus said. "What business is so urgent that you beg audience at this hour?"

"I find myself in a most difficult position," Judas began.

Caiaphus's bushy brows went up a bit. His fingertips came together in his lap and touched one another.

"And your Rabbi? He cannot help you with this weight your bear?"

Judas's eyes looked like a storm at sea.

"He doesn't hear me," Judas said, feeling afresh the stinging humiliation of Jesus' last rebuke.

Caiaphus sighed sympathetically. "I see." Inside he smiled widely, but only careful pastoral concern showed on his face. "It happens sometimes. Our hearts, like our lives, resemble the cycle of the seasons. We can't always dwell in summer. Winter's bite is the very stuff that brings forth the next harvest." Caiaphus voice was oiled, seasoned. It offered assurance that he was well able to back up any promises he might make.

"Your counsel is sought by powerful men," Judas said. Behind him the counting table formed a weighty presence in the room. "You are Israel's guide."

The high priest bowed his head slightly in pious receipt of the flattery. He smiled just enough. "Men often find solace here when their hearts are in turmoil," Caiaphus said. "You are in full confidence, I assure you."

Behind the curtain that covered the door into the next room, the treasurer stood against the wall. His head was cocked to one side in order to hear every sound from the next room. He held his body still as he listened.

"Tell me why you have come," Caiaphus said.

"The first time He looked into my eyes there was honesty. I felt He was a man meant for great things." Judas searched carefully for just the right tone to gain the priest's confidence. "A man sent to set things right, ready to take with Him those who were worthy. In those days, I thought Him to be a man I could follow."

Judas began with how he had been handpicked by the Nazarene. He explained how he had gone, accompanied by his father, to see the man whom all Israel was talking about. Some days later Jesus had gazed into Judas's soul and invited him to join his band of men. Since that day three years ago, they had been together continually. Jesus had demonstrated mysterious powers and passed them on to the men with Him.

"I saw Him make clay from dust and spittle and put it on a man's eyes to make him see." Judas did not omit examples of how this power to heal and cast out demons had flowed through his own hands as well. But the high priest seemed to know about them.

"You still have these powers to heal and such?" Caiaphus asked.

"I do," Judas replied. "Little use they are," he thought.

Caiaphus contained himself entirely, his serene demeanor reassuring the young man as he poured out his tale. As the high priest listened, hearing details that none of his own informants had brought back to him, he realized that Jesus' ability to influence the whole nation was greater than he had realized. He studied the rapt face of the Zealot sitting here before him. The priest also noticed the silver glint of the sicarri, its blade peeking out of the man's clothing as he talked. It seemed to match the cold glint of dissatisfaction in Judas's eye.

As Judas talked, the tone in his voice changed until it carried the full weight of his heart, a burden so dark and heavy it smelled of death itself. All the while, the priest thanked God for this providence. With the groundswell of popular opinion behind them, coupled with their impressive power to heal, Jesus and His band of men were being hailed by many as the new deliverers. To Caiaphus and the temple rulers, not to mention Herod, they were a painful thorn in the side and a threat to the future.

Caiaphus realized that the man who had come to him had merely been biding his time. Judas had ingratiated himself into the band in hopes that the popular new preacher would provide him a stepping-stone to fulfill his own personal ambitions. The high priest intended to give Judas that opportunity before their meeting was over.

Caiaphus shook his head in disbelief as Judas related the endless hours of selfless service he had provided in spite of being passed over time after time in favor of the fishermen. Judas told of Peter and John's incessant vying for the chief seats in the new regime. They were too ignorant to realize that there would be no new regime.

A Peculiar Uneasiness

Judas was bolstered by the priest's understanding attitude. Caiaphus obviously doubted nothing that he told him. The strength of their mutual interest concerning Jesus promised to put to rest the uneasiness Judas felt towards those in Jesus' company. This uneasiness had plagued Judas like an uncomfortable itch inside him, an itch that was impossible to reach with hands that could scratch. This feeling of solidarity with the high priest confirmed, even validated, Judas's feeling that he had done the right thing in coming here.

Judas continued his ongoing discourse on the rebel band. "So then, after all of that, we were just this evening invited to the house of a favored man in Bethany, where Lazarus…" Judas paused, his eyes meeting the priest's again. "…whom the Rabbi called out of the grave…"

Caiaphus was slowly nodding, in deep silent rhythmic motions, as he had been throughout the tale.

"Yes," he said. "I've longed to meet him. It caused some stir!"

Judas raised his eyebrows briefly. "I can only imagine!"

"You had supper with that man this very evening?" Caiaphus asked.

"Yes," Judas replied.

"And," Caiaphus leaned forward in his seat, "does he taste and chew and digest like the rest of us?"

The men broke into controlled laughter.

"He does!" Judas assured him. "Lazarus is quite the mortal, restored fully to all his passions and senses."

"Some of my Sadducee friends would be most upset to hear of it! But even more so, I suppose, if the man were a spirit come back to haunt us!" Caiaphus said. He had approved a secret plan to put Lazarus back into his tomb once Jesus had been taken out of the way. That would stop the Jews from following such fanaticism. If not the fear of God, then certainly the fear of the high priests would be restored.

The priest and the apostle laughed again.

Sliding the gold coin he had snatched earlier from the counting table across the table toward Judas, Caiaphus looked at him with concerned eyes. "Finish your story, friend."

Judas's hand came down over the gold coin. Setting it on its edge, he flicked the coin with his middle finger. It spun rapidly, the whirling metal catching the glint of lamplight as it turned round and round.

"While we were at supper, a young woman threw herself upon Him. She poured an entire box of perfume on His feet." He went on to tell of Mary's tears and gushing praise, which made Jesus stroke her hair and rebuke Judas when he objected to the scene. Judas's nostrils flared and his teeth clenched, knotting the muscle in his jaw. "It's clear there has been something going on between them from the beginning!"

"Lazarus's sister, Mary, and your Rabbi? It is unorthodox," Caiaphus said, his eyes bright. Envy's talons dripped with possibility. It seemed that the last apostle had begun to doubt the morality of his teacher. This was something new! Caiaphus played devil's advocate masterfully. "Perhaps you're being too hard on them. I can understand how her brother's death, much less his being raised again, could have affected her mind, poor child." He paused artfully.

"But He returns there again and again," Judas complained. "Staying with them...just as friends, so He says."

Caiaphus lowered his voice as if he wanted no one to hear his suggestion. "You aren't implying that He has begun to think that He is above the laws of God? Does He believe these fantastic claims that uneducated fanatics are making about His being the next king? Perhaps He feels that it gives Him the freedom to indulge deceitful passions?"

"In spite of all my time with Him, I'll never understand why He does and says certain things," Judas confessed, "things I find difficult to digest coming from a man supposedly destined to lead all of Israel. When I saw the woman, hair loosened and caressing His feet, all of my worst fears were realized in that moment. I realized that the past three years of my life have been a complete waste, no less costly than that alabaster box!"

"When I think of a man such as you being so humbled in favor of a disturbed girl..." The priest clicked his tongue against the roof of his mouth. "It shows that He has little respect for our traditions, not to mention for you or your advice. And after all you've done for him!"

"All of a man's life he waits for something," Judas said, "knowing, having a sure sense, that there is something special for him to do, a particular position of influence to hold...something set aside for him put his whole heart into.

Then he comes so close from time to time that he can almost touch his destiny!" Letting the spinning coin fall, Iscariot put his fingers together near his mouth. "He can almost taste its satisfying sweetness. Until some small thing…" Judas's eyes looked eerie. "…some insignificant event, or unlikely person, steps in the way…" His voice went still.

"You are a smart man, brother Judas," said Caiaphus, "a man with great potential. Your whole future is ahead of you." The high priest spread out his hands. "It pains me that a man so close to the Rabbi and His mission has been left feeling so disillusioned," he continued sadly, "So used. Have you made your concerns known to your Rabbi before?"

"I've tried," Judas sighed. He spun the coin again. "On numerous occasions. But He has others around Him. Dreamers. Impractical men. He listens to them more than to me."

"With so much at stake, why bind yourself to a man whose is certain to fail in the mission to…?" His hands dropped into his lap. "Why give such loyalty to a man who has passed you over again and again in favor of those much less qualified?" Caiaphus rolled his eyes pitifully. "Galileans! Why give unqualified loyalty to a man whose personal vision puts so many others at risk?" Caiaphus picked at the hem of one of his sleeves. "You could leave Him, I suppose, and desert His band of followers altogether."

"And then?" Judas said. "If you recognized me as one of His, others will also. Neither His friends nor His enemies would receive me." Judas looked at the priest expectantly.

Caiaphus smoothed his robes on his lap. "Perhaps you could offer some sign of this change of heart," he suggested.

"My coming here was just such a sign," Judas said boldly. "From this night forward, I sever myself and my reputation from the man whom you yourself say has rejected the fathers, whose words and works, however innocent they may appear, threaten to be the undoing of us all."

The priest rose from his chair and walked around it, his hands clasped behind him, his back to the man at the table. He sighed sadly. "These are difficult times for us all...confusing times...dangerous times. If His claims to be the new king of the Jews reach Caesar..." Caiaphus let the images his words conjured up dance about the room in threatening shadows of future terror.

Judas pictured the Gennesaret during the most terrible storms, with thick darkness instantly falling, the full blast of hell's fury wiping out the noonday sun, making it impossible to know which way was up and which way was down.

"I know exactly what you speak of," Judas told Caiaphus.

"This priesthood"—Caiaphus spread his hands, indicating his residence—"and the shepherding of Israel—my whole family has given up our lives for the sake of it. We live to preserve our way of life and our traditions for our children. My wife's father, Annas, has served faithfully, selflessly. We've paid a great price for it." He paused for emphasis. "It's up to us, Judas, men like myself, men like you!" Caiaphus looked at Judas. "May I tell you my true concerns about your Rabbi?"

Judas nodded.

"He has divided the nation. A house divided cannot stand—you said yourself He preaches it. Since the Rabbi began His teachings, my father-in-law and I and the men of this counsel have often wept together over the great conflict created by Him. Many are unsettled. We mustn't forget them," Caiaphus said. "I fear all those who follow Him from place to place are being drawn into civil war, or worse. If that happens, the Romans would be on our necks!"

Caiaphus's thin lips tightened, his lower one folded over the upper for a moment, and his eyes came back to meet Judas's directly. "Whatever His motivation or His plans, surely Jesus would never desire to be the reason for such a slaughter." The priest stared thoughtfully at the crimson carpet.

Pregnant anticipation filled the room, and its two occupants sat together in silence.

"I can prevent it," Judas swore coldly. "If I accepted the bounty payment then the men from the temple would know I mean business."

Caiaphus suddenly looked aghast.

"You don't think I was suggesting...?" Caiaphus started. Shaking his head dramatically, eyes wide, he continued, "Not a man's own Rabbi!" He paused. "For ransom?"

"As a sign of good faith between us," Judas answered.

"Oh! Oh!" Caiaphus put his hands over his ears.

"I'll need your assurance," Judas stopped the spinning coin flat on the tabletop and looked at the excited priest.

"Assurance?" replied Caiaphus as he brought his hands down.

"All Men Betray"

"There's my own safety to consider," Judas said. "The man who betrays the Nazarene will be hated by as many as will love him for it."

"Betrayal is a strong word, Judas." Caiaphus came back to his chair and sat down on its edge. "Considering the circumstances, I don't know if I would go so far as to call what you suggest *betrayal*. A young man betrays his mother, the only true love he has had, when he takes a wife. A man betrays his brother when he is forced to keep his brother's portion of an inheritance in order to feed his own children, rather than give them up as bondslaves for debt."

"You see, Judas, we are all ruled by circumstance. Not everything is black and white, as we might wish. There are hard choices we are forced to make at times."

Caiaphus touched Judas's sleeve, something he seldom did for fear of making himself unclean by coming into contact with the sin of another. "Betrayal?" Caiaphus said softly. "I prefer to use the word *compromise*. Compromise is the gift of the wise, the great among us. Sometimes compromise is our surest friend."

There was silence again as the last apostle reviewed what had passed between himself and the priest. The high priest's words felt like salve. The absence of the opinion of John and the others, and the fact that Caiaphus did not speak in parables, as Jesus so often did, was refreshing. Things suddenly felt much clearer than they had in the past several months with the apostles.

Judas realized that there were many other avenues for himself and his future, broad pathways of possibility and promise. Here in the presence of greatness, Judas felt nothing of the gloomy forethought that Jesus always advocated. And this man's counsel carried none of the guilt that so often impinged Judas's conscience in the presence of the Rabbi.

At last Caiaphus came behind Judas's chair and leaned to speak in his ear. "Save Him from it, Judas," the priest whispered. He put a hand on the betrayer's shoulder. "Even if it means putting Him in chains for a while. Let Him cool off and have an opportunity to reflect upon His ways. Save yourself. Save us all!" He returned to his own chair and sat down again.

The man behind the curtain held his breath.

Leaving the coin where it lay, Judas said, "What will you give me if I turn Him over to you?"

Behind the curtain, the treasurer smiled and tightly closed his eyes. He clasped his hands together in thanks and victory, wanting to dance in celebration but knowing the noise of his feet on the tiles would give him away.

Judas looked around. The counting table gleamed in the lamplight. "Besides the ransom, I mean." Like a ship in full sail now, he could not be deterred or turned aside; he seized his opportunity by the throat with both hands and squeezed. "I'm excellent with sums. I've kept His moneybox from the beginning. A treasury seat perhaps?"

Hearing his cue, the treasurer suddenly stepped into the room.

"You sent for me, sire?" he said.

Surprised by the man's voice, Judas turned abruptly. The treasurer nodded a polite acknowledgment of him.

"Joses keeps the treasury," Caiaphus told Judas. He raised his voice, showing that the treasurer's appearance was authorized. "This is our friend, Joses!" Caiaphus looked warmly at Judas and smiled just enough to keep his middle tooth concealed. "Judas Iscariot. He has come to help us resolve our troubles!"

The treasurer smiled widely back.

The "Arrangement"

Judas leaned tentatively against a boulder at the bottom of the path that led up from the brook Kidron. The night sky sparkled with a silver dust of stars. Up the path were Gethsemane and the olive press. There, beyond the watchtower near the oil press itself, sitting in the heart of the garden, Jesus would be kneeling or lying face down atop His cloak in prayer. Judas had no second thoughts. The muscles in his jaw flexed with tension. His purse hung heavily at his side.

He stared into the darkness across the valley, expecting at any minute to see the advancing torchlights of the men who were meeting him. Caiaphus had assured him that "the arrangement" was in place. The priest would send two or three men from the temple to accompany Judas to bring Jesus back.

From time to time Judas left the rock to pace back and forth. For three days he had hardly slept. Since the meeting, Judas had one thing on his mind: fulfilling his agreement with the high priest. It was the beginning of a thrilling future. The words of Caiaphus were as firm in his mind as the pillars at the temple entrance. "Save him, Judas...save us all."

Judas had been obsessed with the details of determining the exact time and place. When it was all said and done, Jesus had been the one to determine His own fate. Judas's expression was fierce as he realized it.

"Ironic," he thought. "I didn't have to arrange it all. All that was required was to them where He had gone."

The details were very clear. At a certain point during the Seder meal, Jesus had became agitated. Typically, Peter and John were arguing over which of them would sit at the Teacher's right hand. John was pressing Jesus a little too closely, and the Rabbi suddenly announced that one of them was a scoundrel. Actually, He used the word *betrayer*. Judas choked on his wine when Jesus said it. The others laughed as he spat it upon himself.

The entire table of men went quiet for a moment. They seemed morose until Matthew made some comment about trying to ruin the holiday, which returned them all to eating.

Judas was stunned, fearing Jesus was reading his thoughts as He sometimes did. Like the others, Judas busied himself with his food by reaching for bread. Peter continued to force the issue of who was the greatest, and John said something in Jesus' ear. Jesus, listening to John, dipped a piece of His own bread and handed it to Judas. When Judas accepted it and brought it to his mouth he realized that the fishermen were staring at him in dark silence.

"What?" he managed, in a muffled voice. For an instant he thought Jesus was finally indicating which one would be His chief officer. His mind swirling now, he asked, "Is it me?"

"You said it," Jesus replied. Judas couldn't believe it. Just when he had closed the deal with the temple rulers, Jesus had decided to make Judas His right-hand man.

But it was the angry glare of Peter and John that gave Judas his epiphany. Jesus was not referring to who was greatest. He was suggesting that Judas was to betray him! He had announced it in front of them all! Judas glanced around, horrified. But the rest, besides Peter and John, went right on eating, immersed in their own foolish conversations. As Judas gathered up his things, Jesus simply said, "Whatever you plan, do it quickly."

With those words Jesus sealed His own fate. It was clear that He was ready for a showdown with the chief priests and elders. He had spoken of it all along, only never of when it would come—until tonight. There was no doubt where they would find Him.

Judas knew He planned to spend the night in the garden at the oil press. He sent word straight to Caiaphus to meet him here, just above the Kidron, on the path leading up to Gethsemane. And warned that, for the first time ever, Jesus had told the apostles to arm themselves.

The Fateful Moment Arrives

At last the flaring torches appeared across the valley and flowed towards him in a winding single line. As Judas looked at the glowworm coming down the valley, he wondered at the number of them.

He waited impatiently for the company to reach the place where he was standing. When they were near enough that he could hear their hushed voices, the tramp of their sandals, and the dull squeak of the leather where swords swung on their belts, Judas went down to them.

Caiaphus's servant was in the lead, armed and carrying a torch, with his master directly behind him.

Caiaphus puffed, out of breath, as he stood momentarily on the incline.

"Lead the way!" he said.

Judas looked down the long line of men behind him. He recognized the garb of the temple guard, as well as that of several chief priests and rulers.

"Do we need a entire detachment?"

The servant of the high priest, the same man who had let Judas in the gate at the palace, stood threateningly close to his master. He lowered the torch, putting it directly into Judas face, causing him to step back from the glare and heat on his skin.

"He has twelve." Caiaphus made an arrogant sound in his throat. "Eleven now, armed and expecting us, according to you." The priest's voice was cold as the steel blades that hung on the soldiers' belts. His eyes took on a reptilian look, like a cobra; his great turban gave his head a large, majestic appearance.

It had not occurred to Judas that there could be a fight. With exception of the priests, these men were all armed. There were questioning voices near the back of the line. Caiaphus turned.

"What is it?" he asked those behind him.

"Curiosity-seekers roaming about, asking our business."

The torches made a whooshing sound as they devoured oxygen.

"Well, Iscariot," Caiaphus said. "Everyone is waiting; lead on!"

A dozen pairs of dark eyes gleamed intensely at Judas in the firelight. He turned and led the priests and their soldiers up the hill to Gethsemane.

As they neared the garden the priest said, "How will I be certain which one he is?"

"The man I embrace," replied Judas, thirty pieces of silver bouncing harshly against him. A strange sensation filled his mouth as he said it. It was the taste of bread dipped in the sop, its biting vinegar puckering the sides of his tongue.

The line of men condensed into a mob as the incline leveled out and they neared the entrance to the garden. Caiaphus ordered the captain of the guard to the front, beside the priest's servant.

"Bring another torch. I want to make sure we see the man clearly, so there are no mistakes about His identity. I'll not let Him slip through my fingers again."

Judas led the way on the familiar ground, the captain of the guard right behind him. No one spoke. Judas could feel intense anticipation, like a wave swelling from behind him, rising out of the expectation in the hearts of the men who had been hoping for this moment every day for three years. Only the sound of their feet on the path, their breathing, and the pitch of the flames burning up the night air accompanied them as they approached the watchtower. The light was announcement enough.

When they passed the tower, the son of the gardener, stripped to his loincloth, was bathing. The torch-bearing entourage illumined his nearly naked body, and he left his bath without bothering to put on his other clothing. He ran out to see what was happening.

"What is it?" the boy asked Judas, recognizing him as one of the men who often came there with Jesus. Judas knew him to be the same lad who kept a flock of sheep on the mountain behind the garden. They spoke sometimes, but he had never learned the boy's name. "Your friends are already within," the lad told Judas. He looked at the guards. "Is something wrong?"

Judas simply pushed him aside.

The entourage passed by without a reply.

The boy pursued them.

"Shall I call for my father?" he asked.

"The high priest has business with a man within," one of the Pharisees told him. "It is none of your father's business."

The boy followed them, not knowing what to do.

Ahead of them in the dimness, Jesus and His men had been huddled together waiting, but eventually had fallen asleep. They dozed off with the full realization that tonight was the night that Jesus had spoken of. A heavy fog of gloom and dread had covered them from the moment Judas left the Seder. It was as though every man understood that the great clock of destiny was slowly ticking away in endless, hateful moments.

Judas skirted the main company of sleepy men.

"Humph!" he huffed as he looked down on them. "As usual! All talk and no action!" For a moment Judas for once felt superior to them. He was in control, not merely fetching their supper or finding a place for them to spend the night. But the feeling was fleeting.

The detachment moved less cautiously. Their tramping through the center of the grove awoke Jesus' men.

"Do this quickly!" Caiaphus ordered Judas in a low, stern voice.

"There He is." Judas pointed to a figure kneeling apart from the rest on the opposite side of the olive press. With Judas in the lead, the entourage flowed around the stone pit toward the man Judas indicated.

"Rabbi?" Judas said. His heart beat wildly in his chest. A hot flush crossed his face and his fingertips tingled.

Resting, arms folded over themselves half in recline, just steps away from Jesus, were John and Peter. Peter's lolling head shot up at the sound of Judas's voice.

Ignoring him, Judas spread out his arms, passing the olive press, the words of the priest, like the pillars before the temple, supporting him still. "Save him...save us all."

Jesus had already seen them coming and was rising to his feet.

With a Kiss?

The entourage of armed men and their torches closed in around Him as Judas and Jesus faced one another. His exterior belying the turmoil within, Judas smiled and stepped forward, warmly embracing Jesus and kissing Him on both cheeks, according to custom.

Jesus did not withdraw from the embrace. But as the former apostle came near, Jesus spoke in a voice so low, so calm, it seemed to thunder.

"Would you turn me over to my enemies with a kiss, Judas?"

Before Judas could answer, Caiaphus stepped forward, his entourage and several onlookers crowding behind him. Some of them deliberately revealed their sword hilts.

"Who are you looking for?" When Jesus spoke several of the Pharisees and guards suddenly buckled to the ground. They gasped and looked around in confused fear to see what had hit them. The hair stood up on the back of Judas's neck. Caiaphus himself was sitting on his backside in the dust in front of Jesus. His fine turban had been dislodged and had slipped down over one eye. He brushed the dirt from his hands and righted his turban.

"Arrest him!" the high priest barked, motioning to the temple guard troops and pointing frantically at Jesus as though He would bolt any minute like a rabbit from a snare.

The guard was reluctant now.

"Are you Jesus, the Nazarene?" Caiaphus said with all the authority he could muster, mixed with the angry humiliation he already felt. He scrambled to compose himself.

"I am," Jesus told him simply.

Another invisible hand swept through the soldiers and temple entourage as if loosed by the voice of Jesus. Many of them shrieked and the curiosity-seekers fled. The torch carried by one of those who fled was dropped behind him in his haste. It set fire to the hem the garment of one of the chief priests. The priest shrieked, and one of his fellows came to help him stamp out the blaze. The detachment, eyes wide and grim in the glow of torchlight, shuffled uncomfortably. Some looked over their shoulders in fear, exchanging low, frightened remarks with one another.

By now the whole detachment was in a panic. Several of them threw down their torches and fled into the darkness after the others. The boy from the watchtower stood immovably, still covered in nothing but his linen wrap.

Jesus reached out a hand to help Caiaphus back to his feet.

"Devil's emissary!" Caiaphus spat. He jerked his sleeve away as his servant rushed to help him up.

"What's happening?" Peter rushed into the circle of torchlight, rubbing sleep from his face. He recognized Caiaphus, and then his gaze fell on Judas. Peter scowled, clenching his fists.

"You wretched traitor!" Peter lunged at him. "I should have done this long ago!"

Seeing the unshaven, robust man, with a bulk and an expression similar to a bear robbed of its cubs, rushing toward him, Judas took a step back between two of the temple guards and took cover behind them. They laid hands on the fisherman, who threw off their grip with one heave. Judas sucked in his breath, his own courage draining away. An agonizing feeling, like some great mechanism beginning to spin out of control, a twisting fist, grabbed Judas's gut.

"Arrest him!" Caiaphus forced his servant forward, grabbing him by his garment and pointing at Jesus.

The chief of the guard stepped forward with ropes that the servant yanked away, hurriedly untangling them.

"On what grounds?" Peter shouted.

John entered the circle of light and confusion. He pulled at Peter's shirt to prevent him from attacking Judas and looked back and forth from Jesus to Peter to Caiaphus. He was at a loss for words.

"Ha!" thought Judas. "That's the first time his tongue is not flapping!" Judas felt a hot sense of satisfaction at having the upper hand over John, at least for this moment, after all his taunts.

Just then John found his tongue. "What shall we do, Rabbi?"

The servant of the high priest had the ropes doubled and roughly took one wrist of Jesus to secure it to the other.

Breaking free of John's restraint, Peter took advantage of the moment when priest's servant had his hands occupied. The fisherman seized the servant's sword; its blade glinted in the firelight. Cursing, he lifted the sword and brought it down with a whining slash. The Ethiopian screamed and doubled over. Bodies rushed in every direction.

"He is murdered!" someone shouted.

"Enough, Peter!" it was Jesus again. "Enough! Will you prevent what God has not? I won't refuse the cup He has given me to drink."

Restrained by John, Peter glared at Judas and spat on him. The warm spittle filled Judas's eye and ran off his nose and down his mouth. Judas wiped the disgusting, foul-smelling phlegm on a sleeve. It made his already tense stomach turn over, and he struggled not to retch. More scuffling occurred. When the torches were upright again the servant of the high priest was whimpering, his face glazed with pain and shock, his hands and head dark and wet with blood.

Pushing Peter aside, the rope still hanging limp from one wrist, the Rabbi extended His hand and touched the side of the servant's head. The man cringed, but instantly the pain left him entirely. He had thought he might faint when he felt the wound that completely severed his ear. The ear itself had fallen with a soft, dead thud onto the servant's sandaled foot. Before he realized what it was, he had kicked it off somewhere into the darkness. But now, as his sticky fingers touched the place where the ear had been severed, he felt a new one that had instantly replaced it. The servant trembled uncontrollably, unable to speak. Tears of terror, disbelief, shock, and wonder rolled down his cheeks.

"Bind him!" Caiaphus screamed hysterically.

But the servant took a fleeting glance at Jesus and then looked back at his master. He shook his head no, fingering his new ear, and fled.

"Arrest Him"

"Arrest him!" Caiaphus screeched again, starting to imagine that even this plot to take Jesus into custody was doomed to failure.

None of the armed men moved to do it, even though Jesus offered his wrists. Several of them flinched and closed their eyes tightly, but nothing happened to them this time.

Peter and John stood immobile. The other disciples who had awoken during the melee hung back. Some had fled already.

Jesus thrust His wrists toward the high priest. His eyes met Caiaphus's directly.

Caiaphus pushed another of the guards in front of Jesus. "Bind the Nazarene before He escapes by some other magic!" the priest said. The man looked at Him in trepidation.

Oddly, Jesus chuckled.

At the urging of the remaining temple company, the guard grabbed the hanging rope himself and began to roughly wrap the wrists of Jesus together, knowing all the while that Jesus was well able to undo them if He desired to.

"Seize the rest as well!" The angry high priest pointed a bony ringed finger and turned in a frantic circle, pointing at everyone standing around. Several of the other disciples fled when the order to arrest them was given. One of the guards laid hold of the boy from the watchtower, but the lad struggled free and ran naked into the night.

Jesus, bound and surrounded by His enemies, said nothing else. The soldiers shoved Him towards the path leading out of the garden. His shoulder brushed Judas's as they pushed Him away.

Jesus glanced at Caiaphus, whose rigid expression was tinged with triumph and fear. Jesus met Judas's eyes once more. "You were my familar friend," Jesus said to him in a voice that only he heard.

The guard roughly pushed the Rabbi away.

Judas stood watching the back of Jesus' head in the torchlight. The noisy crowd, now emboldened once again, followed Him down the path like vultures after a fresh kill. John pushed himself in beside Jesus. Refusing to be pushed away again, he clung to Him. Judas's eyes took in the heads of the Rabbi and the disciple; from behind they appeared almost as the same man. So in the end it was John, after all, who refused to be separated from Him.

"It wasn't enough that you stole from us all along! Now you've taken Him away as well!"

Judas whirled around. He was unable to see in the darkness left in the wake of the retreating torches, but he well knew the voice.

"He said to leave me alone!" Judas said to the bulk of shadow.

"I'll leave you alone, murderer!" Peter swore. "For now! But I'll come back for you once I know what they have done with Him." He pushed past the betrayer, almost knocking him to his knees, and followed the mob at a distance.

❦

Judas stayed where he was, his feet frozen to the empty earth as beads of icy sweat rolled off his face. The dancing orbs of yellow light grew smaller and smaller as the company descended the hill. Judas considered where they were going. To appear before Annas surely would be their first step, and then they would go on to Caiaphus's palace to secure the charges before witnesses. Judas imagined John there with Jesus, like Daniel and the angel in the lion's den. He let out a groan of defeat.

Suddenly a searing pain struck the flesh of his thigh. He brushed away his outer garment to see what burned. The sensation was the weight of the ransom, thirty new pieces of silver, each one stamped with the temple seal. A shudder went down his spine. He yanked at the purse until it came loose from his belt and held it up. He looked down the hill after the men who had taken Jesus away and then back at the purse.

His mind went blank. He could not think of what to do next. Some of the coins shifted in the bag and clinked together softly. Before he knew it, Judas found himself running down the path after the arresting party. He didn't know where he was going or what he would do once he got there.

The plotting of revenge and his boiling envy had driven him along since it began. He had assumed that once the affair was finally over, he would be free from all of his inner turmoil over John and the others. All the disappointment and anger and odd foreboding he sometimes felt from Jesus would be gone. Lifted. Resolved. But that had not happened. He had expected lightness and joy, but instead a crushing weight of confusion fell heavily upon him. Black, searing, hot guilt was filling his soul, choking out the very life within him.

He no longer thought about the legends of Judas Maccabee. Neither did he gain a sense of clarity of destiny or direction, which he had believed would come at last. All that remained was a sick, gnawing sense that Beelzebub's eggs had hatched by the thousands in his heart. Their worms had grown and expanded, and were now out of control. They threatened to burst right through his organs and skin and trail their rotten stench down the front of his body. He gasped for air and focused on following the distant glowing flames of the torches. Still, he took great care not to come upon Peter in the darkness.

As he ran, Judas felt himself pass through a veil, as if he were falling through to another dimension. He ran faster, even though one of his sandaled feet had broken a strap in the scuffle and now made an odd slapping sound against his foot with every step. From a distance, he thought he heard a voice. It was a horrible far-off screech, not human, not animal—it belonged to some other creature that was hurtling downward. Stars rushed up past it in the darkness; they seemed to know that the end would come once the fall was finished. It chased Judas down the dark winding path.

⚬

Judas stood up slowly, feeling old and used up. He was completely wrung out. All his faculties, whatever skill or scheming he ever possessed, were all gone. He was a man condemned. Hell's reapers swirled about him. Their lustful, hot breath crept down his neck. Their greedy, grasping whispers exclaimed their delight at receiving him once and for all.

His eyes seemed not to see what was around him anymore, as though an invisible web had been cast from
beyond. An unseen hand beckoned, its talons drawing him
nearer. He followed. Almost peacefully, he removed his
outer garment and folded it carefully. He laid it over the
exposed roots of the olive tree where he had been. He bent
and lifted his foot to reach the sandal strap. The broken shoe
hung limply. Crossing hand-over-hand he unwound the
leather thongs of the useless sandal and coiled them carefully atop the shoe as he set it on his folded garment. He took
off his other sandal and placed it beside its mate.

The earth beneath his bare feet was firm and dry. It felt
strange on the soles of his feet. He had never gone barefoot
as was the habit of baser men, or those too poor to proper-
ly shoe themselves. He loosed his belt and pulled it slowly
through his hand. The tight surface of its braided length
felt rough as it passed between the tips of his fingers.
Turning it around his hand and back over his palm, Judas
pulled, confirming its strength. He stepped onto the worn
path of the garden.

The sun seemed to have died. All light without and
within was gone. He stood in the middle of the path and
numbly looked down the endless corridor of darkness that
wound through the olive trees, down towards the valley,
across the brook, and finally to the priest's house where
Jesus had been taken.

No longer were there sounds of redemption coming
from the temple. No longer was there the noise of unbur-
dened pilgrims happily going home, no reminiscence of
priestly incense, no hum of ecstatic prayer. All was faded
gray, and dark shadows were deepening around him. Nature
itself seemed deathly silent. Even the sound of the birds had
hushed. The last apostle turned his back on the city, shut-
ting it out, hearing only the whisper of his own bare footsteps, the soft pad of them one by one, each foot forced to

move in front of the other over bits of gravel and rock. He counted every step, calculating, adding them up to the sum.

For the first time since he could remember he had no purse at all. It lay on the cold stone of the high priest's palace floor. The contents of it had tumbled out across the stones with none willing to touch the blood money during the high holidays. He had waited out the night, waking and sleeping through the muffled sounds of the intermittent rise and fall of voices from the house of the high priest, where they had moved the quarry to be tried in a secret session of the Sanhedrin.

Images of the Crucifixion

The images that swirled before his eyes were few. Only three. The shadowy bulk of Peter in the dark garden. "Murderer!" His words were daggers. This hairy man had been his bristling nemesis.

The next face shone bright and clear. Its eyes were so deep and full that they spoke with a sound of ten thousand waterfalls. All-knowing. All-loving. Those eyes were also all-sorrowful, but not for Himself. For this scheming, disheveled man with burning eyes and heavy purse who crouched in the shadow of the steep steps leading away from the high priest's house. From there Judas watched them snatch hunks of beard from His face and send Him, bruised and bound, to Pilate.

Also in those eyes were pitiful anathema, a look of eternal separation, as they fell on their once familiar friend. They were eyes that wept because Judas had refused to open when Jesus' patient hand rapped again and again on the door of his heart.

It was then, looking into those eyes, that Judas understood. It was then, after the door had already been tightly shut and the key turned in the lock. It was when it was too late that Judas realized. Of every mention Jesus had made for the past three years that the Son of Man would be betrayed, not one had been an indictment. No! Every one had been an invitation, a clear call to turn aside before it was too late. He had tried to tell Judas to step off the path of destruction and turn from the jealousy that, like a jackal sniffing out a hare, hunted Judas down. Those eyes had warned him to escape from the jaws of jealousy, but now it was too late.

The last image was that of the indignant, scornful Caiaphus, with Annas jeering in the background. "What is your guilty conscience to us?" they had said.

Slowly, mechanically, Judas walked to the edge of the grove. He stood for a moment in the cover of olive foliage. A lost sheep grazed in the shadow of a rock, its bell tinkling softly. The shepherd, if he knew the lamb was lost, had not yet come to find it. There would be no other witnesses. Judas slipped out from the trees and moved straight up the side of the hill to the ridge. At the top, a lone tree, half again the man's own height, perched strangely overlooking the brow. Its silhouette outlined by the brightening sky behind it, it bent down, frozen, crooked, its surface swept smooth by years of wind. The tree extended a single arm, a strong branch that stretched perpendicular to the surface of the earth beneath. It stuck out over a tumble of rocks and dry yellow grass that dropped into the ravine below.

Judas passed the boulder where the sheep grazed. It looked up at him blandly, chewing, and let out a single bleat. Here, on other days, Judas had stopped to chat with the young shepherd. The boy would fold his skinny, sun-darkened arms around his knees, while his busy fingers fidgeted with the sides of his frayed garment. Shepherd's crook resting against him, the boy was a fixture atop the rock, watching his flock or eating his lunch.

In the jagged crevice below, which divided the mountains, piles of refuse lay scattered. Faded, rotting bits of old torn garments tumbled among the discarded wooden ribs of broken crates. Shards of shattered vessels, irreparable, tossed aside, littered the ground. A useless sagging cart with one leaning wheel, its missing spokes grown through with several seasons of weeds, teetered on its edge, and bleached bits of bones lay scattered here and there.

There was only the smell of the wind. Clean, dry. Its sound occasionally whistled softly. His hair lifted slightly from around his face as Judas stood facing into the barren wilderness. Without hesitation, he flung one end of his belt over the branch of the tree and caught the knotted end again in his hand. Almost losing his balance on the steep incline, he pulled the belt through itself and formed a perfect loop. As he slid the belt out farther on the arm of the tree, his bare feet slipped under him momentarily. Judas leaned back and pulled the noose over his head, down around his neck, and tightened it until, numbed from these last hours, his pulse throbbed at his temples once more. Standing erect, his ankles twitching unsteadily, he swallowed hard and leapt into the ravine.

Whirling wildly, the great weight of his body pulled mercilessly on his spine. His tongue was bitten through, and its flesh and blood filled his clamped mouth. Clamped shut once and for all, as it should have been the night before in the garden, the week before in Caiaphus's chamber. The metallic taste of his own blood filled his throat and overwhelmed his senses. He panicked completely, trying to lift his head above the noose, but his arms hung down uselessly, as if they were unattached somehow. They refused to help him.

Pain and retching, cut off by the stricture at his throat, exploded inside his helpless body. He could smell his own death fast approaching. The rope that constricted his neck burned deep and relentlessly. He screamed but no sound came out. It made no difference. No one would hear his cry of anguish anyway. His hands were numb. Swelling, they hung down as though the fluids in his veins would burst right through the ends of his fingers. His frantic gasps for breath, sharp with blood, wet with pleading desperation, spat upon his face.

All the while the vista before him pitched from side to side, rocking wildly. Each swing made him feel as though his head would burst from his body. The noose, like a rudder on course, turned him slowly around until he was forced to face the garden, the temple, and his sin.

He thought he heard the clanking sounds of sacrificial irons moving the carcasses of bulls over the fire as asphyxiation closed in. The sear of flesh hooks lifting meat from the boiling pots pierced his thighs and the sides of his body. Their points scraped the surface of his bones and sent streaking fingers of agony up his spine.

Smoke drifted upward from the edifice of the holy place in the heart of the city. Swallows flew. A black circle closing in from the outer edge folded upon his tunnel of vision.

He could not feel the involuntary twitching of his feet as they kicked uselessly. They kicked for their last time against the goads, against the empty air, until, finally, they were still.

Only the hem of Judas's torn shirt flapped softly against his thighs. The rest of it, loose, hung off one bare shoulder. His head leaned to one side; his eyes stared out of nothing into nothing; they seemed almost childlike.

A thin, blackened line of blood trickled from the corner of his clamped mouth. The rest of his features, intermittently obscured by tangled hair that freely flew about in the breeze, looked down, staring blankly from above the noose.

Rising from the temple square, a shofar blast sounded.

The Lost Sheep

Just after midday, the young shepherd finally came hurrying up around the side of the mountain in frantic search of his renegade sheep. The shepherd stopped briefly, and, pursing his lips, blew a sharp, high whistle into the sunny air.

Then, cupping his hands beside his mouth, he called; his young, worried voice was shrill and frightened. Over and over he repeated the name of the missing lamb. The boy would call and stop and listen, but he heard only the sound of the wind, not the tinkling of the bell that hung around the wandering sheep's neck.

The shepherd berated himself for letting the animal escape again. This time when he found it he would be forced to do what he had hoped to avoid. He would break its leg, and then maybe it would learn not to wander from his side. Coming upon the steep incline towards the brow of the hill and the vista of wilderness beyond it he worried.

"I hope it hasn't gone there," he told himself mournfully. "I may never find him before the jackals get to him!"

A shadow from high above, between the shepherd and the sun, passed over him. He sucked in his hurried breath and looked up sharply, shielding his eyes against the noonday glare. Vultures, two of them, carrion scavengers floating high in the sky, circled over the far side of the hill. His heart beat furiously as his worst fears threatened to be realized. Picking up his pace, the lad struggled up the incline, pulling himself along with the help of his shepherd's crook. It made a hollow sound with each strike upon rock and soil. Coming over the top at last, the shepherd straightened up. His breath came fast and the high; white sun beat down as his squinting eyes searched intently for the lost sheep.

Suddenly, the lad froze, his face filled with horror. There before him, where the mountain fell into the ravine, was the reason for the circling vultures. The shepherd's rod fell from his hands as he ran forward. The man on the tree was familiar. A laughing, handsome fellow who gave him a denarius from time to time for no reason at all. The lad stumbled and fell and scraped a knee but struggled up again until he finally reached the tree. Over him the branch creaked as the man's dead body turned gently in the wind.

The shepherd struggled to push the limp weight of the man up, attempting to lift him and loosen the rope at his neck. But the man's useless, heavy legs only flopped off of the lad's thin shoulders. The boy wrapped his bare arms around the knees of the hanging man, frantically scrabbling on falling rocks to stay upright on the incline. Again, he tried to lift him up and undo the noose from his neck. Once, losing his balance completely, he clutched the grisly form to keep from falling into the ravine himself. The boy swung helplessly out over the cliff, dead man and shepherd twirling together wildly on the end of the dead man's belt.

His own skinny legs flailing, with the creepy feel of the hair and cold flesh of the hanging man's legs against his own cheek, the boy was finally able to hurl himself back onto the hillside and scramble up. Terror and confusion gripped him, together with rushing guilt that he could not bring the man down from the tree. The boy began to cry uncontrollably.

"Why did you do that?" he whimpered through closed teeth, his nostrils wet and flaring with every breath. His ribs quivered beneath his brown skin. His frustrated hands, fingers outspread, clung to his sides. His nose ran and tears drew lines down his dirty chin. At last the boy screamed at the dead man, "I can't help you! You're too heavy!"

Staring at the man on the tree, he backed away. He was unable to avert the gaze of his crying eyes from the figure hanging over the ravine until he tripped over the crook of his fallen staff. Collecting himself, he looked for the last time at the ghastly figure of the man whose name he didn't know. Then, turning his back, the lost sheep forgotten, the shepherd ran down the hill.

Summary

Judas's offense led to fraternizing with the enemy. Jealousy married jealousy to annul three years of close fellowship. Judas had been privileged to witness the sick being healed and the dead being raised. Anger and guilt over his own sin (he had been discovered to be a thief) nullified his personal bonds with men he had held as close friends. Eventually, jealousy caused him to deny everything that had been sacred in his life.

Jealousy commandeered Judas's weaknesses. His act of betrayal exemplifies a primary characteristic of jealousy: dissolution of respect, loyalty, and love. Jealousy allows treachery to become an option for action.

It would appear that Judas carried the baggage of the things that threatened or offended him into his relationships and experiences with Jesus and the eleven disciples. That fellowship exposed the weakness in Judas's character, but he doomed himself to destruction when he surrendered himself to his jealousy. The jealous Pharisees provided Judas an opportunity to even the score. He believed that fraternizing and plotting with the Pharisees was a means to justify himself and get back at those whom he envied. Judas married his jealousy to that of the Pharisees to form an unholy alliance against the Son of God. Jealousy caused Judas to become what Jude described as "a cloud without water, foaming up, raging evil against honor, reserved for wrath and utter fall."

Bonnie Chavda is a minister's wife, mother of four grown children, and an ordained minister, who has devoted more than 27 years to help God's people experience living encounters with the Lord. In addition, Bonnie has been involved extensively in international missions and serves as associate pastor of All Nations Church in Charlotte, North Carolina.

Bonnie is a published author of many inspirational articles and a contributor in the Women of Destiny Bible. She serves as advisor to a national women's magazine (*SpiritLed Woman*, Strang Publishing) and enjoys creative writing on the side. An energetic, straight forward, conference speaker, Bonnie's approach to the Bible and to faith continues to inspire thousands in their walk with God.

For other books, audiotapes, or other resource material from the author, contact:

Mahesh Chavda Ministries International
P.O. Box 411008
Charlotte, NC 28241
(704) 543-7272
FAX: (704) 541-5300

E-mail: info@watchofthelord.com
www.watchofthelord.com

Books by Mahesh Chavda

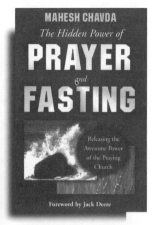

THE HIDDEN POWER OF PRAYER AND FASTING

The praying believer is the confident believer. But the fasting believer is the overcoming believer. This is the believer who changes the circumstances and the world around him. He is the one who experiences the supernatural power of the risen Lord in his everyday life. An international evangelist and the senior pastor of All Nations Church in Charlotte, North Carolina, Mahesh Chavda has seen firsthand the power of God released through a lifestyle of prayer and fasting. Here he shares from decades of personal experience and scriptural study principles and practical tips about fasting and praying. This book will inspire you to tap into God's power and change your life, your city, and your nation!
ISBN: 0-7684-2017-2

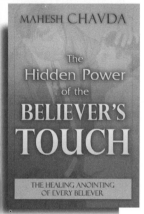

THE HIDDEN POWER OF THE BELIEVER'S TOUCH

Here is the fatal blow to the belief that God does not heal today. Through the power of his personal experience and the strength of his biblical insight. Mahesh Chavda reveals how the healing compassion of our Lord reaches the hurting masses simply by the believer's healing touch. Written with compassion, humor, and insight, *The Hidden Power of the Believer's Touch* affirms that the healing anointing and the gifts of signs and wonders are not reserved for "super saints" or the specially gifted, but are available to every believer who carries the compassion and love of the Lord Jesus.
ISBN: 0-7684-1974-3

THE HIDDEN POWER OF SPEAKING IN TONGUES

Almost 40 years ago John and Elizabeth Sherill introduced the world to the phenomenon of "speaking in tongues" in their book *They Speak With Other Tongues*. The book was an immediate success as thousands were touched by the power of this spiritual gift. *The Hidden Power of Speaking in Tongues* again explores this spiritual experience powerfully prevalent in the early Church. This much-maligned and controversial gift was a practical part of their worship and intercession and seeks to be rediscovered in our day. In a day of spiritual poverty, Chavda challenges the Body of Christ to experience afresh the secret dynamic of "speaking in tongues," as he removes the veil covering this glorious gift.
ISBN: 0-7684-2171-3

Available at your local Christian bookstore.

Additional copies of this book and other
book titles from DESTINY IMAGE are
available at your local bookstore.

For a complete list of our titles,
visit us at www.destinyimage.com
Send a request for a catalog to:

Destiny Image® Publishers, Inc.
P.O. Box 310
Shippensburg, PA 17257-0310

*"Speaking to the Purposes of God for This
Generation and for the Generations to Come"*